Series by Julie Johnstone

Scottish Medieval Romance Books:

Spellbound Hearts
The Lairds Magical Lass, Book 1

Return of the Highlanders
Secrets of a Highlander's Heart, Book 1
Tangled Up with the Highlander, Book 2
The Highlander Burns for Vengeance, Book 3

Wicked Willful Highlanders
Highlanders Hold Grudges, Book 1
Highlanders Never Surrender, Book 2
Highlanders Never Forget, Book 3

Of Mist and Mountains Series
Highland Hope, Book 1
Highland Reckoning, Book 2
Highland Prize, Book 3
Highland Heartbreaker, Book 4

Highlanders Through Time Series
Sinful Scot, Book 1
Sexy Scot, Book 2
Seductive Scot, Book 3
Scandalous Scot, Book 4

Highlander Vows: Entangled Hearts Series
When a Laird Loves a Lady, Book 1

Wicked Highland Wishes, Book 2
When a Highlander Loses His Heart, Book 3
How a Scot Surrenders to a Lady, Book 4
When a Warrior Woos a Lass, Book 5
When a Scot Gives His Heart, Book 6
When a Highlander Weds a Hellion, Book 7
How to Heal a Highland Heart, Book 8
The Heart of a Highlander, Book 9
Christmas in the Scot's Arms, Book 10

Renegade Scots Series
Outlaw King, Book 1
Highland Defender, Book 2
Highland Avenger, Book 3

Regency Romance Books:

Scottish Scoundrels: Ensnared Hearts Series
Lady Guinevere and the Rogue with a Brogue, Book 1
Lady Lilias and the Devil in Plaid, Book 2
Lady Constantine and the Sins of Lord Kilgore, Book 3
Lady Frederica and the Scot Who Would Not, Book 4

A Whisper of Scandal Series
Bargaining with a Rake, Book 1
Conspiring with a Rogue, Book 2
Dancing with a Devil, Book 3
After Forever, Book 4
The Dangerous Duke of Dinnisfree, Book 5

A Once Upon A Rogue Series
My Fair Duchess, Book 1
My Seductive Innocent, Book 2
My Enchanting Hoyden, Book 3

The Laird's Magical Lass

Spellbound Hearts, Book 1

by

Julie Johnstone

The best way to stay in touch is to subscribe to my newsletter. Go to https://juliejohnstoneauthor.com and subscribe in the box at the top of the page that says Newsletter. If you don't hear from me once a month, please check your spam filter and set up your email to allow my messages through to you so you don't miss the opportunity to win great prizes or hear about appearances.

If you're interested in when my books go on sale or want to be one of the first to know about my new releases, please follow me on BookBub! You'll get quick book notifications every time there's a new pre-order, book on sale, or new release. You can follow me on BookBub here: www.bookbub.com/authors/julie-johnstone

Chapter One – Freya

1265
Dunvegan Castle
Isle of Skye, Scotland

My step-mama was an evil witch.

I had long suspected it with her deceitful ways and wicked intentions, but this night seemed to be proving my suspicions to be true. I stole a glance at my da, disappointed not to see some sort of horror on his face. Was he really that blind? She even looked like a witch tonight, dressed in a long heavy cloak. It surprised me that a woman as scheming as she was believed the silly whispers that the spirits of the dead rose up on the night of Samhain to find new souls to snatch and take back to the netherworld. If that were true, which it most certainly was nae, it was ridiculous to think a cloak could protect her from evil spirits.

I brought my gaze back to her as she had finally ceased talking, and she arched her eyebrows at me, waiting, I knew, for my response to the unbelievable words she'd uttered. Berry stain covered her cheeks, nose, forehead and under her eyes. The tightly pulled hood of her cloak cast strange shadows on her sharp nose and red-stained skin. Had I met her on the stairwell, I would not have recognized her.

"I willnae wed him," I finally replied to my step-mama's

ludicrous words. But my voice was less steady than I'd intended. My da was my protector and yet when I looked to him for assurance, he would not meet my gaze. His avoidance sucked the air from my lungs and left burgeoning panic in its place.

"Ye will," Yennifer replied, shoving her hood back and sitting on the edge of my da's desk. She moved like a ghoul. The thought was uncharitable, but true, nonetheless. She reached out and took my da's hand, causing the heavy material of her cloak to slide up her arm and reveal her skeletal frame. The woman never ate at supper. She was too busy complaining about my sister or me to put food in her mouth. I frowned as she squeezed my da's hand.

It took me a moment of swallowing past the large lump that had lodged in my throat before I could speak. "Da?"

His eyes met mine, finally. I started to release my pent-up breath, but it got stuck again in my chest as remorse darkened his gaze. Sweat instantly dampened my underarms and palms. *Nay. Nay. Nay. This couldnae be happening. Da wouldnae allow this. What had Yennifer said? How had she convinced him to agree to this?*

He began to speak, but I didn't hear him. My thoughts raced, and I tugged on the high bodice of my gown. I couldn't breathe. Why couldn't I breathe? It was winter, but the heat in the solar was oppressive. A hard yank loosened my bodice enough for me to gulp in some air. Da would not betray me. I knew this to my core. He was my protector. He always had been. This was the man who had given a vow on Mama's deathbed to allow me and my newly born sister to choose our husbands when the time came. This was the da who had come immediately to banish the nightmares that tortured me when my mama was no longer living to do so. He was the man who had allowed me to sit on his lap as he held council meetings to plot intricate battle maneuvers even after he wed Yennifer and she had insisted women had no place in council meetings.

I needed to remind him. Speak to him in private. Make him see Yennifer was plotting, always plotting to gain power for the clan that Bran would one day rule when Da died. I shuddered at the thought of my stepbrother ruling us MacLeods. His core was rotten, though Yennifer somehow managed to persuade Da otherwise.

"Freya." Da's gentle tone brought my attention fully back to the moment. His gaze was fastened to mine, still full of remorse. It twisted my insides into knots. "Did ye hear me, lass?"

My words wedged in my throat, so I shook my head as I struggled to push them out. "Might I speak to ye alone?"

"Nay," came Yennifer's sharp reply. "Yer da has already explained things to ye."

I glared at her. "What did ye say to convince him of this?"

"Freya," my da said. My name was a sigh from his lips that made me feel suddenly a burden to him.

The room began to spin, so I squeezed my eyes shut until the movement ceased. When I opened them again, his hand was resting on Yennifer's leg. Unblinking, I stared at that hand, thinking upon what Vanora's and my old nursemaid used to say. *Lust and power were the rulers of all men.* There was my answer. Yennifer has used desire to persuade my da that this wedding was somehow for the best. I just needed to make him see otherwise. To remind him of his given vows. "Ye promised Mama on her deathbed that Vanora and I could choose our husbands, as she chose ye."

The wind whistled outside, filling the silence for a moment. Da removed his hand from Yennifer's leg and rested his palm flat upon his desk. Then he started drumming his fingers. I'd watched him do this many times when he was considering what to say. "Ye do nae need to remind me of my vow to yer mama. But it was given in more certain times, lass. I could nae have anticipated how things would change." His words were like a hand squeezing my throat, cutting off my air once more. He exhaled a long breath and then said, "Ye love our clan?"

He was leading me somewhere. Likely to a conclusion I would not care for. I'd seen him do it to grown men, to powerful lairds his equal. Yet I had no choice but to answer or stand like a petulant child. I was no child, so I nodded.

"I know ye would do anything to protect our clan. Our way of life."

I stared at the fire crackling in the grate. I did not want to answer, yet not answering would get me nowhere. "Aye." I shoved the word out between my clenched teeth. This is how it went. Da asked a series of questions that somehow led whoever was attempting to defy him to acquiesce to his wishes. I was no fool. I would not walk merrily down this path that led to my sacrificing myself in marriage to a man who thought himself my superior. Who believed my sole purpose was to serve him in pleasure and providing heirs. Who would forever dismiss any counsel I might offer, opinion I might have as inconsequential, unknowledgeable.

"Do ye recall why we are warring with Clan MacDonald for control of the channel?"

"Of course," I said. "Whoever controls the channel has all the power in the Highlands because they can leverage the route for trade and military advantage." I felt a twinge of pleasure at my display of political knowledge. See Da? I wanted to say. Ye made the right choice allowing me to sit in the counsel and observe, no matter what Yennifer thinks. Perhaps if I showed him more of my knowledge, more of how I could serve the family other than as a sacrifice at the wedding altar? "That channel is the gateway between the Isle of Skye, Inner Hebrides, and the north-west Highlands." I knew it wasn't normal for a lass to be educated on the intricacies of power struggles between clans, so I wanted Da to see he had made the right choice in educating me.

The slow, self-satisfied smile that turned up Yennifer's berry blackened lips made me stiffen. I'd made a tactical error. Somehow, I'd walked into the trap that Yennifer had set for me. I tried to think through what I'd said, but the past felt jagged, disjointed, a series of flawed images. She was watching us, watching him, and her thin lips curled higher in anticipation.

"Colin MacDonald raided Eilean Donnan a sennight ago, drove yer stepbrother's troops and his warriors—our men—out. He was let into the castle by MacDonald's treacherous bitch sister. MacDonald now has control of the stronghold."

I frowned. "I thought when King Alexander demanded the handfasting between Bran and Laird MacDonald's sister he gave equal control of the channel to both our clans."

"He did," Da said. "But the MacDonald is greedy. He does nae want to share control. He wants his clan to be all powerful."

"So he has attacked Eilean Donnan?"

"Aye, and he killed many of our warriors and drove out the rest."

"That means he broke the treaty between our clans!" I grimaced that my voice had risen despite my effort to control any reaction.

Da nodded, and Yennifer stared at me, her lips pressed into a smirk.

I tried to grasp at the strings of my control, but they were breaking one by one. I inhaled a calming breath, to consider, think, go forward with care, and yet words slipped from between my lips. "Then King Alexander will send troops to aid us and take the stronghold back. He said so!"

"The king has changed his mind, as kings do." Her smug tone made me want to throttle her.

I glanced to Da for confirmation, and he nodded. "But that cannae be so! The king decreed the handfast was for peace and shared control!"

"Aye, I recall what he said, Freya."

"Then he will send troops to aid us!" There were no more strings of control to reach for. I was striding toward panic. "We did nae break the treaty! MacDonald did. And King Alexander vowed he would send troops to aid the wronged clan. We are the wronged clan!" I was huffing with righteousness.

"It seems yer being learned in the political mechanisms of men is a good thing after all," Yennifer said. The satisfaction in her voice pitched my stomach downward. I was a fool. A novice, trying to outwit a seasoned manipulator.

Da, always the peacemaker between Yennifer and myself, cleared his throat and said, "MacDonald has made a claim to the king that Bran broke the treaty first. He says it was our clan who attacked his castle, who nearly burnt Dunscaith to the ground."

"The king cannae believe that of ye, Da. Ye are the most honorable man I ken."

Da gave me the patient smile that I recalled from so many occasions as a child. When he'd told me Mama had died birthing Vanora, but I had not understood it meant I'd never talk to her again, so I'd asked every morning for two sennights to talk to Mama, see Mama. And he'd explain all over again that I could not because death meant never speaking face to face with someone again in this life.

"MacDonald claims his sister overheard Bran planning the attack on Dunscaith," Da said. "And the king says he will nae pick a clan to aid unless he's certain of who is lying and who is truthful. That means he leaves us to battle for control of Eilean Donnan once again and whoever gains control this time, has full control of the channel."

I hitched my brows. "Did Bran do that?"

Da gave me a sharp look and said, "Do nae question Bran's honor, daughter."

I pressed my lips together on reminding my da that Bran had once nearly drowned me. And as a young lad, when he and Yennifer had come to live with us, he had teased smaller boys mercilessly, and he now ruled the MacLeods under him with fear, not respect. Da knew these things, but Da was blind to Bran's faults, because Da was so loyal.

"To do so is dangerous," Yennifer hissed. "Bran answers to yer da as his laird, follows yer da's orders. Do ye see?"

I could not reply for a moment. It was not a stalling tactic. My lips had gone cold with understanding and fear of what it meant. If questions were raised about Bran's honor then people might start to question Da's. Might conclude that mayhap Da had given Bran the order to attack Dunscaith. That would mean Da had entered Bran into the handfasting, into the treaty, never intending to keep it, but likely to make it seem his intentions were honorable so MacDonald would lower his guard. Da would never have done that. I could not say the same about Bran, and yet I had to admit that Bran had never failed to follow Da's leadership. I nodded. "MacDonald is lying."

"Aye," Da said, "but we do nae have the proof. Eilean Donnan is nearly unbreachable, given where it sits. I need a strong ally to aid in taking it back."

"Why can nae Bran wed another then to gain an alliance to aid us in taking Eilean Donnan back?" I demanded. "I assume his handfast with Katherine MacDonald was nae consummated if ye are demanding I wed Donald MacKinnon."

"I am nae demanding, lass. I am asking ye to help me, our clan, because ye love me, yer family, and yer clan. And I am in talks for Bran to wed again, but I do nae ken how long negotiations may take or if we will even be able to come to an agreement, and I need an alliance now. I did nae break the treaty, lass. I want peace. MacDonald wants power. Control. He will use Eilean Donnan to cut off our passage between the island and the mainland. He will do this until we submit to his control or starve. Or he may simply allow enemy vessels to pass through the channel to destroy our home."

I wrapped my arms around my midriff and squeezed myself. My future stretched before me as a hound to my master Donald MacKinnon. My stomach roiled. Finally, I swallowed past the hard knot of doom. Our clan had yet to regain full strength from the years of war with the Mac-Donalds. I knew this. To attack Eilean Donnan and gain it back my da was correct that we would need an ally who believed they'd control the channel with us. And if Donald MacKinnon wed me, Clan MacKinnon would not only gain shared control of the pass, they'd gain a strong political alliance with my clan as well and that could put land in their hands and coin in their coffers.

My head hurt, and I whispered, "Mayhap MacDonald will nae cut off the channel or aid other clans to attack us? We do nae ken for certain." After all, the MacDonalds had not had control of Eilean Donnan until a sennight ago.

"Every indication is that he will," Da answered.

My stomach clenched and a wave of nausea rolled over me. I inhaled a long breath to try to settle my stomach. "And if I refuse?" I asked, each beat of my heart pounding in my ears.

Yennifer and my da exchanged a long look that made my stomach do a flip. "Yer da would nae ever force ye, Freya. But fearing ye may selfishly refuse—"

"Yennifer," Da said, his tone a gentle chastisement.

Yennifer stiffened but gave a curt nod. "Fearing yer wish to nae wed Donald could possibly bring ye to refuse, yer da and I spoke to Vanora. She is willing to wed for the sake of the clan's safety."

Bile rose in my throat as I gaped at my da. *Vanora! He would wed Vanora!* She was a child yet, and every bit as silly as her thirteen summers allowed. More so! It seemed she fancied herself in love with someone new every other sennight. No doubt she now currently fancied herself in love with Donald MacKinnon.

"What did ye say to Vanora?" I demanded, looking between Da and Yennifer. "Did ye weave fanciful tales of Donald's bravery and honor? Did ye tell her how wonderful her life would be?" I pointed at my da, my finger shaking. "Ye would sacrifice Vanora for power?"

"Listen to her insolence!" Yennifer crowed, jerking upright. "I warned ye husband that ye allowed too much opinion from her. That ye needed to control her."

"Enough!" Da slammed his first on the desk causing his wine goblet to rattle and red wine to slosh over the rim to spill crimson drops on the dark wood. Da stood as well, towering above Yennifer.

A deep red rose to the surface of his skin, coloring his cheeks in a splotchy manner and a vein bulged by his right eye. "I'll join ye at the festival in a moment," he said to Yennifer, dismissing her without saying the words.

"As ye wish, husband," she replied with a nod, "but try nae to tarry too long. All the other clans will have arrived, and the ceremony to mark the festival beginning of harvest end can nae be started without ye." With that, Yennifer brushed past me with a cool look, and Da sat on the edge of his desk and faced me.

"I hope ye ken me well enough to realize I would nae ever sacrifice ye or Vanora for power."

A large lump settled in my throat, and I nodded. The reasonable part of me knew this to be true. I knew Da sought to protect us all but did Yennifer? I had no doubts that she'd be willing to sacrifice Vanora and me for power for my da, which meant power for Bran and her, and I greatly feared she knew just how to manipulate my da into thinking it was all for the safety of the clan. But what could I do? If I did not agree to wed Donald, my foolish sister would. I could not allow that. I was Vanora's protector, her older sister. The grief that sometimes hit me for the loss of my mama rose in me and tears slipped out of my eyes.

Da's face softened, and he moved around his desk to cup my cheek with his warm, rough palm. "I love ye daughter. I ken I ask a lot of ye. I ken ye are angry about us speaking with Vanora."

I stared at him, seething on this regard. "That was meant to manipulate me."

"I am sorry. 'Tis nae for power for the sake of power. 'Tis to protect us all."

I needed to leave before I said horrid, hateful things I could never take back. "May I go?"

"Aye, but ye should ken that Donald is on his way here. I'll be announcing the joining of our families tonight. Ye will be properly nice to yer soon to be husband."

I clenched my teeth on railing at Da. Knowing he would gain my consent; he had sent for Donald. It may be for the clan protection, but I felt manipulated. "I will be properly nice," I repeated, purposely leaving off the part about the soon to be husband. If there was a way to get out of this, to protect my clan without sacrificing the rest of my life, I was going to find it.

A skeptical look settled on Da's lined face. "Ye have accepted yer fate?"

I did not believe my fate was to wed Donald, so aye, I'd accepted that. I nodded without a twinge of guilt, only determination.

"Go then," he said, waving a dismissive hand at me.

I rushed out the door and down the torch lined passageway toward the stairs. My footfalls clacked against the wood and echoed in the empty passageway. The solitary sound of my flight made the hairs on the back of my neck prickle and gooseflesh pepper my arms underneath the heavy material of my winter gown. I rubbed at them absently for a moment, feeling silly about my uneasiness. And yet, I gathered fistfuls of my skirts to quicken my steps as if I believed that the ghosts of the lost souls roaming about on this night could snatch me.

I was brave, not cowardly. It was simply my anxiousness to get to the beach and find Vanora and my friends and speak to them. Vanora needed a proper lecture and possibly a threatening about her rash agreement to wed Donald if I would not. And I needed my friends' counsel. I currently had no ideas how to aid my da, my clan, without sacrificing myself, but four minds would be better than one to come up with a solution.

When I reached the top of the stairs, I spotted Vanora walking backward up the stairs holding what looked to be a looking glass. She was flanked on either side by Katreine's sisters. "Vanora!" I bellowed, all my frustration erupting.

"Oh!" Vanora cried out and jerked around. "What are ye doing inside still?"

I marched down the stairs, huffing and fuming. Glaring at her, I said, "The better question is why on earth would ye agree to wed Donald MacKinnon if I willnae?" Her cheeks splotched instantly red, but I was not feeling merciful even in the face of her embarrassment. She opened her mouth, but I cut her off. "Ye have fixed me good this time, Vanora. Unless I can find a way out of it, I will be trapped into wedding Donald to help Da and the clan."

Vanora frowned. "Would ye nae wish to help Da and the clan nae matter what?"

"I—I—the point is, yer agreement has taken away my option nae to agree! To protect ye, ye foolish child—"

"I am nae a child!" she said, stomping her foot and proving my point.

I eyed her foot purposely before drawing my gaze to meet hers once more, and she was now glaring at me. "To protect ye, I had to agree, and now I must come up with a solution to aid Da and the clan that does nae involve my wedding Donald."

"I think he's handsome," Vanora said, her tone ringing with adoration. The twins nodded their agreement.

"A pretty face masks his dark heart!" I bit out. "Do nae agree to anything else without talking to me first." Vanora stared with that stubborn streak which only rose for me.

"Vow it on Mama's grave!"

"Fine!" she huffed. "I vow it."

I started to brush past them, saw the looking glass clutched in Vanora's hand, and paused with the suspicion this somehow boded trouble for her, which meant trouble for me. "Whatever are the three of you doing?" I demanded.

Vanora's cheeks burned redder than they had been. "Euphemia says if we walk backwards holding a looking glass we'll see our next—"

Euphemia clamped a hand over Vanora's mouth and blurted, "Hound we shall own!"

I eyed the known mischief maker. "What are ye really hoping to see?" I asked, sweeping my gaze over the three of them.

"Our next lover," Millicent pronounced with an air of authority I knew to be false.

I hitched an eyebrow. "Hmm…" I said, tapping my lip. "Last I saw Katreine at the king's castle, she said yer mama had left the two of ye home"—I motioned between Millicent and Euphemia—"because she feared ye would embarrass her at court, because ye were still too shy to speak to boys."

"Katreine is a liar," Millicent huffed.

I plucked the looking glass out of Vanora's hands and said, over Vanora, Millicent, and Euphemia's loud protest, "I will tell yer elder sister ye think so when I find her at the festival."

Millicent went pale. I had to bite my cheek not to laugh. After ten years of friendship with Katreine, I knew well her temper. I was certain it was even more forceful with her pesky younger sisters.

"Do nae do that," Millicent said, her tone pleading.

"I'll consider keeping silent, but ye must tell me why

the three of ye were walking backward up the stairs holding this looking glass?"

"To see the man we will wed in the looking glass."

I frowned. "Where did ye get such nonsense?"

"Morgana," Vanora said, exchanging a look with Millicent and Euphemia.

"Morgana is here? At our stronghold?" I could not keep the awe out of my tone. I'd only ever seen the witch in person once, and that was when I'd gotten lost in the dark woods I was not supposed to be in ever without Da and a score of warriors.

All three of them nodded.

"Where?"

"Near the herb trail on the east side of the castle," Vanora replied.

"How do ye ken it was her?"

"She told us," Vanora said. "In exchange for showing her where the herb garden is."

"Whyever would she want to ken where our herb garden is?"

"To save her mama."

"Are ye making this up?" I demanded.

"Nay!" Vanora cried out, crossing her arms over her chest. "She said she'd come for an herb that only grew in our herb garden. In exchange for promising nae to tell anyone she was here; she told us how we could discover who we would wed, if we held up a looking glass and walked backwards up or down the stairs."

"Fine," I replied, a hope forming. "Go on with the three of ye and get to the festival."

"Are ye nae coming?" Vanora asked.

"I'll be along after I put yer looking glass up," I supplied.

"Might I have the looking glass back?" Vanora asked,

eyeing it.

"Absolutely nae," I replied. "Morgana duped ye," I supplied. It could be true, then again, mayhap it wasn't. And I was anxious to see if it wasn't or was. Maybe I would not see Donald, then I could rest easy and enjoy the festival and my friends who I so rarely got to see with their living a good distance from my clan. "Now off with ye before I lose the little bit of patience I have left."

Vanora pressed her lips together, but said, "Come along. She can be horrid to deal with when she's vexed at ye."

I listened to them argue over who was worse to deal with, myself or their sister, as they tromped down the stairs. When I could hear them no more, I held the cracked looking glass up and backed down the steps, taking care to go slow. I got all the way to the bottom of the first flight, and all I'd seen in that looking glass was me. Maybe, I wasn't concentrating hard enough.

I focused all my thoughts on what my husband might look like, whilst also fervently hoping I did not see Donald. I concentrated so hard my head began to ache, and my vision blurred from my intense, unblinking staring. I shuffled backward down the sharp curve in the stairs. Suddenly, two men appeared in my looking glass. Gasping, I jerked around, my foot caught in my gown, and I slid forward off the edge of the step to collide into the tallest of the men. The hard hit knocked the air out of my lungs.

Solid arms wrapped around me for a moment before the man set me to the side of him while righting me. Heat singed my cheeks, neck, and chest as I stared at them. They had on hooded cloaks like Yennifer had worn and had their faces stained with berries just as Yennifer had. I resisted the urge to scoff at two men believing in tales of the dead rising to snatch their souls. My gaze moved from their faces to their cloaks, and I immediately recognized the emblem of a small, simple crown with an armored hand holding a cross that was sewn into the shoulder of their cloaks.

MacDonald warriors!

Panic sent me scrambling backward, feet scrabbling on the wooden planks as I held the looking glass in front of me like a weapon. "I'll scream!" I hissed through clenched teeth, my voice rising to an unbecoming pitch that made the blood rush to my cheeks.

"Ye already are, ye daft lass," said the tallest of the two men.

I glared daggers at him, eyes narrowing into slits. "What are ye doing here?" I demanded, trying to inject as much authority as I could into my shaky voice.

"We're emissaries from MacDonald," the same man supplied, his tone bordering on insolence. I made a derisive noise, a sound caught somewhere between a gasp and a scoff, and he hitched an eyebrow at me, not hiding his amusement. "Ye've a frog caught in yer throat, do ye?" he asked with a lazy drawl that made my skin prickle.

"Yer amusing," I replied, letting my voice convey the sarcasm that my words had not. "I'll ask again. Why are ye here? Has yer lying, thieving, honorless laird come to his senses and sent ye to surrender Eilean Donnan?" The heat in my cheeks intensified as I threw the words at him like stones.

"Nay. My b—" The shorter man gave a shake of his head before continuing. "The lying, thieving, honorless, foolish laird has sent us with an offer for the laird's eldest daughter," the man blurted.

For a moment, my mind went blank, and I was certain that I had misheard. Then clarity returned like the shattering of glass, and I felt the blood drain from my face. My lips parted as did the taller man's for the barest of breaths, before he clamped his mouth shut and visibly clenched and unclenched it, as if uncertain what to say next. My nostrils flared like those of a tethered mare. The notion of being wed to my family's enemy was a horror worse than being wed to Donald himself. "If yer laird wanted to make an offer for my laird's eldest daughter he should have at the verra least sought out the laird's eldest daughter. She's a mind and a mouth of her own, and she is more than capable of answering any question he was to pose to her! But here's a little hint: her answer would be nay, so do nae bother to seek her da out." The disgust in my voice was uncontrolled, shocking even to me. I turned to stalk away, fury propelling my feet, but a hand clamped on my elbow like a steel vise.

Anger burst from me like a thunderclap, and I jerked around, tugging my elbow free of the tall man's grip. "How dare ye touch me!" I spat, my voice reaching a shrillness that echoed in the hall like a scream.

The man gave me a steely look and slowly peeled back his fingers one by one. "Beg pardon." How was it possible to beg someone's pardon with the right words yet convey the message that you were not sorry at all? I opened my mouth to hurl an insult, but he spoke. "I simply wished to ken if ye are the laird's eldest daughter?"

"Do ye think if I was the daughter of the laird I'd be stuck inside during this festival cleaning that spoiled woman's bedchamber?" I was amazed how easily I'd thought of the lie and spit it out. But I had no intention of standing here any longer. My da would not accept this envoy's offer. That much I knew. It was too late for that. The MacDonalds had broken the treaty, and Da would not enter one with them again. Without waiting for a reply, I turned away, not caring what the stranger might have said. All I cared about was finding my friends and getting their counsel on how I could possibly avoid wedding Donald.

It wasn't until I stepped into the inner courtyard, breathless from the confrontation, that I realized I was still clutching the looking glass, my knuckles white and tight around its polished frame. In an explosion of anger, I hurled it into the darkening woods, its gleam catching the last breath of dusk before disappearing into the tangled night. I started away but stopped dead with a sharp intake of breath.

What had I done? In one reckless moment, I'd thrown away the only thing my sister possessed of our mama's! I turned back, my heart drumming a frantic beat. The courtyard lay ghostly and bare, shadows stretching ominously across the stone. And then a woman appeared from thin air, seeming to float just above the ground, holding Vanora's looking glass.

"Morgana," I murmured, the witch's name falling from my lips as gooseflesh prickled along my arms.

The witch's silvery purple eyes shone at me from across the courtyard. Her presence was spectral, eerie in the sepulchral light. "Ye lost this," she said, a smirk twisting her lips.

"Ye lied to my sister and her friends," I flung out, each word a desperate volley to mask my own fear. I was vexed that all I'd seen in the looking glass was the two envoys, and I needed to know the truth. Morgana's eyes turned hard; sharp, twin daggers aimed at my heart. I backed up a step, realizing too late the mistake I'd made in calling someone like her a liar.

She snapped her fingers with a commanding flick, and my hand opened without my doing it, the looking glass flew straight into my palm, my fingers closing around it like a trap. I could feel my eyes widen with shock, my heart drumming, wild and untamed, as if it might escape my chest. "I do nae lie," Morgana said. Her voice was a low jagged edge, each word jabbing me with all the weight of her wrath. "Those words were nae for ye, the looking glass is nae yers—'tis yer sister's."

Her disdainful sneer made me feel small, a scolded child whose complaint had been dismissed. Yet still, something brash made me press Morgana, a defiance borne of desperation. "I saw two men in the looking glass. Envoys from the MacDonald laird. I ken I will nae wed those men. I wish to see who I'll wed."

"Do nae wish to see the future, Freya MacLeod." Her tone was a warning like the thunder before a great storm. "Such a gift is a burden." With that, she waved her hands, and I was forcefully shoved back from her by the air. "Go now," she said, whipping her hand in a circle, so that my body was turned away from her. "I have many herbs to find, and they are hiding from me."

The wind pushed me across the pebbled stones so that I slid more than walked. I held my breath, heart racing, but as I reached the end of the path the wind was suddenly gone. Fearful to turn back, I started toward my friends once more, my steps quick and earnest. They were my only hope, the only faces I could trust, unless some magical solution fell into my lap and offered a relief that seemed more distant and impossible by the moment.

Chapter Two – Colin

"*D*o ye think that was the laird's eldest daughter?" Connor asked beside me.

I dragged my attention from the shadowy passageway the lass had stalked down and glared at my younger brother. He shifted from foot to foot; a sure sign Connor already realized he'd made a grave error by almost revealing who we were. Despite my telling him more times than I could recall to think before he spoke, he continued to allow his temper to rule his tongue. "Aye, I do, ye clot-heid," I grumbled and glanced back down the passageway once more.

"She lied," Connor said, half-snarling.

"Aye. It runs in her family." The lass had perfectly fit the description of Freya MacLeod that Katherine had gathered in her time with Bran. Just saying the man's name enraged me. This clan had cost me all I was willing to pay, and yet my da's words as he lay dying in my arms rang in my head now. *Try for peace until ye see for certain there is nae another option. War means lives lost. Ye will be laird. Yer duty is to protect our clan. Save their lives.* This was my last attempt. Too many that I loved had been lost to this war.

"Well, I did nae think the day would come I'd agree with anything a MacLeod would say, but Katherine told us the MacLeod warriors described Freya MacLeod as having the most compelling eyes of any lass," Connor said, "and they were right."

He stared at me, waiting I assumed for me to agree. "I could nae tell ye what her eyes looked like," I offered with a shrug.

"Liar," Connor responded. "Ye're one of the most observant men I know."

"I do nae care about the lass's eyes. She's a means to peace. 'Tis all." Freya MacLeod's eyes were a strange combination of brown, gold, and light green. I did not like that I could recall that, and I cleared my throat, trying to rid myself of the heavy guilt.

"Ye ken Magy would have laughed at ye for feeling as if agreeing a lass had lovely eyes made ye disloyal to her."

I nodded, while staring at the flash of pity in my brother's eyes. The knot in my throat was immediate and familiar. I got it every time I talked of Magy, but that was better than the consuming rage that had nearly destroyed me. I still had the rage, but it had become a weapon I wielded against others, not myself. "I ken it," I finally answered, when I was certain my voice would not reveal a hint of the sadness that was my constant companion. "She did nae have a jealous bone in her body," I added, even as her face danced before my vision. She'd been dead for three summers, another casualty of the war with the MacLeods, but her image in my mind was still clear, though not as bright as it had been, and that worried me. Was I forgetting little details about her when I'd vowed at her grave that I'd never forget a thing about her, never replace her, never love another?

"We should have just snatched the lass and been done with it."

I scowled at Connor until he shifted once more. "I want to annihilate all the MacLeods as much as ye, brother. More so, but I must try for peace one more time."

"Why?" he demanded, the word bit out.

"Because I am laird. Because we have lost Da, Mama, Magy, and so many others to this war. And war brings death. Because I promised Da I would try every avenue I could think of for peace until I'm certain there's nae another way."

"Mark me, brother," Connor said. "There's nae another way. Do ye honestly think Laird MacLeod will join in another alliance with ye when they broke the first one?" No, no I didn't, and I opened my mouth to say as much, but Connor spoke before I could. "I think they made that alliance keening they would break it."

"I'm nae sure." I had thought about this a great deal. "And unless I am certain, I have to try for peace and make the offer."

Connor's nostrils flared. "Do nae tell me Laird MacLeod did nae ken his stepson was going to attack Dunscaith."

"I did nae tell ye that," I said. "I havenae once uttered that in the dozens of times we've discussed it since our stronghold was attacked and half burned. I told ye I am nae certain, but I lean toward the fact that Bran did nae ever intend to keep the alliance. I believe he intended to gain a foothold in Eilean Donnan by pretending he would honor the alliance. Whether Laird MacLeod kenned of his stepson's intentions is another matter. If I enter an alliance again, I will be the one who resides in Eilean Donnan, and nae the MacLeods, so we will be the ones who have the warriors to control the channel there. That will have to be part of the alliance, and I will be watchful and careful."

Connor shoved a hand through his hair even as he glanced around. His attention came slowly back to me. "I'm sorry, brother. Being amidst our enemies makes me tense."

"I understand," I said.

"Ye do nae fear someone will recognize us?"

"Nay." I motioned Connor to follow me up the stairs where the guard below had told us we could find Mac-Leod's solar.

"Their smugness prevents them from believing we're bold enough to walk into their stronghold, just as I told ye it would. Besides that, our faces are stained, and we have on the cloaks, and we will stick to the plan of pretending to be envoys from the laird of our clan."

"Ye."

I nodded. "Aye. Me."

"And when MacLeod rejects the offer?"

"Simple," I replied. "We snatch the lass Freya. I will use her as a means to end this war. If he wants his beloved daughter returned, he'll need to confess to his and his stepson attacking Dunscaith, so the king will support us. And allow us to rule the channel on our own."

"We should just snatch her," Connor said, shaking his head. "This other way, this offer of marriage for peace, is too much trouble. Ye do nae even want to wed again!"

"If I could think of another way to gain an alliance without gaining a wife, I would." I didn't want any woman but Magy, and she was beyond my reach forever. "And I will try the honorable way first."

"Honor be damned," Connor growled. "MacLeod is nae honorable."

"I must be able to live with what I've done, brother, and know I tried for peace in all ways, before I snatch a lass and use her."

Connor paused at the top of the stairs and faced me. "What if he does nae agree to the terms of the confession?"

"What da would nae do all he could to save his daughter?"

"Ye will nae kill her," Connor said. "Ye're nae a murderer."

"Nay, I'm nae like the MacLeods," I said, thinking once more of Magy. "I do nae kill innocent women. But I will keep her at our stronghold."

"You would keep a lass against her will forever?"

"I do nae imagine the lass will wish to return home to a da who refused to give the confession to get her back."

Connor snorted. "I do nae imagine that spitfire lass we just met will believe ye."

"I do nae imagine I care."

"Do ye think her pleasing to the eye?"

The abrupt change in topic didn't surprise me. Connor had a habit of jumping around from topic to topic with no warning.

"I did nae take note."

Amusement trickled across his features. "Liar."

I was lying. The lass was pleasing. More than pleasing. Some might say bonny with the long fiery hair and the light, interesting color eyes. And she was quick-witted.

"Well, if by some strange gift of the gods MacLeod does agree to another alliance and to wedding his daughter to ye, at least she will be pleasing to bed."

"It would be a duty, done once, to consummate our union. Nae anything more."

Connor shook his head. "Ye do nae make sense to me."

"That's because ye have nae ever felt for a woman as I did Magy."

"I loved Magy as a sister," Connor protested. "Ye ken I did."

"'Tis nae the same, but I ken."

Connor got a thoughtful expression for a moment. "I can nae imagine being with one woman, bedding only one woman, the rest of my days."

I chuckled. "And that, brother, is why ye should nae ever take a wife," I said as we reached the top of the stairs.

"We are in agreement," he said. "Now, let us go waste our breaths and time, *John*." He winked.

"Trying for peace one last time before snatching a lass is not a waste of anything, *Doughall*," I said, using his fake name I'd given him.

A hard knock later, and a bellow to enter from within, found Connor and me standing in front of Laird MacLeod— the man who had led the battles that killed my mother, my father, and my wife. My blood roared instantly in my ears, and I had to struggle against curling my hands into fists. It was a good thing the guards had taken our swords for the meeting with MacLeod. I feared if I'd had mine upon me now, I would have plunged it into his heart.

I forced myself to bow, as an emissary would, though the gesture cramped my stomach with distaste. Connor followed suit as MacLeod watched us with narrowed eyes. He did not offer us a seat, and the upturned slight snarl of his lips told me there would be no peace this day. But I would see it through. "What is it that yer laird wants? Has he come to his senses and decided to surrender the castle?"

I clenched and unclenched my teeth until I felt I had control of my temper. "Nay. He wishes for peace, and he extends an offer of another alliance through a marriage of himself and yer eldest daughter. Ye say it was nae yer warriors who attacked Dunscaith, so ye should want peace as well."

"Nae with a man who broke the treaty."

"He believed ye to have broken it first." They had. I knew they had, given what Katherine had overheard. If only there was a way to prove it.

"Well, he was wrong. Ye can relay to yer laird," MacLeod said, sneering the word laird, "that Eilean Donnan will nae be his holding once my daughter weds Donald MacKinnon, and we take the castle and lands together. Then we will rule the channel, and I will wipe his name, yer clan, from history." I was positive that had been the man's intentions all along.

That was ill news about the impending wedding of Freya MacLeod and Donald Mackinnon. That would align the two most powerful clans in the Highlands against me. I could wed another, but then we were back to war, with two more clans dragged into it. I had to stop the alliance. I knew no other way than to snatch the lass as I had planned. There were no avenues for peace left. What I had to do filled my mouth with sour distaste. I considered myself honorable, and kidnapping a lass was a dishonorable action. But I was cornered with enemies closing in, and I was unwilling to lose another person I loved, another person I was responsible for, to this war.

Chapter Three – Freya

I paused halfway down the seagate stairs and stared through the white mist that now covered the twilight sky. My heart thumped from my hurried steps, and my breath came in short gasps. Each exhalation sent a little white puff from my lips. I swept my gaze over the dozens of tents below me on the beach, through the crowds of revelers and over bonfires. My vantage point was high, but I did not see my friends. I did smell something delicious, though. The savory scent of roasted meat drifted to me making my stomach growl and mouth water.

I was just about to give up the cause and descend into the merry chaos, when I spotted Katreine, Elena, and Muireall huddled together on a log near the lapping waters of Dunvegan Loch. They were gathered in a circle around a woman who rested on her haunches beside a fire. Orange flames slashed through the shadows of the looming night. The woman's long white hair flowed down her back and over her shoulders to graze the ground on either side of her. Something about the scene made my scalp prickle, but I shook off the odd sensation. It was simply lingering wariness from my encounter with Morgana. I wound carefully down the narrow steps toward the beach, into the throng of people, weaving in and out, making greetings, but not stopping to talk. I did pause at a fire pit to help myself to a stick with chunks of perfectly cooked rabbit meat skewered on it. Food would help me think better how to solve my problem.

"Thanks, Egrid," I said to the plump head of the kitchens, blew her a kiss, and continued toward my friends.

Their excited faces and enthusiastic waving pushed away my worry for a moment and warmed me. Everything was going to be fine. They'd know what to do. If not, surely the four of us could think of a solution together. They were scooting over to make room for me as I reached them. I sat down beside Katreine, and she plucked a chunk of the rabbit meat off my stick. She paused, the meat near her lips, leaned toward me and whispered, "'Tis a Summer Walker." She motioned to the woman in the center of the circle. "She claims she travelled through the Dark Forest alone and came upon Morgana." A tap came on my shoulder, and I leaned back to see Elena and Muireall grinning at me from the other side of Katreine.

"We missed ye!" Elena said in a low tone. Nevertheless, a chorus of people hushed her.

"Same," I whispered and then turned my attention to the Summer Walker. Only a Summer Walker would be brave enough to move through the Dark Forest unaccompanied, and foolish children—like I had once been—and well, I suppose a desperate person might. Was it a Summer Walker's hard life that made them brave? I liked to think of myself as more fearless than other women, but I had not faced the sorts of hardship a woman without a true home or clan to protect her had. I imagined that sort of life called for a special kind of bravery, and I found myself leaning in to hear what the woman had to say. I could use some advice on bravery.

"As I was saying before the latest guest joined us—"

"That's nae any guest. That's the laird's eldest daughter,

who will soon belong to me."

Donald's nasally voice made me rigid. With a hefty amount of dread, I drew my gaze to him. He stood with half a dozen of his men on the outside of the circle, behind a log. He gave me a smug look that made my insides tangle into knots. There stood the man who would have the ability to control me, unless I found an acceptable solution quickly.

"Ye can nae own another truly," the Summer Walker said.

Donald laughed. "Of course, ye can, woman. 'Tis the law of man's land."

Every word out of Donald's mouth increased my certainty that I could never be his wife.

"Freya, come to greet me!" he demanded.

Greet him? I glared at him. Our impending union hadn't even been announced yet, and if I could help it, it never would be. "I'm nae yers yet, Donald," I said, through clenched teeth. "And ye're being rude. We were in the middle of listening to a tale, so go on with ye. I will see ye later." *Or not.*

"Ye'll nae be talking to me like that when we're wed," he growled.

"If ye say so," I bit out, knowing full well when my insolent behavior reached my da's ears, I'd likely get a sharp lecture and be required to beg forgiveness, but I'd take my chances. Chuckling erupted amongst Donald's friends, turning his face red, and sending him stomping away.

Beside me, Katreine poked me in the side. I knew before I turned my head her way, that all three of my friends would be gaping at me, which they were. "We'll discuss it later," I whispered, knowing full well they wanted an accounting of whether I was to wed Donald. "Please continue your story," I said to the Summer Walker who gave me a nod.

"As I was saying, I passed through the Dark Forest a sennight ago, and there I did see Morgana at the Twisted Tree of Life—"

"She lives there!" someone called out.

"In an underground cave," someone else in the group inserted. "With her mama, the red witch!"

"Shh!" I said, wanting to hear the rest of the story. Something about it, stirred an odd excitement in me.

The Summer Walker smiled gratefully at me. I knew from previous years with others of her kind, she would likely offer one tale and then ask for coin to offer another. That's how these travelers survived. Some sold wares, others sold their skills, and the ability to weave a convincing tale was a skill like any other. Perhaps a greater one since so few people could do it.

"There I did see her with her magic goblet of gold, which she set to a crooked man's mouth. He made a wish, drank from the goblet, and his spine straightened right before my eyes," the Summer Walker exclaimed.

Laughter erupted around the circle and people stood. "Ye need to work on yer story telling skills," a man called out, tossing a chunk of bread at the Summer Walker before he turned and left. One by one people departed with various discouraging comments and having tossed things at the woman. A half-eaten meat stick. A smooshed mince pie. A piece of thread. It was not long before Katreine, Elena, Murieall, and I were the only ones left. The poor Summer Walker looked as if she were on the verge of tears, so I fished in the inner pocket of my gown, touched on the single coin in there, and rose.

"Is that yer first time making up a tale?" I asked in a gentle tone.

"I did nae make the tale up," she said on a sigh as she

took the coin. "Do ye see my hair?"

I nodded.

"'Twas the color of the sun afore the ban-druidh Morgana turned it white for spying on her."

My lips parted in surprise. Beside me, Katreine, Elena, and Murieall gasped. "Ye were nae making up a tale," I blurted.

"Nay, I was nae. I truly did come upon Morgana in the Dark Woods at her home when I was traveling through the woods on the way here for the Samhain festival two nights ago."

"And ye really saw her straighten a man's spine?" Elena asked. The tremor in her voice and excitement on her face made me think she might have her own problems she needed to fix.

"Aye," the traveler said while nodding. "I heard him beg a wish of her, and she said she was nae in the habit of granting wishes for men unhappy with their lot. Then he pulled out a ring and said that his mama had saved Morgana from drowning when she was younger, and Morgana's own mama had given her prized ring to his mama for the deed with the instructions that when the woman, or her unborn child who would then be grown, was ready for her wish, they were to return the ring in exchange for their heart's desire. The man's mama had departed the earth, and the man's one wish was to be able to stand up straight. Morgana placed her hands on either side of the man's face, determined he was telling the truth, then disappeared into her cave. When she returned, she was holding a glowing goblet. She dipped it in the fairy pool and then told him to drink from it, and that his wish would become his reality."

My heart raced as I listened to the Summer Walker. Her words drifted on the breeze, swelling in my ears, filling my head and heart like a melody I had hoped to hear: a sign that my deepest desire, my chance to wed for love, was not lost. But only if I dared. Only if I could drink from Morgana's magical goblet. The goblet! Morgana would never allow me to touch it. I would have to steal a drink from it without her knowing.

Then my wish could come to pass. But Morgana wasn't in her cave. She was here, in the gardens, searching for an herb to save her mama. If I found the goblet, brimming with its enchantment, and drank before she returned home, she'd never know it had been used. The plan seemed perfect, as perfect as the tale the Summer Walker had spun. But there was one more problem: Morgana's mother. She could be there, and she was a witch just as Morgana was. I had no notion if she was ill, injured, or if Morgana had some vision of a sickness to come. I had to have help if I was to dare it. I knew just whom to ask—or rather, which three people to ask—for help.

Chapter Four - Freya

y plan to "borrow" the magical goblet was likely unwise, but desperate as I was, I was willing to take a risk. I was counting on my friends either to come up with a new strategy with me or risk getting themselves into trouble by aiding me. It was a big thing to ask of them, but again, I was desperate. I strode as fast as I could through the thick crowd of people on the beach, with Katreine, Elena, and Murieall on my heels. I was the tallest of our group, so I had a natural lead.

"Freya!" Elena huffed as we reached the edge of the woods that touched one side of my home. These were the woods that led to the Dark Forest, that led to Morgana's home, that led to the glowing goblet that had to save me from wedding Donald. "Freya!" Elena bit out again, but this time, her loud voice caused several people to turn their attention our way.

I whipped around to face my friends, and Elena, who was the closest behind me, stopped just in time not to barrel into me. "I promise I'll explain as soon as we're out of earshot," I said, pitching my voice low.

All three of them nodded, much to my relief. If I had been them, and one of them had abruptly said, "follow me" right after the Summer Walker had told us of the magical goblet, and then they had charged off without any explanation, I would have demanded one before leaving all the festivities behind that I had traveled so far to come to. Then again, I thought, as I turned around and doubled my pace toward the woods, maybe I wouldn't have. Maybe, I would have followed any of them without question, just as they were doing for me. That's what years of true friendship brought—unwavering loyalty.

When I got to the edge of the woods, I finally felt like I could stop, like I could breathe. Donald had likely gone straight to my da to complain about my rudeness, so I needed to seek out the goblet before my da sought me out. If I was to be punished by being confined to my room, the chance to "borrow" Morgana's goblet would be gone. It wasn't as if I could show up at the ban-druidh's home and ask to use the goblet to get my wish. I'd heard what Morgana had said to the man with the crooked spine before he had produced the ring given to his mama. I had no such favor to leverage, and I had no doubt she'd be unwilling to grant me my wish.

"All right, Freya," Elena, the most outspoken of us, said, "clearly something has occurred since last we saw ye at the king's court."

I turned toward my friends and told them quickly of all that had transpired with Yennifer and my da. When I was done, they looked almost comical to me with their gaping mouths.

"Vanora is just as foolish as my sisters!" Katreine cried out.

"Aye," I agreed.

"And Yennifer surely convinced yer da to wed ye off and use Vanora to manipulate you," Elena added.

"Yer da has been bewitched!" Murieall added.

Gratitude for their support warmed me, and I started to nod, but I paused as an unwanted truth invaded my head.

"I'm positive it was Yennifer's idea to ask Vanora to wed Donald if I would nae," I said, my thoughts turning. "She knows I would die for my sister." My friends nodded. "The problem is," I said, forcing myself to face the truth, "my da would nae have asked me to wed Donald if he were nae desperate to protect the clan. He must make an alliance to win the war against the MacDonalds. He must take back Eilean Donnan, so they do nae cut off the sea passage to us."

"Surely, there is a way to win the war without yer having to wed Donald," Katreine said.

I nodded as hope made my pulse tick up. "I might have thought of a way."

"What are ye going to do?" Murieall asked. She was the most cautious of us, so if anyone was going to object to my plan, it would be her.

I took a deep breath, prepared to beg for her help, unless one of them had a better idea. "I'm going into the Dark Woods—"

Murieall's eyes grew wide with her dismay. "There are all sorts of ruffians in the Dark Woods," she said. "I do nae see how—"

"God's blood, Murieall!" Katreine, who didn't have a trace of caution in her body, protested. "Let Freya speak. I imagine she is going to tell us what she's intending us to do."

"Us?" Murieall squeaked.

"Aye," I said. "I need yer aid."

"What do ye need, Freya?" Elena asked.

"Well, ye all heard the Summer Walker's tale about the goblet."

"Ye're going to steal the goblet!" Katreine exclaimed.

"Nae steal," I protested. "I'm going to borrow it. I'll

return it after I drink from it and get my wish."

"Morgana will turn ye to stone if she catches ye!" Murieall cried out.

I scowled at her. "Morgana will nae catch us, if we hurry. She's here at the castle."

"Why do ye keep saying us?" Murieall's hand clasped her neck, as if she were imagining it in a noose, likely from getting in trouble for going into the Dark Woods with me. They were forbidden to us all, so it made sense. Thieves and worse dwelled in those woods and had been known to pillage and plunder, but I didn't plan to linger. The Fairy Pools and Twisted Tree of Life were on the edge of the woods.

"I need ye to keep a lookout for Morgana, and if her mother is at their home, I'll need someone to draw her out if need be, so I can borrow the goblet."

"Ye want us to trick a ban-druidh!" Murieall exclaimed.

"Stop blabbering like a bairn!" Elena said, her tone gruff. "I'll gladly aid ye, Freya."

I smiled gratefully and gave her a quick hug. "Thank ye."

She nodded. "I've my own wish I'd like to make."

"Ye do?" I asked, surprised.

"Aye. I wish to have the power to destroy the clan that killed my family," she said, her tone hard and unforgiving. A pang of pity went through me. I reached out and squeezed her hand.

"Ye mean we could also drink from the magical goblet if we aid ye?" Murieall asked.

I hadn't thought about that possibility until this moment, but I didn't see why not. "Aye. We should all get a wish. What's yers?" I asked Murieall.

"My mother has the lung disease," she whispered, tears

filling her eyes. "I want to wish for her life to be spared."

"Oh, Murieall!" I cried out, my heart twisting. I pulled her into a hug. "Ye'll get the first wish. Why did I nae ken this?"

"She took ill after I saw ye at court."

"Katreine, will ye go with us?" I asked.

"Well, I'm nae going to be left back here at the festival to make excuses for the lot of ye. I'm a horrid liar, and if anyone came looking for ye, I'd certainly get ye in trouble. And I, well, I do have a wish," she said, color flooding her cheeks.

"What is it?" Elena asked.

"I wish I were older than Millisandre."

I frowned. "Why do ye wish to be older than yer sister?"

"Because she is to wed Alec."

"Ye still think ye love Alec Buchanan?" Elena asked.

"I do love Alec, and the only reason he's chosen Millisandre as his future wife and nae me is because, as the eldest, my sister, will inherit our home when Da passes. 'Tis nae fair. If I was the eldest, I would inherit the castle, and then Alec would have chosen me as his wife."

I opened my mouth to argue, but Elena gave me a shake of her head. She was probably right. Even if I had the time to try to convince Katreine that if Alec really loved her then whether she inherited a castle or not would not matter, I doubted I could convince her of that. "Then ye shall drink from the goblet as well," I said. "But we must make haste. I do nae ken how long Morgana is going to linger in the garden, though she did say she searched for herbs hiding from her."

"Then, let us go," Elena said.

The woods from my home to the Dark Woods was not dense and the late afternoon light filtered in. The ground was flat and easy to traverse, and the temperature was not too cold, yet still I had a foreboding. "Is this foolish?" I asked, as I led the way hand and hand with Elena along the winding trail.

"Most definitely," Elena said, "but I would do just about anything to destroy the Campbells, and if I had the ability to read minds—"

"Oh, I would nae want the power to read minds," Katreine said, her tone ominous.

"Well, I'd nae want to get older," Elena snapped.

"I only want to get two summers older," Katreine shot back. "I'm going to be verra specific when I wish."

"Do ye really think we'll get these wishes?" Murieall asked, the hope in her voice so keen that I paused and turned to smile at her.

"I do. The crooked man got his." Above us, a large flock of birds suddenly burst into flight, their wings flapping in a frenzy, abandoning the canopy of trees like they were chased by some unseen force. A ghostly presence seemed to haunt the forest, and the idea that this creature might already be prowling, while we were all weaponless, urged me to quicken my pace. "Hurry," I bade the group, and we rushed to the bridge that led from my clan's land to the unclaimed expanse of the Dark Woods. We raced across the rickety, weathered bridge, each step louder than the last, and entered the tangled, eerie brush of the woods. Over-head trees loomed thick and oppressive, sucking away the light and swallowing us in shadows. All I could see were ghostly outlines, the skeletal shapes of the trees, and the faint figures of my friends swallowed in a sudden mist. The temperature plummeted, and biting cold cut through the air, a chill that rattled me. Silence descended on the woods like an unseen fog, a silence that spoke of absences—as if creatures dare not exist here, as if life itself was banished.

"I'm scared," Katreine whispered, grabbing at the back of my gown. I glanced over my shoulder to find her and Murieall huddled together with Murieall holding onto the back of Elena's gown.

"Do any of ye have a weapon?" I asked, cursing myself for the foolishness of not bringing one.

"I've my dagger," Elena said. She stopped, tugged up her skirts, and unsheathed the dagger that I knew her older brother had given her. She gripped it, holding it high as we continued to walk along the trail which grew narrow, steep, and winding.

"Freya, do ye ken the way?" Katreine asked from behind me.

"Oh, aye," I said, trying to sound braver than I was currently feeling. "My da takes us through the Dark Woods on the way to the king's court." Of course, Da always traveled with at least three dozen armed warriors, so we'd never met trouble, but I kept that tidbit of information to myself.

The trees lining the edges of the narrow path grew increasingly thick and dense, walling us in with their dark trunks, creating a nearly impenetrable barrier on either side. Branches laced themselves overhead, twisting and tangling, forming a canopy that dipped low enough to scrape at us as we passed. They seemed insidious in purpose, almost as though they wished to halt our progress and trap us here. I could tell by the clenched, painful grip of Elena's hand in mine that I was not the only one who felt this, and her quickened breath had the timbre of unease. The ground beneath our feet changed treacherously, too. What had been a smooth trail turned rough and uncertain, becoming a network of gnarled and twisted vines that snaked back and forth, looping over the path like treacherous serpents eager to trip us. Thick roots jutted up from the earth, ripping open the ground with raw force and adding to the entanglement.

I stumbled over them, barely catching myself, and then a moment later, Elena, too, tripped, my grasp on her hand the only thing that kept her from falling. The cold bit deeper with every step, and our breath came raggedly. Our hands, twined together, grew cold as stone, the chill seeping deep into our bones until we could barely feel each other's touch. Shadows deepened around us, and I felt a hollow stirring in my chest, a flicker of something like fear. Elena's voice came in a whisper, almost swallowed by the darkening air.

"I do nae like this place," she said, her words tinged with worry and a shivering disbelief. White mist curled from her lips in perfect circles, swirling into the night air like tiny ghosts. I had never seen anything quite like it, and my breath froze in astonishment.

"I thought the Fairy Pools were supposed to be a place of beauty near yer home," Katreine said.

"Aye, they are," I answered. "That's the main fae pool where all the fae now live. This fae pool, near the bandruhids Twisted Tree of Fate, was home to the first fae our clan ever knew of."

"What happened to her?" Elena asked.

"Well, according to legend, she fell in love with the first laird of our clan and her da, the fae king, was powerfully vexed, because it was a forbidden love. Eventually, she convinced her da to allow her to wed the MacLeod laird, but permission was only granted on the condition that she had to return to the land of the fairies after twenty years with her human husband. When twenty years came and she had to go, she gave a flag to her husband."

"My mama told me this legend," Murieall said. "Ye all call it the Fairy Flag."

"Aye," I said, climbing the hill that led to Morgana's cave. "The fae told our laird that if a great time of desperate need came to our clan, if he waved the flag, help would arrive—but thrice could he do this. She warned that on the third waving, either the clan would have total victory over their enemies or would be destroyed."

"How many times has the flag been waved?" Elena asked.

"Nae any yet," I answered, then looking down the trail, I realized we'd come to the cave. Beyond it, was the fairy pool where we would dip the goblet. "We've arrived," I said, my heart pounding. "Katreine and Murieall, ye two stay here and stand guard. If ye see anyone approaching, give a loud whistle. Ye can whistle, aye?"

"Aye," said Murieall.

I nodded, wiping my suddenly damp palms against my skirts. "If we do nae come back—"

"Do nae say such a thing," Katreine hissed.

"Well, if we do nae, tell my da where we went. I hate to ask it of ye—"

"We'll do it, but ye are coming back," Katreine said.

A moment later, Elena and I approached the cave as quietly as we possibly could, barefoot, trying to not even stir a leaf or crack a stick. We'd worked so hard to get this far, and I knew if we were caught now, it was over; I'd never get this chance again. We sneaked upon the entrance, and I dropped to my hands and knees to peer inside. I could see straight into the cave where that witch Morgana and her mama lived, where we'd heard they kept the one thing I needed to change my life. I squinted my eyes to be sure it was true. I could hardly believe our luck. The cave was completely empty. I waved Elena forward and we both ducked inside. In the center of the cave was a small table cluttered with all manner of tiny bottles, herbs, twine, roots—too many things for my mind to sort through, but the one thing I did immediately fix my gaze upon was the golden goblet. That had to be it, though this goblet was not glowing as I'd been told it would.

"Do ye see it?" I asked Elena.

"Aye," she whispered as I had. "Do ye think it's a trick?"

It felt like one. I'd been certain we'd encounter obstacles, but we had not. I looked around the small cave. How could two witches possibly live here? There were no beds that I could see, no chairs to sit upon, no wardrobes for clothes, nothing that made a place a home. There was a fire on the far side of the cave that appeared to be built into the actual stone, and as I took the scene in, I realized there were a set of bloody footprints on the floor of the cave. That foreboding I'd felt earlier stirred again sending shafts of ice through my veins to my heart. "Something seems amiss," I whispered, motioning toward the floor and the bloody footprints.

"Let us make haste," Elena returned, the fear in her tone matching the unease coursing through my body. I made a dash for the table, grabbed the goblet, and gasped as it immediately began to glow.

"Elena!" I said, excitement now running stronger through me than fear.

"I see!" Elena answered, gripped me by the hand and dragged me toward the cave exit. I was entranced by the glowing goblet and the possibility of changing the course of my life. "We've got it!" I shouted, forgetting the need to be quiet.

Elena shushed me, but it was too late. I'd unleashed

noise. Birds squawked overhead. An owl hooted from somewhere, and Katreine bellowed, "Coming!" Within a breath, she and Murieall appeared, racing down the trail, skirts in fists, glancing behind them as they ran. They stopped in front of Elena and me, both gawking open-mouthed at the goblet.

"There's bloody footprints inside the cave," Elena said, and the words broke through whatever momentary trance gaining the goblet had cast upon me.

"Come on!" I rushed out, swiveling toward the trail that led to the fairy pool and taking off without waiting for a reply. We had come this far, and I did not intend to lose my chance to make my wish. I ran up the trail, which twisted to the right then spiraled to the left before straightening out to climb steeply upward. On either side of the path, the normal trees of the forest gave way to thick thorn bushes that ripped and clawed at the wool of my skirts as I ran. The roots and vines underfoot rose from the ground with ancient fingers and caused me to trip several times, but I was not the only one. Behind me came declarations of dismay, but I did not stop. I could not.

As I ran, the rough ground beneath my feet grated against the soles of my shoes, wooden branches and tangled roots poking and prodding. The air was thick with the scent of damp earth and fresh rain, the musty smell of old tree bark and the sharp scent of crushed thorns from the bushes. I pushed myself faster and harder until my side pinched sickeningly from my pace and my blood pounded in my heart, my neck and my head. Finally, I reached the end of the trail, and the woods parted to a rolling glen where bright moonlight shone down in a dazzling shimmering display. I blinked in shock. We had been travelling longer than I'd realized. The breeze carried a mist toward me to dampen my face and rushing water buzzed in my ears. I'd seen the fairy pool once before, but as I ran toward it, I was awed all over again by how high it was. The waterfall that dumped into the pool seemed to be coming from the heavens themselves.

I didn't stop, until I stood in front of the bottom of the fall at the pool. Dropping to my knees, I dipped the glowing goblet into the frigid waters, filled it up, and started to bring it to my lips when I remembered my promise to Murieall to allow her to drink first. "Here," I said, starting to extend it toward her, but she pushed the goblet back to me.

"Ye drink first," she said, nibbling on her lip.

Ah, she was scared and wanted to see what might happen to me. I didn't take offense. I raised the goblet to my lips and concentrated on the wish that I'd been crafting while we walked to the witch's cave. I wished to see my future, so I could manipulate it to be able to marry for love and know the man I wed loved me in return. Liquid filled my mouth as I made my wish. I swallowed it down, coldness numbing my tongue, coating my throat, and making an icy path to my belly. When I was done, I passed the goblet to Elena who did exactly as I had. Katreine came next and finally Murieall. Just as Murieall lowered the empty goblet from her lips, sun shone down upon us, and we all gasped in unison as we looked toward the sky.

"How can it be daytime?" I whispered. Da would surely be looking for me. And my friends' das would be looking for them.

"The goblet must cast magic that made us lose track of time," Elena answered.

"Aye," came a rage filled tone from behind us.

The three of us swiveled around, our eyes wide with disbelief. There stood Morgana, holding a limp woman draped over her arms, whose long, flowing silver hair perfectly matched Morgana's. Dread rumbled painfully in the pit of my stomach and twisted it into tight, hard knots. The woman had to be Morgana's mama. My hands began to tremble, my fingers twitching at my sides.

Morgana's eyes started to glow and blaze. Their fiery gleam lit up the forest, and suddenly she released her mama, who floated gently as if made of air. My mouth parted in shock, and I was rooted to the spot, paralyzed as Morgana raised her hand carefully to her midriff, palm face down, and slowly lowered her hand to her side. She seemed to pull her mama to the ground by an invisible string. The woman lay unmoving on the ground, eyes wide, mouth open, and the bottoms of her feet were bloody and ragged. Her stare was empty, distant. I had no doubt she was dead.

"The four of ye have killed my mama." Morgana's jagged tone sent a ripple of fear through me, causing a pain as if I'd been cut deeply with a serrated dagger. I clutched at my side as she glanced from her mama to us, sweeping her gaze over us, then locking it on me. "Ye are thieves," she said, her attention staying fixed upon me. Her voice thundered through the forest. Did she know taking the goblet had been my idea? It was my plan, my fault. My foolishness.

The others said nothing, all of them overwhelmed by Morgana's ferocity. Words tried to form on my lips but died there, withering in my throat with the terror of my guilt. It washed over me, pouring relentlessly, in waves.

I took a deep breath to explain, but Morgana's hand cut through the air, and she opened her index finger and thumb before pressing them together. My lips immediately came together of their own volition. Terror spread like a vine through me, and I attempted to raise my hands to my lips to try and pry them open. Once again, Morgana raised her hand to her midriff, and when she lowered it, my own hand was driven down by my side. I cut my eyes to either side of me, my fears confirmed. Elena and Katreine were in the same predicament, but Murieall had only one hand at her side. The other was stuck at her midriff still gripping the glowing goblet.

"Ye are intruders," Morgana hissed, her voice cold and exact. "Ye took what was nae yers to take and in so doing, ye took my mama's life."

"We only wanted—" Murieall began.

"I ken what ye wanted," Morgana thundered, the words assaulting my eardrums and making me whimper. Her breath slivered white from her mouth like a serpent about to strike us from the depths of her soul. She came to stand in front of me, so close I could see the flair of her nostrils, and the heat of her breath fanned my face.

"Ye want magic?" she demanded.

I could not speak or move to answer, though my blood rushed through me like a raging river. "I'll give ye magic!" she said, her voice holding an ominous quality. Her eyes lit silver round the rims, but the center, the center danced with flames. "Drink from the goblet, Freya, and taste the magic." The goblet flew from Murieall's hand into mine, my hand jerked upward to my mouth, and water appeared in the goblet. Suddenly, I was swallowing and coughing as the liquid slid down my throat, until the goblet was empty once more.

Her eyes impaled me, and a cruel smile twisted her lips. She raised a long bony fingers to my cheek and ran the tip of her nail down the right side of my face, leaving a stinging path as she did. "Freya MacLeod, ye wished to see yer future, so ye could manipulate it to be able to marry for love and ken the man ye wed loved ye in return."

My eyes grew wide with shock. She knew exactly what I had been thinking when I'd drank from the goblet.

"I give to ye the gift of sight," she whispered, white smoke swirling from her lips to mine. My lips parted and smoke filled my mouth with a sweet bitter taste. My thoughts swirled, banging into each other, making me dizzy. I was choking. I was going to die. "Ye will see things afore they occur. And ye will have the power to manipulate futures. But nae yer own. Yer greatest wish will be yer greatest misfortune."

I was dizzy with fear, but I did not fall. I was locked in place, and there I stood, as one by one, Morgana took each of our wishes and twisted them to curse us.

Chapter Five – Colin

I couldn't steal what was missing, and Freya MacLeod and her three friends had gone missing. I did what any man scheming to take a lass to save his clan would do—I joined the search for her. And when I found her, I was going to take her, wed her, and then send a raven with my terms to her da.

We searched through the night with the party we'd been assigned to, but to no avail. And as the sun came fully in the sky to bring another day, horns began to blow, and shouts rang out through the forest.

"They've been found!"

"They're alive!"

"Return to the castle."

"What do ye want to do?" Connor asked beside me, low enough that only I could hear.

Horses stampeded past us from other parties of warriors who'd been out looking for the four missing lasses. I wanted to end the war, so there was only one thing to do. "Return to the castle."

Connor made a derisive noise and threw up a hand. "We can nae snatch the lass with her entire clan looking upon us!"

"I ken that, brother. We'll take her when nae anyone is looking."

I gathered my reins to head to the stronghold just as

horses galloped past us with the MacKinnon banner waving at the front of the line. Irritation flared to see Freya MacLeod on the front of Donald MacKinnon's horse. She hung in front of him like a limp rag. What in God's name had happened to her? On the horses behind her, three other women were seated in front of warriors. One stared ahead at nothing. One sat crying. The last lass was gnawing on her nails and babbling.

I urged my horse onward, its hooves pounding the terrain as we charged through the forest, branches snapping in a blur around us. Connor rode close behind. Together, we burst from the dense line of trees and barreled into the wide expanse of the inner courtyard, a swirl of chaos and activity that halted for a moment at our arrival, all eyes turning to witness our dramatic entrance. MacLeod warriors jostled and shouted, their voices rising in surprise, while scores of men from visiting clans—each bearing unfamiliar tartans—milled about, intent on their own intrigues and maneuvers.

Some clutched weapons they had been inspecting; others worked to repair armor, or strategized in small, conspiratorial knots. The clang of metal and the hum of conversation stilled and hushed, everyone suddenly attuned to the dust and urgency of our approach. Faces registered shock and curiosity, as though confronted with a strange and unexpected sight, a pause stretching through the throng like a breath before an exhale. An astonished silence washed over the bustling courtyard, all eyes wide and locked upon us.

I slowed my panting beast, as did Connor, and when we were halted, he turned to me. "This does nae bode well for the plan to snatch the lass unbeknownst to anyone."

I nodded, surveying the scene and thinking.

"What's our plan?" Connor asked, voice pitched low as chaos erupted around us. People poured into the courtyard, shoving and pushing, their curiosity to see what had happened to the lasses overriding any sense of decorum.

"We wait for an opening to do what we need, and if one does nae come quickly, we will have to depart and regroup."

"I'm glad to hear ye say that," Connor replied.

I scowled at him. "I'd nae endanger us."

"Nae if yer thinking logically, ye would nae, but ye have nae always been known to think logically."

"I do nae need ye to remind me of my mistakes," I bit out. "They haunt me. Believe me."

Connor nodded and then fell silent as we both turned our attention to MacLeod who was aiding his daughter off the destrier.

"Where the devil have ye been?" he demanded, but as he did, the woman who'd been on his heels pushed her way past him and grasped Freya. "Ye selfish, selfish fool!"

"Yennifer," MacLeod snapped. "Let Freya answer my question."

I couldn't tear my gaze from the lass. Her eyes were rounded like a cornered rabbit, and there wasn't a hint of color on her face.

"I—" she started.

"I found her in the Dark Woods," MacKinnon interrupted. "The lot of them were wondering around lost."

"Why the devil would ye go into the Dark Woods alone?" MacLeod demanded. When Freya didn't answer, MacLeod grasped her by the arms and stood face to face with her. "Answer me, daughter." She stared at her da, her expression transfixed. What exactly had happened to the lass and her friends in the woods?

One by one the three lasses that had been with Freya were aided off the destriers they rode, and each lass looked every bit as dazed as Freya. They were all daughters of lairds, and from what I'd gathered, close friends with Freya.

"Answer me!" MacLeod now shouted. I wasn't certain if his temper was snapping out of frustration or worry for his daughter, but either way, the way he shook her sent me back to when Katherine told me about Magy. How one of the MacLeod warriors had shaken her so hard she had cried out. I heard a cry then, and I was not in this courtyard. I was at Dunscaith three years ago. But this time, in my thoughts, I had not chased our enemies into the woods. I'd stayed on the castle grounds, so that when the MacLeods had breached the outer courtyard, I'd been there to drive them back before they'd ravished Magy and then killed her.

MacLeod shook the lass yet again. Or was he shaking Magy? I squeezed my eyes shut, and when I opened them, it was the MacLeod lass I saw.

"Why did ye go in the woods?" her da demanded.

"We went to borrow Morgana's magic goblet," one of the lasses standing behind Freya said. The lass stepped forward, gave a curtsy to MacLeod, and, twisting her hands in front of her said, "We all had wishes we wanted to come true." Her words had dropped low, and her gaze darted around before focusing on the far side of the courtyard. I followed her line of attention and found a man striding toward us, too young to be her da, mayhap her brother?

"We heard a Summer Walker speak of a magic goblet that would grant ye yer wish if ye dipped it in the old fairly pool and drank from it," said the lass with bright red hair and face full of freckles who had stepped forward.

"Foolish lasses!" MacLeod swore, releasing his grip on his daughter. He pointed at her. "Ye're lucky ye were nae injured venturing into the woods as ye did on a ridiculous whim! I told ye nae to go into the Dark Woods without escort. All is well that ends well," he boomed, and the crowd in the courtyard fell silent. "I was going to save the announcement for supper tonight, but seeing as how MacKinnon rescued my daughter, we will celebrate their betrothal tonight. They will be wed in a fortnight."

"Nay." The forceful word split the moment of quiet after the announcement and drew my gaze back to Freya, who seemed to have finally snapped out of her stupor. She was staring at Donald MacKinnon with a look of horror. "I can nae wed him, Da. I'm sorry." Her hand fluttered to her neck. She backed away from MacKinnon when he stepped toward her and closer to her da.

"Do we need to call Vanora down here?" the woman Yennifer asked.

I picked up on a threatening undertone, and I supposed the lass did too. She flinched. "Nay. Nay!" Her gaze started to glow, making my belly clench at the sight. The gold became brighter. The green more vivid. She pointed at Donald MacKinnon. "If ye wed me, ye will murder yer da."

Immediately, a hush fell on the crowd. I stilled myself at her words.

"Do nae be ridiculous!" Mackinnon replied, his tone curt and his expression a thunderous sky.

"Ye must listen to me!" She ran to him and grabbed his hand, tilting her head to stare up at him. "Yer da will attempt to ravish me, and ye will kill him! I saw it!"

"What do ye mean ye saw it?" her da demanded.

She released Donald's hand and took a deep shuddering breath as she turned to face her da. "I've been cursed," she said, raking her hands through her hair before pressing her fingers to either side of her temples. "I did nae want to wed

Donald. Ye ken it," she said, circling her arms around herself and rocking back and forth on her heels. "I wished to see the future, so I could manipulate it. I wanted to wed for love, and I thought if I saw the future I could destroy yer enemies and wed as I wish!" She pressed her fingertips to her eyes and tapped them. Her agony was so acute it took my breath. "We took Morgana's magic goblet," she whispered. Tears spilled down her face and she patted herself on the chest. "I have been cursed." Her voice was choked. Raw.

"Cursed?" the woman Yennifer asked in a curious tone.

"Do nae be ridiculous!" her da thundered.

"She speaks the truth," the red-headed, freckle faced lass said. "We took the goblet without asking and when the Morgana came back from gathering the herbs she needed to make a potion to put in the goblet to save her mama, who was wounded, the goblet was gone, and her mama died. Morgana cursed us."

"Ye have nae been cursed," MacLeod, growled. "Enough of this foolishness!"

"Da," Freya cried out. "Ye must listen to me! The witch twisted my wish into a curse. She gave me the gift of sight," she said, her voice shrill. "But nae how I wanted it! I—"

"Sight for the future is a gift!" Freya's stepmother crowed.

Freya shook her head so violently I feared she'd do damage. "Nay!" she said, her tone hard. "Nay. Morgana told me I will see things afore they occur." Freya looked up at Donald again. "When ye found me, and ye touched me to put me on the horse. I saw yer future if ye wed me. Ye will kill yer da. It will divide yer clan. And ye will be killed by one of yer own. A dagger to the heart."

The silence of the crowd erupted into furious whispers. My own pulse had sped, and I looked to my brother. Our gazes locked, and I could see by his excited expression he was thinking what I was. If this was true, if Freya now had the gift of sight, we had to snatch her today. Before someone else did. She would be the key to ending this war. She would tell me how. And when.

"I do nae believe in magic," Donald said, like the fool he was. "I make my own future. And I would nae ever kill my da."

"I have the sight!" she bellowed at him. "The witch told me so! She said, I will have the power to manipulate futures but nae my own. That my greatest wish will be my greatest misfortune. I am trying to save ye!" The lass's tears streamed down her face now, and I felt a twinge of pity for the daughter of my greatest enemy.

The wind picked up suddenly, swirling and gusting and carrying the whispered words to my ears.

Seer. Site. Future Maker. Prize.

MacKinnon heard the whispers. It was obvious by the scowl upon his face. "Stop yer lies, Freya."

The smack of her palm connecting with his cheek rang out in the courtyard and pitched it into silence once more.

"I'm sorry," she rushed out. "But ye must hear me. Ye must listen."

Before anyone could react to what she'd done, another smack rang out. Heavier. Harder. Freya cried out and went careening to the left from the force of Donald's blow. She careened right into me. Our gazed locked for one brief second, before I set her aside and charged at him.

Aye, she was my enemy.

Aye, I intended to use her.

But nae any man had the right to hit a woman.

And then I saw Magy. Battered. Broken. And all I could think was how I'd failed her.

My control snapped, and I charged MacKinnon. My fist connected with his jaw before my arms were seized, and I was shoved to my knees. Around me, chaos erupted, sparked by the lass's words, Donald's actions, hers, and my own.

"Take Freya to her chambers," MacLeod ordered a guard.

The guard grabbed her in a firm hold and propelled her away, but as the lass was being forced out of the courtyard, her wide, frightened gaze was locked on me.

"I demand retribution for this man hitting me," MacKinnon snarled, pointing his sword at me. "I will have retribution, or ye will nae have yer alliance!"

MacLeod hesitated a moment before nodding. "Take him to the dungeon to await his punishment." As the guards jerked me up, Connor stepped toward us, but I shook my head. If I was going to escape the dungeon, Connor needed to stay out of it to aid me. I was dragged through the crowd of frenzied, chattering people, down a set of stone stairs, and shoved into a small dungeon. The iron door was slammed and one of the warriors who shoved me in said, "We'll send yer head back to yer laird."

"I do nae think so," I replied, an odd sense of mirth rising in me, despite now being locked in the dungeon to await my head being lopped off. I'd come to get peace or snatch a lass. Instead, I'd recklessly interceded to protect the lass I'd intended to use. And might possibly lose my head for it. Plans had gone awry.

"Do ye doubt that my laird will take yer head?" the guard snarled.

"Nay. I doubt yer laird's ability to return it to Laird MacDonald."

"Oh, he'll receive it, all right. And he'll be sorry he sent ye."

"I think he's likely already sorry," I replied. Sorry I'd interceded like a clot-heid.

"That's better," the guard bit out and stomped away.

I watched the guards disappear up the stairs as thoughts tumbled in my head. In Freya's effort to help MacKinnon, she had just sealed her own fate. She would not be safe. She'd be hunted by men wanting to use her. It wasn't lost on me that I was one of them. Though currently, my opportunities were limited.

The need to escape tore at me, as I stood in the dimness, trying the bars in vain, the cold metal unyielding beneath my fingers. Each failed attempt at the stubborn lock felt like an eternity slipping away. With a grudging resignation, I slumped onto the damp stone floor, the chill seeping through my clothes and into my skin. A scent of mold and decay hung in the air, a reminder of the forsaken place I was now in. I had never before found myself in need of rescue, never been the helpless one. It had always been me who took charge, who saved others from dire circumstances.

Now I could only cling to the hope that Connor would come through for me. He was my only chance. Would he manage to steal a key? Could he sneak down here without raising suspicion? As the hours stretched into years, minutes stuttering into decades, I counted everything I could to avoid counting the time. Drops of water tumbled from above, tiny creatures that splattered against my head and shoulders, running down my spine. Rats scurried by with unfettered freedom, each one a reminder of the growing futility of my efforts. I named aloud every person who relied on me, every soul I could not bear to fail.

Why had I been so foolish to intervene? The question gnawed at me, but what choice had there been? There was no other option. Not for me. Could I have stood by a silent witness to the cruelty unfolding? I closed my eyes and saw once more the image burned into my mind: MacKinnon's hand raised to Freya, slapping her so hard that I thought I heard the blow echo between these same walls now caging me.

My muscles tensed at the memory. No, I could never have stood by. I knew this even as irritation rose up within me, mingling with the sensation of being trapped in this useless, precarious position I had gotten myself into. The impatience I felt earlier swelled to an anxiety filled with fear for everyone else. I couldn't stop myself from pacing the minuscule space, back and forth, back and forth. Connor and the others needed me. Each of them was counting on me to come back to them.

What if Connor could not release me? What if he were caught in the attempt? My worry clawed at my insides like the sharpened talons of some angry bird, and I could feel my normal control slipping. Cursing, I leaned my head against the bars and squeezed my eyes shut.

I jerked upright at the sound of footfalls, and on the staircase light flickered, casting twisting shadows. Freya MacLeod emerged from the darkness, and I blinked, certain I was imagining things. But no, no, there she still was. She had the cell key in one hand and a torch in the other. It danced across her face, illuminating her large eyes. My body reacted strangely to her appearance. I was surprisingly and keenly aware of the curves of her lush figure hinted at under the fine material of her gown. I forced the unwelcome recognition away.

She took a deep breath, and I could see her chest rise with it. I didn't know why she was here, but she was nervous. "I do nae ken who ye are, but when I collided into ye, I saw a vision of ye," she whispered.

I believed in magic. I hadn't always. I'd been a denier. But the cost of my disbelief was the one woman I'd ever loved. The scar on my forehead suddenly burned. The weight of it was like a physical burden. I raised my hand to rub at it, and the skin was hot, tender, and rough to the touch. It was a constant reminder of my past mistakes and the price I had paid. Freya's eyes tracked my moves from the other side of the dungeon door. "What did ye see?" I asked. The sound of my breathing filled the silence that fell for a moment.

She sucked her lower lip between her teeth for a moment, thinking, I suspected, on exactly what to say. As her lip released so did her words. "A battle is coming to yer home even as ye are here."

A sliver of apprehension coursed through me.

Freya moved to me and stuck her hand through the slit in the door. "Take my hand," she said, urgency underlying her words.

I did not hesitate. Her intent seemed earnest and grave, her words like a solemn spell. I took her delicate, trembling hand in mine. She curled her fingers around my palm, holding it with a desperate strength, as if to seal our fates together by a touch. Her eyes began to glow, luminous and wild like twin moons in the dark sky of her face. "Ye need to get to Eilean Donnan. Ye need to get there now," she urged, her voice rising with frantic insistence, as if each word could conjure the very speed of my journey. "If ye do nae, ye're sister will be taken." Her voice cracked with anguish, with dread, with the weight of what she feared. Freya shuddered, a violent tremor that rippled through her body like a strong wind. "And she'll wish... she'll wish to the gods for death."

My heart banged to get out of my chest. "Who's coming? Who comes to my stronghold? Who will take my sister?"

Freya's eyes locked on mine, her gaze so bright and fierce that I wanted to look away until the intensity burned itself out, but I didn't. I held her stare. "Bran. Bran comes. Yer sister will think to sacrifice herself to save yer clan." She blinked then, almost as though purging the sight from within herself, and when she opened her eyes, they had returned to their normal color. She pulled her hand away, the warmth of her touch gone cold. "Ye are my enemy."

Her words struck with their truth.

Her gaze became a dark accusation, as if daring me to deny her words. "I ken who ye are now."

I nodded. I had learned long ago the power in silence. To hold your tongue was sometimes to wield a sharpened blade. To wait was often to conquer.

"Consider my debt to ye paid," she tossed the words like stones. "Ye intervened for me, and now I have done the same."

"This debt is done," I replied, choosing my words with care, measured and deliberate. There were other debts that I could not wipe clean. Debts of death. And destruction.

I gripped the bars with my hands, my temples throbbing with the urge to be released. "Let me out."

"Nae without yer vow that ye will leave peacefully and nae take me with ye." Her voice was softer, almost tender, but no, she was negotiating.

"I can nae give that vow."

"Then ye will die," she fired back and locked her eyes with mine. "My da will take yer head. Ye can count upon that. Yer refusal to give yer vow will damn yer sister to a life of pain and suffering." Her words were a quick, sharp volley.

I did not want to give that vow, because I knew if I did, I would keep it.

"Ye waste precious time ye could be reaching yer sister."

She knew exactly how to prod me to take what she offered, give what she demanded. "I give ye my word," I bit out between clenched teeth, feeling them grind.

She pulled out a dagger. "In case ye forget yer vow—"

"I'll nae." The words were a bitter vow upon my lips.

She pointed the dagger at me. "I will gut ye if ye do."

The lass was surprisingly ferocious. "I have nary a doubt ye'd try. But I am a man of my word."

"Ye're a MacDonald, so I doubt that verra much, but given yer sister's life is at stake, I will take yer word this time. Behind the dungeon door is a secret path. Take it. It will lead ye to an underground tunnel that will take ye all the way to the loch. With the festival going on, yer departure will go unnoticed."

I needed to find Connor, but I'd keep that information to myself.

She turned the key and opened the door, raising her dagger and backing away. "Do nae tarry," she warned, turned and gasped at the site of Connor standing there.

He stepped toward her, as if to grab her. "Nay, brother," I called out. "I gave my word. Go on now, lass."

She didn't hesitate. She raced up the stairs and was gone.

"Ye're a fool," he thundered. "She was in our grasp."

"Aye," I agreed. "But if my word can nae be trusted, I'm as bad as MacLeod and his stepson."

"Yer honor will cost us Eilean Donnan," Connor growled.

"I hope nae," I replied, only just noticing that Connor

had my sword sheathed with his. "How did ye get my sword?" I asked.

"I did nae," he replied, unsheathing it and extending it to me. "'Twas at the top of the stairs by the dungeon door. Do ye think the lass—"

"Aye," I interrupted. Not only had she freed me, she'd tried to ensure I would escape with my life. I owed her. I just didn't know when or how the debt would be called in.

Chapter Six - Freya

My first marriage lasted a sennight.

I wished I could say my visions had not come true, but they had. Swiftly. And violently.

My da did not believe in magic and fearful for our clan, for our survival, had wed me to Donald whilst promising me if Donald ever laid a hand on me again, Da would come for me.

Donald had not believed my vision either.

I wagered Donald would be a believer in my visions now—if he were alive, but he wasn't, the fool.

Laird MacKinnon had come for me. Just as I had seen. Just as I had said. Old man. Lecher.

He had climbed on top of me and would have taken me as clumsily and thoughtlessly as his son had, but Donald had stumbled into our bedchamber after drinking in the Great Hall half the night. He'd stabbed his da in the heart with a dagger—just as I had told him he would. That was all I had seen transpire with my own two eyes. The rest, I'd heard after I'd managed to escape the castle unnoticed in the uproar. I had intended to try make my way back to my home, to my da's protection, but there had been no need to make the attempt on my own. Da had sent men for me. They'd met me on the trail I'd been fleeing down.

I sat on my bed, staring at my bedchamber door. I was sick of this room, but Da had ordered me to stay in here as he continued to question each member of our clan, searching for the traitor who had freed the MacDonald "emissary", as he still erroneously believed Laird MacDonald to have been. I felt guilty about that, but nae so guilty that I had admitted anything. Laird MacDonald had risked himself to help me, the daughter of his enemy, and though I fully believed he had been at my home for nefarious purposes, I did not regret freeing him to save his sister.

I was loyal to my clan, but I'd seen in my mind's eye how Bran would have tortured Katherine once he retook Eilean Donnan. I could not allow the woman, sister of our enemy or not, to be a casualty of a war she had not started.

So here in my bedchamber I remained, where Da felt I was safest, as he searched for the traitor who didn't exist and sought my next husband. Da believed in my visions now and had promised this time to allow me to choose a man who's future I did not fear. I had demanded his vow not to allow Yennifer to threaten to use Vanora to force my hand ever again. He had given it, knowing, I was certain, that I had concluded that there was no choice but to sacrifice myself so the clan would not be destroyed by MacDonald.

My gut twisted at the prospect of another marriage, but Da still needed to protect the clan and win back Eilean Donnan and my own interference had prevented Bran from doing that. I had tried to use my powers to see my da's future, the course of attack he should take to win the castle on his own, but as Morgana had said, my powers were my curse. I only saw blackness when I looked for visions that might help my clan or myself.

The creak of the door jerked me from my thoughts. The door swung open, and Vanora flounced in, eyes sparkling with mischief and a conspiratorial smile curving up the corners of her mouth. I waved her over with an impatient motion as the guard who had been assigned to watch my door shut it.

Vanora dropped upon my bed, the soft feathers sucking her in and the bed tilting ever so slightly. She held out a sweet treat to me, which I eagerly plucked from her hand and popped into my mouth. Sweets were my weakness. "What is occurring?" I demanded.

"Great lairds have been streaming into the castle all day to make a bid for yer hand! They all wish to wed ye now that word has spread that yer gift of sight is real! Is it nae wonderful? Da has been speaking with lairds all day! Mayhap, ye will get to wed someone ye desire?"

I tugged my hand away. "These men want me to use me," I muttered. "And this is nae a gift!" I tapped my eyelids. "It's a curse. I only ever desired to be wanted for myself, and now there is a string of men here who want me for what they hope I can do for them."

The door swung open with a loud creak, followed by the thud of the guard assigned outside my bedchamber door hitting the ground. And in my doorway a stranger with a shiny bald head and beady, dark eyes appeared. My heart raced at the sight of him, and I scrambled to my feet, pulling my sister behind me. I noticed the unmoving guard outside the doorway, his body sprawled awkwardly on the floor. The stranger's presence was imposing and unnerving. I caught a whiff of the man—a mix of leather and mead with an underlying hint of something sinister.

As he thudded into the room, my sister's slight frame trembled against my back as I stood ready to defend us. "Who are ye?" I demanded, my voice catching.

He smiled, displaying rotted teeth that made my stomach clench. "I'm about to be yer husband, lass."

I opened my mouth to scream, but he tore across the room, men streaming in behind him, before I could get any words out. He clapped a sweaty palm over my mouth, jerked me to him, and ordered one of his men to contain Vanora. It was a needless order. She dropped into a dead faint before the warrior reached her—ever the skittish cat. My own legs threatened to stop supporting me. When a man wearing the simple unadorned dark brown wool habit of a priest entered my room, my legs did buckle, and my heart plunged.

This was my fault.

I had taken something that was not mine to take, and Morgana's mama had died because of my thoughtless actions. We had not meant harm, but nor had we thought beyond ourselves. I had wished to control my future, I had wished to wed for love, and now, I could see clearly, those wishes would never come true.

My arm throbbed where the stranger with the rotting teeth gripped it. I would have protested, but if he let me go, I was certain I'd fall. I had no desire to appear weak in this moment. The priest moved to stand directly in front of us. From somewhere deep inside of me, in a reserve of mettle I had not known existed, I found the will to make my legs lock in place as the priest said, "Laird Matheson, are ye ready to begin the ceremony?"

His answer was a grunt, and the priest launched into the vows. My stomach knotted with each word he spoke, and perspiration dampened my back, my underarms, and my upper lip. When Laird Matheson finished his vows, the priest looked to me. I pressed my lips together when asked to repeat my vows, and I glared at Laird Matheson and the priest.

"Ye do nae want to attempt to defy me, lass," Laird

Matheson said.

"I will nae wed ye," I growled. Where were my da's men? Why had no one come to save Vanora and myself? I looked to the door, and Lord Matheson chuckled, and at my feet, Vanora moaned and started to stir.

"If ye're looking for someone to come to yer rescue," Laird Matheson said, "ye should nae. Yer courtyard and great hall are filled with men vying to wed ye. Yer da is verra busy, meeting with prospective husband's for ye."

He would be sitting in his solar, working to make the best alliance for our clan. Meanwhile, I was about to be taken right out from under his nose. A mocking smile curled Laird Matheson's lips. I suppose my realization of what was happening showed on my face. He gripped my chin, and I drew back, but there was nowhere to go. He had me locked in place. He brought his face a hairsbreadth from mine. "Ye are a beautiful lass. A foolish one, too."

"And how, pray tell, do ye think me foolish?"

Vanora moaned again, and I willed her to stay silent and still, so that she might be forgotten in this horror. But, of course, she did the opposite. She pushed herself upright, looked up, and opened her mouth, as if to scream, but Laird Matheson barked, "Secure the lass." The two warriors standing to the right of us had Vanora in their grasp, jerked to her feet, and one smacked a hand over her mouth. Vanora's eyes went wide, and her arms flailed for a moment, before she was contained.

"Do nae hurt my sister!" I hissed.

"Or what?" Laird Matheson mocked. "What will ye do?"

"I swear to ye," I seethed, my head pounding with fear and rage, "if ye harm my sister, I'll kill ye!"

Laird Matheson threw his head back and laughed even as his grip on my chin grew so tight pain danced up the sides of my jaw and made my eyes water. "I'm glad to see ye will be a spitfire wife." He covered my mouth with his in a hard, punishing kiss. My stomach roiled, and I had to fight the instinct to gag as his hot, wet lips moved against mine.

It was not my first kiss, but it was every bit as unenjoyable as the kisses Donald had forced upon me. I willed a vision to come. Something I could use to convince the man not to wed me, but nothing came. Tears burned my throat, but I swallowed them down, refusing to show weakness. When he broke the kiss, he released my chin and waved a hand at the warrior who was covering Vanora's mouth. "Put yer dagger to the child's neck," Laird Matheson said.

"Nay!" I cried out, trying to jerk out of his grip, but it was useless. Laird Matheson was much stronger than I was.

"Ye will wed me," he said, his tone unbending, "or I will have my man slit yer sister's throat. I do nae want to hurt her," he said. "I only want ye and the power ye will bring me with yer gift to see the future."

I was a fool. I'd stolen the witch's goblet and been cursed for it, and then I'd marked myself for ruin when I'd announced it in front of an entire courtyard of people. I'd ensured that a tide of men seeking power would come for me—each believing I could deliver it into their greedy palms.

Laird Matheson's warrior set the tip of his dagger to Vanora's smooth, white skin, and within a breath, a drop of blood appeared and rolled down Vanora's neck. Her frightened gaze met mine and widened with a silent, desperate plea. My thoughts spun chaotically in my head as I tried to find a solution, turning over ideas and discarding them as quick as they came to me.

"I can nae conjure a vision on command!" I said. "I may nae even have one to help ye."

"Ye'll conjure one now, or yer sister will die." He inclined his head toward Vanora, and the man with the dagger at her neck pressed harder, cutting off her air. Her face paled as she gasped for breath, and tears flooded her eyes and rolled down her cheeks. She whimpered softly, a sound that tore at my heart. I wanted to rake my nails down Matheson's face. I wanted to gouge his eyes out. Or gut him with the dagger his man held to my sister's neck. I wanted to gut him with my own bare hands.

Instead, I placed a palm on his cheek and concentrated with all my might. Visions danced on the edge of my mind, but none were clear. Fog clouded everything. I forced myself to breathe slowly. Cool air moved in and out of my nostrils. I blocked all noise except the beats of my heart. *Thump. Thump. Thump.* The fog lifted slightly. Out of the darkness, an image formed, then two, then three. My head throbbed, but more visions cleared the canvas of my mind until I saw five images.

I met Laird Matheson's gaze. "The Campbells will attack yer castle. Raise the bridge. Boil sludge and burn the men attempting to scale yer wall. Then ye will be the victor." A wave of exhaustion hit me, and I started to move my palm, but Laird Matheson grabbed me in an unrelenting hold.

"What else?" he demanded.

I stared into his eyes as disgust curled in my belly. Greed was the fastest downfall of any man. I did not need to put my palm back on his cheek. Another vision hit me in the gut. "Ye will ride through the mist the night the battle is over to see yer lover—wife of Laird Campbell. If ye do this, ye will ride off a cliff to yer death."

"Do nae give me lies because ye worry I'll give attention to another."

"I welcome yer turning yer attentions to another," I flung out, which got me slapped. The hit was hard and sent my head in the other direction and put unwanted tears in my eyes. I blinked them away before I turned my face to his. The metallic taste of blood filled my mouth. He'd split my lip. "If ye do nae heed me, ye will die."

"I do nae believe ye." He slapped me again, first one side of the face, then the other. The sharp crack echoed in my ears and wobbled the floor beneath me. More tears blurred my vision, but I would not let them fall. I blinked rapidly and saw Vanora. The knife had pricked her neck, a single drop of blood running down her skin. I gasped.

"Will the blood ye see next be dripping from her lifeless body?" Matheson pushed me away with a cruel smile.

I looked at Vanora, remembering the time we were small and she sliced her arm open. I pestered the healer until she taught me how to dress the wound and kept it up long after Vanora had grown tired of the whole ordeal. I could not lose her. When I did not speak, Matheson drew his hand back to slap me again.

"Ye do nae strike fear in me with yer bluster!" The words exploded from my mouth.

His face hardened at my words, and he struck me once more. This time, my knees buckled. I fell, catching myself on my hands and knees. I breathed in through my nose, the floorboards just below them. I forced myself to stand, and when I straightened up to look at him, I saw more clearly this time. Blood flowed freely down Vanora's neck, and the fear on her face sent a sharp pain through my heart.

"I'll wed ye," I blurted. I had no other choice. But at least I knew this smug man would soon be dead. "Ye do nae believe me now," I said, my voice hoarse. "But ye will."

He chuckled and signaled toward the man with the

dagger. "We shall see if ye speak truth." The man pulled the knife away from my sister's neck. Matheson nodded once more, and I felt a sharp tug on my arms. Two men dragged me from the room, Vanora soon following.

Chapter Seven – Colin

I stared out of my solar window to the battered bridge of Eilean Donnan. Parts of the bridge had crumpled. That had happened when I'd stopped the attack from Bran MacLeod. One guard tower had been destroyed when MacLeod and MacKinnon had attacked us. Fires had scorched the gardens and stables when MacLeod had attacked with Laird Sinclair. Every time Freya was wed again, I lost more ground in the war against her father and whichever clan he had made a new alliance with. Many of my men were dead and many of those who remained were sick. All were weary, tired of war. Provisions were low and morale lower.

We needed hope. We needed a weapon. I needed Freya—before she was wed yet again to someone only too willing to make an alliance with her father.

The knock at my door was not a surprise. I'd been waiting all day for my brother to return.

"Enter."

The door creaked, heavy footsteps fell, and then a long breath was taken. "She's on the move."

I did not need to ask who "she" was. We'd been tracking Freya's every move since the day we'd fought her brother off, just as she'd told us to do. I knew every man who had taken her. Each of them had gotten to her moments before me. And each had died exactly as she had predicted. I presumed the latest was not any different. Still… "Did Sinclair die in the great hall?"

"Aye," Connor replied. I turned then and met my brother's grim gaze. "By fire. Exactly as the whispers on the wind say the lass predicted. Why do ye think he did nae listen to her? He was her third husband! The others had been victorious in battle but losers to death—just as she saw."

"Too smug," I replied. "These men were too smug. I will nae be smug. I will be careful."

"If we get to her before anyone else."

I nodded. "What did yer spy tell ye?"

"She fled three nights ago with her sister Vanora in tow at the witching hour when chaos erupted after Sinclair died. As always." I resisted the strange urge to smile at the news of the lass's cleverness. Well, she was mostly clever. She kept managing to escape only to be captured again by predators hunting her for her power. It seemed they used her sister every time to force Freya's hand. I hoped I did not have to do the same. Once the predators had forced her hand, they had sought alliances with her father. He'd agreed each time. The men who snatched her did not want to make an enemy of one the most powerful lairds in the Highlands, and MacLeod had used each alliance to attack Eilean Donnan and weaken us further. I was hunting her, too, so I supposed that made me a predator as well.

"What else did Ailas's raven say?"

"Ye still have nae acknowledged my cleverness in planting a spy in Sinclair's stronghold."

"Ye're verra clever to have thought to send the lass ye were bedding to be a lady's maid to Freya," I replied, my tone as brittle as my mood.

Connor winked. "Was that so difficult?"

"Connor, I'm nae in the mood for yer antics."

"Fine. The lass and her sister are taking the Dark Forest to her home by way of the ice path. Her da sent men to aid her, but she had already fled, fearful they'd nae reach her in time."

"Of course he'll nae," I grumbled. "And he'll make yet another alliance with whoever takes her. The man choses power over his daughter every time."

"I suppose this means we will nae any longer be offering to trade her for a confession?"

"Nay currently. I'll use her to leverage for peace—an alliance between them and us, sealed by marriage. And if MacLeod will nae have peace, I'll use her to destroy him."

"So ye will wed her?"

I nodded. "Aye. She must be mine, so that by the laws of our land, nae anyone else has a right to take her. And the wedding will give me the right to attack if they do."

Connor nodded. "It's settled."

"Aye." It felt like a weight upon my chest. My wedding another was something I'd vowed never to do after Magy died.

"Are the horses readied?"

"Aye, brother. Ye ken we're nae the only ones hunting her."

"Aye, but we have the advantage of knowing where she's heading and the path she's taking."

Chapter Eight – Freya

The laird hunting me and his men caught us at the edge of the path to Morgana's cave.

I could see the cave at the top of the ice path. Once we were there, I was going to beg her to take away this curse. And if she refused then Vanora and I would head quickly home. I stepped a tentative foot on the ice that never thawed when hands snaked out of the dark and wrapped around my waist. With a jerk and a twist, I was rotated to face a beast of a man. Behind him on horseback sat his four companions.

My first thought as I stared at them was that I should have listened to Vanora when she'd said she heard horse's hooves. I'd dismissed her insistence as her normal skittishness. In my defense, I had paused briefly to listen, but nothing sounded in my ears beyond the roar of my own blood pumping desperation to my limbs, heart, and head to reach the witch and beg her to take my gift from me.

My second thought was direly belated.

I should have headed straight for home. Now, I was not only going to be saddled with this heinous curse, but I was also going to be forced to wed once more. The truth of the matter was plain enough by the one man in the brown priest's habit. I shuddered at the thought and my insides knotted with dread.

I wanted no part of having a husband ever again. What I

had to show for my past marriages was scars, seen and unseen, and a rage that burned so hot I was being scalded from the inside and out. Men took what they wanted. Roughly. Cruelly. Threateningly. And I had no choice but to submit to the pokes, pinches and slams of their bodies into mine. The grunts like swine. There was no pleasure. I was their wife, their property.

And my da—my teeth clenched in frustration and confusion. I knew he had not chosen the husbands for me beyond Donald, and I knew he must have thought he had no choice but to make alliances with the men who took me and wed me, yet, knowing these things, I could not help but feel abandoned by him. And then I felt guilt. He was laird. He was trying his best to defeat the MacDonald—the man I had aided—to save our clan. Yet, questions had begun to pepper my mind. Had he tried hard enough for peace? Had MacDonald refused? Then again, Da could not trust the word of a man who had broken the alliance once before. And yet, I could not forget how MacDonald had attempted to defend me.

"Freya Sinclair do ye willingly take Laird Buchanan as yer husband?" the priest demanded.

I blinked, realizing I'd gone far away. I struggled to focus, but my mind was trapped in sludge. Each thought took a great amount of energy to form. We'd travelled for three days, barely sleeping, with nothing to eat but berries. Escaping had taken a toll, but not as great a toll as my life as a wife. I was surprised to find my arm extended and a cord wrapped around my forearm to bind it to Laird Buchanan. I clenched my teeth to stifle my sudden desire to giggle hysterically. I was being wed again, and I had not even truly been aware it was already occurring.

"Nay," I said as I had at my other three weddings.

Again, a dagger came to Vanora's neck. She didn't flinch anymore. Our eyes locked, understanding passing between us. I'd grown more timid and she'd grown bolder. Strange that. I swallowed the bitterness clogging my throat. "Nay willingly, but aye." I couldn't make myself be totally cooperative, but I would capitulate the required amount to protect Vanora.

The priest began the ceremony, and I allowed my mind to wander to the dreams I had let go of, dreams of wedding a man I loved who loved me in return. I no longer wanted any man.

My arm was suddenly jerked, and I looked to the right to find Laird Buchanan glaring at me. "Say yer vows."

Time moves slowly when you are waiting for something good, some hope. But bad things? They come at you with the speed of a violent storm wind. "I Freya MacLeod—nay, Matheson…" I did giggle then. It erupted out of me, forcing my clenched teeth open, demanding to be released. What was the last name that had been forced upon me?

"Sinclair," Vanora supplied, drawing my gaze back to my sweet sister. She winked at me, and I smiled back. There was the hope I had to cling to. In darkness, if you looked long enough, there was almost always a sliver of light to guide you through the roughest parts.

"I, Freya Sinclair, do pledge to take this man as my husband." Those were not the vows. I knew very well they were not, but they were close enough in my estimation. The priest seemed to agree as he nodded and pronounced us wed. We were not by the laws of our land. I shuddered at what was to come next. It was the consummation that would make me Lady Sinclair.

Was this to be like the first three times I'd been wed? I had not cared for being thrown upon a horse and ridden home to the safety of their castle to then be immediately bedded. But given the alternative of being bedded here on the forest floor, I prayed to be tossed onto the horse like a sack of grain. And in an attempt to make the outcome true, I tried to twist toward the riderless horse to mount it, but I was immediately jerked back around, and my newest husband said, "Nae so fast, lass."

I frowned. "Are we nae riding hard toward yer home to gain the protection of yer castle?"

"Nay before I bed ye," he replied, dragging me away from his men. Behind me, Vanora's gasp reached my ears. My entire body stiffened.

He stopped and turned to face me, brown beady eyes finding mine. "Aye. Yer visions for yer other husbands started after ye were wed and bed."

"Nay," I countered, my rising hysteria making me hot all over. "My visions do nae have anything to do with my being wed and bedded." I'd not been wed when I'd had the vision of Donald killing his father, but I could see by the disbelieving look on Laird Buchanan's face that my words fell on deaf ears. He yanked me to him, lifted me, and tossed me over his shoulder like a sack of grain I had only a breath ago wished to be treated as. Another wish gone awry. The air left my lungs in a whoosh as his shoulder dug into my stomach, and all the blood in my body started a painful slide toward my head with each of Laird Buchanan's heavy-footed steps toward the woods.

I'd been bedded by three men and never had it brought anything but pain. I knew it was coming, but I needed time to gather my courage to face it once more. I was pulled upward so fast that the world tilted. Then I was slung to the ground with such force that my head hit, bounced upward, and stars danced in my eyes. Pain exploded in my head and a high-pitched sound rang in my hears.

This man was different than my other husbands. I sensed the danger in his already aggressive moves. His smell of death. The way he looked at me as if he would devour me. I was the prey, and he was the hunter. My duty was to protect Vanora, and yet when he ripped off my underclothing to gain entrance into my body and spread my thighs with a force that left my inner thighs screaming, the things I knew shifted.

I could not, I would not be used and abused without a fight. He yanked my arms above my head with one hand and pressed them there, his palm against my wrists. Sharp pebbles and sticks dug into the sensitive flesh of my hands.

My heart pounded a beat that was surely leaving bruises on the inside of me as Laird Buchanan yanked down his own braies and there was proof of his dark heart. He was aroused by the promise of the pain to come for me. Fear filled my mouth with a metallic bitter taste, and blood pumped hard through my veins to pulse the one by my right eye and between my collar bones. I had only one way to fight that I could think of. As he started to lower his body, I jerked my knee up to hit between his thighs. He grunted, but before he could roll away, I brought my knee up again and once more.

He released my arms, fell to the side, and I did not waste a precious breath. I scrambled to my hands and knees, then hand over hand for a breath, till I gained my feet to run. Was I thinking logically? No, no. Logic had no place now. Self-preservation had taken over. I raced down the path away from him, feet pounding against the hard frozen dirt to send jolts through my body that rattled my teeth. The thick gnarled roots in the dirt dug into my feet as I ran through the thin soles of my shoes. Cold air burned my lungs making each breath hurt, while tree branches, bare from winter's kiss, scraped my arms and legs, opening my skin to leave lines of blood.

"Ye bitch!" came a roar from behind me, which made me cry out in fear and push my legs so hard they burned with the effort of my escape.

"Ye're going to pay for this!" came another bellow from Laird Buchanan. It was closer and louder and ratcheted up my fear so that the ache in my chest moved down my stomach to make a solid block of ice there. I looked back as I ran to judge how close behind Laird Buchannan was, and that was a terrible mistake. My foot caught a root, and I flew forward onto my stomach. Pain erupted on contact in my chest, stomach, and head. I no more than got my hands under myself to push up again, when Laird Buchanan grabbed me from behind, flipped me over and hit me so hard with the back of his hand that my head jerked to the side, my lip split, and blood filled my mouth.

I dug my hands into the dirt, gaining fistfuls, and threw it at his eyes. With a roar, he hit me again, my head jerking the other way, and my cheek throbbing. Then I was shoved back onto the ground and his heavy boot, smelling of a stable, pressed upon my chest as he looked down at me. "I'm going to show ye what happens to disobedient wives."

"And I'm going to show ye what happens to vile husbands," came a deep voice from behind me.

"He's nae my husband," I managed to mutter before my world went black.

Chapter Nine – Colin

I'd never taken pleasure in killing a man, but this time could be the exception. I had a breath to glance at Freya. Her lip was split and bleeding. Her dark lashes lay against her pale cheeks—a mercy, at least, that she'd been rendered unconscious. A small gift from the gods. Her gown was tattered. Her hair knotted. I drew my gaze to the man who would have ravished her on the ground, dirt and roots digging into her body. I imagined plunging my hand into his chest and ripping out his heart. I did not feel shocked by my thoughts. My anger was the only thing I could feel. It pulsed within me, numbing all else.

The man took his boot off Freya's chest and glared at me. "Who the feck are ye?"

"I'm the man who's going to kill ye," I replied. I could attempt to teach this man a lesson about hitting women, but men like him were beyond changing. "I'll be fair about it," I added. "Ye can try to best me, and if ye do, well then, the gods have spoken and off with the lass ye go. Yer name, if ye please," I said, as I withdrew my sword, and he his.

"Laird Buchanan," he snarled. "And ye are?"

"Laird MacDonald," I offered, raising my sword.

"I'm going to kill ye, MacDonald, and then feck this here lass whilst I rule over the Isles," Buchanan offered, pointing his sword toward me. "And then I'm going to kill that man," he said, waving his sword toward my brother.

"I'm afraid I can nae allow ye to do that," I replied. "I'm rather fond of my brother. Come on then." I motioned him with my palm to come at me. I'd been in enough combat in my lifetime, to understand I was better than most. My da had me training from a very early age when most lads were sleeping or eating or running through the forest wielding swords fashioned of sticks and defeating made up enemies.

Buchanan lunged then, snapping my attention to him. I brought my sword up to deflect his initial hit and was surprised by the power behind his swing. It was greater than most men, but I knocked the hit away with effort. He came again wish shocking speed, striking low, so I had to jump not to be struck across the leg.

"Colin, do ye need aid?" Connor called.

"Nay!" I responded, swinging as I did to strike at Buchanan. I caught him across the arm, slicing into his skin, leaving a trail of crimson with my blade, but it didn't seem to slow him.

"Ye're certain?" Connor demanded, as I ducked and blocked another swing.

"Aye," I growled. This fight would be fair. I'd not have my brother's help besting this man. If I was to win, it was the will of the gods, and if I was to lose, that was the gods' will as well.

Buchanan lunged forward, skimming his blade along my left side, almost gutting me. A cry split the air. The lass had awakened. Buchanan turned toward Freya, and I seized the opportunity. I struck him in the gut, my sword going deep. With a grunt, he dropped to his knees as he released his sword. He looked toward me, eyes wide with the surprise of a man who knew death was close. His hands came to my sword, his fingers closing around the blade. Instantly, blood dripped from his hands, my razor-sharp blade having cut into his skin.

"Mercy," he pleaded, the word a ragged gasp of desperation.

"He does nae deserve mercy," came words hard as stone.

I glanced toward Freya. She stood now, arms wrapped around her waist, a far enough distance from us to run if needed. She was a shattered object, put back together hastily, the pieces not quite fitting. Her face was swollen and bruises already purpled her skin.

Fear glinted in her eyes that I might indeed give this man mercy. "What sort of mercy?" I asked, thinking now of how Elizabeth had told me that Magy had begged for her life and that of our unborn child. "If ye're asking for the sort of mercy ye were offering Freya, then ye'll nae get any. If ye're asking for mercy from one warrior to another, I'll make yer death quick."

"Make it quick then," he said. "Take my head."

"Verra well," I said, pulling my sword from his stomach, so I could use it to take his head.

I saw my mistake in the curl of his lips and the flash of a dagger. There was no time to correct, though. The dagger struck hard, but not true. It plunged into my left arm, but with my right, I drove my sword into his stomach once more, and this time I twisted until he howled, and fell backward to the ground. I moved over him as he lay there panting, blood and saliva coming from his parted lips. "This will be a verra slow death," I told him.

"'Tis exactly what he deserves," the lass said, moving to stand beside me and look down at him. "Ye would have raped me." She spit on him. "Ye die the death of a man without honor." She bent down then and set her splayed hand on his heart. Silence fell for one moment and the temperature seemed to drop before her eyes started glowing, and she said, "Ye will nae enter Valhalla. Ye will dwell on the other side of the doors with all the dishonorable men. That is what awaits ye, Laird Buchanan. I have seen the vision."

She rose and turned to me. I saw it then in the stiffness of her spine, the jutting of her chin. There was steel underneath the shattered pieces, and that's what had kept her alive.

"Come," she said, looking between me and Connor. "Ye must aid me in saving my sister."

I frowned. "Aid ye?" What the devil was she thinking. She barely looked as if she would be standing much longer.

She nodded, stepped toward me, and before I knew what was occurring, she pulled the dagger out of my arm. I jerked in response but managed to hold in my curse. I'd had much worse injuries in my life, but that didn't make this any less painful. She reached toward me again, and I flinched backward, which curved her upper lip into a smile. She grabbed the edge of my tunic, and with a strength that surprised me from such a wee lass, she ripped along the edge of it that had been frayed in the fight. She then used her teeth to tear it all the way off and wrapped the material around my arm to stop the flow of blood that was trickling warm from the wound Buchanan had inflicted. "This should hold ye until ye can kill the rest of the men."

"The rest of what men?"

She looked at me as if I were a simpleton. "Buchanan's men, of course. They hold Vanora down the path." She pointed behind her.

"Vanora?"

She frowned and suddenly swayed where she stood. "Ye best nae let my sister ken ye asked who she is. I doubt she'd take kindly to yer nae kenning her name." As the words left her mouth, she swayed again, but this time, she tilted so precariously, that I grabbed her arm to steady her. She did not even glance to where I held her arm. She did, in fact, not even seem to notice. Clearly, what she had endured this day had muddled her thoughts as well as battered her body. How had I not noticed? Well, I had been busy. I studied her for one moment. Blood smeared her face, but it was her eyes, dull and void of emotion that were the biggest indicator. I thought upon what I'd just witnessed happening to her. It was possible, she had endured much worse.

"I remember now, lass," I said, gentling my tone as she sagged against me.

"There are three men and a priest." She laughed then and swiped the back of her hand over her forehead to leave a smear of blood. I glanced at her hand and saw it had deep gouges in it that were bleeding. "Priests are men," she said, laughing again, but it was a hollow, humorless sound. "Three against four," she said, holding up her dagger, pushing off me, and folding like a wave crashing down. I caught her before she hit the ground.

Her head lolled backwards to expose the long slender column of her neck, and her eyes closed. Her eyelashes, surprisingly dark for her red hair, fanned the top of her cheek bones. She was light, too thin, as if she either had not been fed enough or did not eat purposely. Still, even with all her bruises and cuts, she was a lovely lass. Shame that I would add to her misery stirred, but I dismissed it. Shame did not compare to the need to keep my clan and our home safe and in our control, and I would never hurt this lass.

"Ye want me to stay with her or come with ye?"

"Come with me," I said, laying her gently down. "I do nae ken how trained these warriors are," I said, glancing toward Buchanan to ensure he could offer her no harm. One look confirmed he'd never harm anyone again. Death had been quicker than I'd hoped, but given the circumstances, it was for the best.

As we walked down the trail, Connor said, "She did nae remember ye."

"She will," I said, knowing her mind had not been all there moments ago.

"Do ye think she'll be so grateful ye saved her that she'll willingly wed ye?"

"Nay," I said, "I think she'll want to kill me."

"Then ye best sleep with one eye open so the lass does nae plant a dagger in yer heart."

"Aye," I agreed. "I fear ye're correct."

Chapter Ten - Freya

I was swimming, kicking, thrashing, arms and legs wheeling. Yet no matter how hard I struggled, I seemed unable to reach the top of the water, unable to break through to the surface. Arms flailing, I kept getting close. I would poke my fingers up, so tantalizingly near to the world above, and a breeze would hit them with a promise of escape, the promise of air, but then I would be dragged back under.

The first time, it was my da who pulled me below. Gripping me steady, a strong hand wrapped round my ankle. I fought him with all I had in me. I was kicking and screaming, incomprehensible words bursting from my mouth, coming out as bubbles and glugs that rose to the surface through the depths of the warm loch waters. I went up again. Kicking furiously, I shot upwards, my lungs pressing against my chest, my breath short but not yet urgent, not yet dire. This time, with a desperate shove, my entire hand broke above the surface. I couldn't see under the murky water, but a hand clamped around my leg again and wrenched me back down.

I came face to face with Donald. I pummeled his chest, frantic, but it was useless. He dragged me down, down, down. The water grew cold and dark, darker still, and the pressure in my lungs increased. My feet touched ground at the bottom of the vast loch, and mud squished between my toes, gritty and thick, like it would trap me forever. Donald slid his hand around the back of my neck, gripping hard until pain throbbed there, as he'd done so often in the bedchamber when *guiding me*, as he'd called, it to please him. And then he disappeared as suddenly as he'd come.

The pressure in my lungs increased, hurting me and scaring me, and causing my heart to pound. I didn't want to die here, trapped underneath the surface of the loch water. I kicked hard, clawing to the top, breaking the surface, seeing the distant shore, but it was a brief moment, before hands circled my waist and back under I went to find myself staring at my second husband. Laird Sinclair gripped my hair and yanked my head back, making my scalp sting and burn. His teeth sank into my shoulder breaking the surface of my skin. He liked to leave his love mark, he said. That was no love I wanted any part of. He too disappeared, but he slowly faded away.

My lungs screamed at me now and the need to breathe drove me up toward the surface once more. I sliced my hands through the water as quick as my arms would allow and kicked as if demons themselves were behind me nipping at my heels. As I neared the surface, Laird Buchanan appeared, reaching toward me and terror caused me to scream, kick, and flail my arms attempting to back away from him before he could reach me. He grasped my neck, drew me toward him, and set his mouth over mine, sucking the little life left in me. My limbs grew heavy, my mind groggy, and my heart slowed to the thudding beat of the dead. I had no more fight. What I needed was someone to battle for me long enough for me to regain my strength.

Freya.

The one word came from above me.

I looked up toward the surface, suddenly so near once

more. Above, Laird MacDonald battled with Laird Buchanan. How had they gotten there? They swung their swords, the clank of metal hitting metal reverberating sound below the surface of the water to me. A dagger appeared in Laird Buchanan's hand, and he threw it, hitting Laird MacDonald in the shoulder, but the man didn't even blink his eyes. He plunged his own sword deep into Laird Buchanan's belly, then he looked straight at me, as if he could see I needed help, as if he would help me.

Swim to me, he said, reaching out his hand. *I'll pull ye up. I'll nae let ye slip back under.*

"Freya!"

The urgency in my sister's tone, startled me so that I blinked, and there she was, standing over me, hair lying in soft curls around her face, dark smudges under her eyes gone, and a pretty pink healthy flush.

"Yer awake!" she said, grinning. She leaned down to hug me and pressed a kiss to my cheek.

The kiss certainly felt real. Was I awake? I looked around the room. I didn't know this place. Beyond the bed I lay in there was one wardrobe, a table that appeared to hold a wash pot, and a wash tub that looked to have seen better days. There were no tapestries on the walls to make the room inviting, no rushes on the floors to help keep the warmth from the fire that was burning in the grate in the room, and the bed was lumpy. No, this was not my bedchamber at home.

"Freya?" Vanora leaned close, concern dancing in her eyes. She set her hand upon my forehead, and her warmth immediately seeped into my skin. I was indeed awake, but not at home, and my mouth felt full of cinder.

"Wine," I croaked, barely getting the one word out.

A woman came forward, holding a goblet in her hand. I

frowned, unsure if she was a vision or real? Had I lost my mind? She stopped beside Vanora, and I stared, because something in her eyes was so familiar. They were the blue of the loch after a storm came through and the sun finally graced the sky again. They were bright, bold, and mesmerizing, and I could have sworn I'd seen them before, or a pair of them that looked just like hers.

She reached behind my neck, sliding a gentle hand there to cradle my head as one would a bairn's, and then ever so slowly, she brought the goblet to my lips. "Drink," she said.

I didn't normally care to be ordered about, but this was one order to which I gladly capitulated. As the wine filled my mouth and cooled the burn in my throat, I felt instant relief. When I was finished, I pushed the goblet away, looking between the stranger and my sister, and I attempted to sit. My arms trembled with the effort, and both the stranger and my sister made a move to aid me, but I said, "I've got it." My voice sounded ancient like a door that had gone ages without being opened. "How long have I been asleep?"

"Three days off and on," Vanora said, sitting on the bed beside me. "I was worried, but Katherine said yer body and mind were simply taking time to heal."

"Are ye Katherine?" I asked, looking to the woman with the eyes that seemed familiar.

"Aye." She offered a kind smile that reached her eyes. "I'm Colin's sister."

"Colin?"

"Laird MacDonald," Vanora supplied, sounding pleased enough to do so. Her tone eased a bit of the trepidation building within me for waking up in a strange place. If Vanora had been ill-treated, I'd hear it in her voice and see it in her eyes.

"Ye lied about my stepbrother," I said to Katherine.

"Nay," she replied. Her lips pressed into a hard thin line. "I did nae lie. Bran and yer da attacked Dunscaith."

"They would nae have broken the treaty," I insisted. My da is honorable." He had done things I'd hated, but he'd done it to protect the clan. "Yer brother broke the treaty!"

Katherine's brows dipped into a deep frown, and she gave a little shake of her head. "Ye confuse me."

"I dunnae doubt it's hard, given ye are a MacDonald." I was not feeling charitable at the moment.

Her nostrils flared, but she took a long breath before speaking. "Ye have survived four unwanted husbands—"

"Three," I corrected her. "My marriage to Buchanan was nae consummated." Thanks to her brother, but I was in no mood to give the man any credit. Aye, he'd rescued me, but he'd done so to wed me himself. To use me. I had no doubts about this.

Katherine nodded. "I believe ye are cunning, but I can nae equate cunningness to yer willingness to believe lies. My brother had to take Eilean Donnan before yer da and stepbrother cut off the trade route to our clan. And he came for me. To save me. Once he knew the manner of man yer stepbrother was, he would nae leave me with him."

I snorted at that. "Yer brother took Eilean Donnan to control the trade route."

"My brother does nae have a wish to control the trade route," she snapped, frowning at me. "He simply wishes to live in peace and have equal access to the route and nae have it used to control our clan."

"Oh, aye?" I said, letting all the sarcasm I felt come through in my tone. "Then I suppose yer brother will be returning me to my clan."

"I can nae do that," came a velvet-edged deep voice.

"Exactly as I suspected," I muttered, looking immediately to the door where the response had come from. In the threshold, consuming much of the space with his powerful arms above his hands to clasp the top of the doorframe, stood the man Laird MacDonald. My mind flashed for a second to our first meeting on the stairs when I was holding the looking glass. I'd seen him and his brother when I was trying to ascertain who my future husband might be. I inhaled a sharp breath. Was it Laird MacDonald? Unease rippled through me. I did nae want another husband at all, but especially nae other one who wanted me for my sight.

But another memory hit me. His tackling Donald when Donald had slapped me. And Laird MacDonald saving me in the forest when Laird Buchannan tried to ravish me. I recalled the vision I'd seen of him saving his sister. "Ye saved yer sister," I said, feeling immediately foolish. Of course he had. But it was still strange to me, my visions. I hated them for what they'd done to me, but here, here was something good that had come from them.

"Aye," he said, nodding.

I thought about my vision. Katherine had been captured and blinded in one eye. Her dog had been blinded in one eye as well. And her servant. I looked to her, curious just how correct my sight was. "Do ye have a dog and a servant who is close to ye who would lay down his life for ye?"

"Aye. Dyamant is my dog. Jon is the stablemaster who had known me since I was born. He'd lay his life down for me."

"Why do ye ask?" Laird MacDonald inquired, lowering his arms. I could not help but stare at him. He wore only braies, no tunic, and his body was the most powerful I'd ever seen. He was crafted of sinewy muscle and broad shoulders, as if he'd spent every moment of every day swinging a sword. His abdomen looked to be hard planks fastened together. And he moved with the easy grace of a man in expert control of every muscle of his body. "Lass?"

Heat singed my cheeks when I realized I'd been staring. I swallowed my embarrassment. "They are things I saw in my vision of the future if ye did nae rescue Katherine."

"That sounds like something yer stepbrother would do," Katherine said. "He's a violent man."

I wanted to deny it, but I had no great love for Bran. He'd been the sort of boy who was mean to the hounds and stray cats at our stronghold, and who had mercilessly teased other boys who were not as strong as he was, so my vision had not shocked me. I knew why Da had put Bran at Eilean Donnan. Bran was ruthless, but surely Da would not look the other way if he knew Bran had ill-treated Katherine. "My da would have stopped yer ill treatment had he known of it," I said to Katherine, wanting to defend Da.

Vanora nodded but Katherine snorted. Laird MacDonald took a step into the bedchamber. I pulled the bedcovers underneath my chin. I was aware they were no protection against a man, still, I could not help myself.

"What makes ye think that?" Laird MacDonald asked. "Yer Da did nae stop the ill-treatment against ye? In fact, he wed ye to Donald after he saw the man hit ye."

I could not deny that last sentence, and it shamed me and angered me. "My da told Donald if he ever laid a hand on me again, he'd attack his castle and gain me back."

Laird MacDonald's disbelieving snort increased my anger. "Yer da chose power over yer safety. Was his plan to attack the castle and rescue ye *after* ye were harmed again?"

I glared at the man, not liking the doubt his question raised in me for my own da. "Ye do nae ken my da!"

"I ken him enough," Laird MacDonald said. I didn't like

the quiet surety in his tone. "He fought my family for years for the stronghold because he craves power."

"That is nae true. My da craved peace."

Laird MacDonald cocked his eyebrows. "Is that what ye tell yerself, so ye do nae have to face that he keeps choosing power over ye?"

"Colin," Katherine said, and I heard the warning in her voice to her brother, as if I was some fragile flower she needed to protect.

"I do nae need ye to protect me," I snapped at her, then turned the full force of my ire on her brother. "Ye think yerself better than my da?"

His stare was unblinking, unapologetically arrogant. "I think I'd nae ever allow my sister to wed a man that hit her."

I felt my nostrils flare at the subtle blow he'd delivered me. "Ye allowed her to handfast with my stepbrother." I made a guess that Bran had hit her, given her earlier comment.

A dark cloud settled on his face. "I did nae ken yer stepbrother's temperament when I did nae protest the handfast. And when I did come to know his true nature, when Katherine finally revealed it, I came for her."

I made a derisive sound from my chest. "Ye came for Eilean Donnan."

"Aye," he nodded, surprising me with his honesty. "Because yer da and stepbrother attacked Dunscaith and broke the treaty between our clans." I scowled. So much for honestly. "But I would have come simply for my sister."

I forced myself to unclench my jaw to speak. "My da did nae order such an attack. He would nae ever break a treaty he agreed to. He has honor."

"Then Bran broke the treaty, and yer da needs to ken it."

"Lies," I muttered. "Bran follows my da's orders."

"As I said," Laird MacDonald replied, sounding smug, "yer da broke the treaty."

I tensed all over and looked to the stand beside me for something to throw at the insufferable man. Vanora squeezed my hand and that drew my attention back to her. "Tis a gift from the gods that Laird MacDonald was in the Dark Woods when we were and stumbled upon ye and aided ye."

I laughed at that, which set an injured look upon Vanora's face. "I'm sorry, sister. Ye are young. And sweet." Refreshingly open to seeing the good in others. And still naive, despite how she had changed and become less afraid, stronger. "Laird MacDonald being in the woods was nae a gift from the gods." I speared him with what I hoped was a glacial look. He stared back, unblinking and looking unaffected, be damned the man. "I do nae ken what lies they have fed ye while I slept, but Laird MacDonald was only in the woods to hunt me, so he could capture me, and use me to keep control of Eilean Donnan and defeat Da. Is that nae correct, Laird MacDonald?"

"Vanora," Katherine said, rushing toward Vanora and I to take her hand. "Why do we nae go gather some refreshments for yer sister from the kitchen and let her and my brother speak?"

"Nay!" I protested, alarmed by the thought of being alone with any man.

Katherine cocked questioning eyebrows at her brother, and I understood then that she would do as he bid. Did she do it out of fear or out of earned loyalty?

"Would ye wish for yer sister to be subject to all we may say to each other?" Laird MacDonald asked.

I hated him. Or the anger coursing through me certainly

felt like hate. Of course, I did not want to be the cause of Vanora thinking every man was evil like I did. But that wasn't the only reason I wanted her to stay. I did not want to be alone with him. My gaze fell to the edge of his braies. I knew what lie under there. He hadn't attempted to wed me yet, but maybe he cared not for doing so first? I could feel the furrow of my brow, the way my breath had increased, and the coverlet now under my chin. I blinked, only realizing I had pulled it all the way up to cover me, as if that would offer any protection if he wanted to take me.

His hard expression softened, and it felt like I was suddenly stripped bare, all my shame and fear on display. I despised the weakness and him for revealing it and seeing it.

"I'll stand by the door," he offered to me, "but I would speak with ye alone."

I begrudgingly nodded, as I saw no other good choice. Vanora exited the room with Lady Katherine, and when Laird MacDonald immediately took a step toward me, I scrambled backward to press my back against the headboard of the bed while my heart threatened to thump out of my chest. "Ye promised!" I hissed.

"Aye. And I intend to keep it. I wanted to give ye this," he said, reaching down toward his thigh, grasping the dagger sheathed there, and extending it to me by the hilt. I stared at it; sure it was some sort of trickery. He smiled slowly. "'Tis nae trickery."

Did the man read minds?

"Nay," he said, chuckling. "I did nae read yer mind." I gasped. "Ye're the only one with the power to see into the future here," he said.

I took the dagger and wrapped my fingers around the cool metal of the hilt. "I'm surprised ye would give me a weapon. Are ye nae fearful I'll plant it in yer black heart?" I asked, allowing a smile, I hope conveyed the unfriendliness I felt, to curl my lips upward.

His gaze did not become hard at my display of anger but surprisingly softened a bit. "I would earn yer trust. And I'm a watchful man."

I snorted. "It will take more than a dagger to earn my trust. Let me go. Better yet, give me an escort back to my home."

"I can nae do that, Freya," he said, taking a step toward me.

I motioned at him, alarmed but also surprised by the remorse I thought I heard in his voice. My alarm won out, though. "Back up as ye said ye would, please."

To his credit, he did so without question. Though he probably did so because he had considered that it would be harder for me to hit him with the weapon he'd given me.

"If ye will nae send me home, then I presume I was correct that ye were in the woods hunting me." He did not reply, only stood and stared with a closed expression, which stoked my ire. "To use me for my sight."

Interest flickered across his features. "Do ye have control of yer sight?"

That these words were the ones that conjured the first real interest I'd seen, infuriated me more. It was always about my sight. I could tell him I was gaining more every day. That would be somewhat true. I could not always force the visions to come. Nor could I always get them to come when I wanted them too, but I was getting better at it. The one thing that I could not do at all was conjure any visions of my own future. When I tried I still saw black. But instead of saying any of that to my enemy, I said, "Wouldn't ye like to ken."

"I would," he said, surprising me yet again with the

honest answer. He started to step forward, then drew his foot back as if remembering his promise. I would not soften. He did not deserve gratefulness. "Freya, I do nae want to use ye, but if I must I will."

I glared at him until my eyes burned. I did not care that he sounded as if he truly meant what he said. How he sounded did me no good. Actions spoke much louder than words. My heart drew into a tight ball of anger inside of me for all I had endured at the hands of men. "Ye can nae make me do yer bidding, Laird MacDonald." I knew the words rang hollow, but I flung them anyway. I refused to just march willingly into another marriage.

He looked down for a moment, his hand shoving through his hair as if he were contemplating a distasteful task. When his gaze rose to meet mine, I could see regret there. It did not comfort me. It set ice in my veins. "I'm sorry to say, lass." His words were gentler than they had been, and that made me tense. Something bad was coming. I knew it in my gut. "I am truly sorry to say I do believe there are ways to get you to do as I wish."

Vanora. He would threaten Vanora. He was just like the others.

Chapter Eleven - Colin

"I should kill ye," the lass growled.

She was annoyingly lovely when angry. I frowned at the errant, unwelcome thought. And yet, though I didn't like noticing her appearance, I did. I had to force myself to focus on her words and not the way her tawny eyes shimmered with the heat of her rage. I nodded. "I can understand how ye would feel that way, given what ye have endured."

She pointed my dagger at me. "Ye do nae have any notion what I've endured."

I thought of Buchanan hitting her and how he'd intended to abuse her. "I've a small one, but ye're correct, only ye know the dark details." She gave a little shudder that stirred my protective nature. I wanted to kill Buchanan all over again, and I wouldn't lose any sleep at all if it had been me to kill her other husbands as well, but the gods had seen to that themselves.

"I would throw this at ye without remorse," she said, waving the dagger as she kept it pointed in my direction.

"But ye are a poor aim?" I guessed.

She made a derisive noise at that. "Why do ye think that? Because I am a woman?"

"Nay. Women can learn to throw daggers, if taught. My own sister is better than most of my warriors with the dagger."

Her eyes widened at that news, and her lips parted with her obvious surprise. "Did she learn in secret?"

I shook my head. "Nay, I taught her." She gave me a dubious look that made me want to laugh. When was the last time I'd felt like laughing? I cast my mind back but could not recall. "So why do ye nae throw the dagger at me?"

"Because I do nae ken how," she said, looking at once irritated about that fact and embarrassed. The lass was a strange combination of strength—she had to possess it to have endured what she had—and fragility, to be so easily embarrassed about things.

"I could teach ye," I offered surprising myself and clearly her.

Her eyes grew rounder, and she gawked at me, but then her eyes narrowed. "I'll nae be here long enough for ye to teach me. I ken ye wish to wed me to use my visions."

"I do nae wish to wed ye," I said truthfully.

She burst out laughing at that, then slapped a hand across her mouth, as a horrified look came to her face. She was an interesting surprise, but it did not matter. This would be a marriage of necessity. Slowly, she peeled her fingers back from her mouth. "I do nae want ye to think I laughed because I believe all men want to wed me for me." A frown suddenly puckered between her brows. "Or really any man," she said. "Men are users."

I was about to contradict it, but I did not currently have the right to do so. I had not been a user. Now, necessity dictated that I must be. "I imagine there are many men who would wed ye if ye did nae have this gift."

She gave me a black layered look. "'Tis a curse, nae a gift. And if ye do nae wish to wed me, why are ye?"

I inhaled a long breath to order my thoughts and choose

the right words. I did not want a wife, but I would have one. So I would be honest and do my best not to hurt her. I'd be respectful and ensure my clan treated her with respect. And I'd protect her, house her, and feed her. She could even keep her sister with her, if she wished. "I need peace," I said.

"Ye expect me to believe that?"

I shook my head. "Nay. I do nae expect ye'll believe much of anything I say for a good long while. But that does nae make my words less true. I entered the original alliance to gain peace with yer clan."

She snorted then said, "Lies."

If she didn't look so fragile and frightened in the giant bed with the covers pulled up to her chin, I would have stalked to her and given her a much-needed shake. Instead, I counted slowly to ten in my head. I could argue with her— pointless—or ignore her outburst. I chose the latter. "When yer brother or da or both broke it, and I stormed Eilean Donnan, I lost many men."

She opened her mouth no doubt to say something cutting, but she closed it, pressed her lips together, and finally said, "I'm sorry for yer loss of men for yer dishonorable decision to break the treaty."

I don't know why her combining her sympathy offer with a poke at my character amused me, but it did, and I stood struggling not to smile for a long moment before I finally gained control and attained the proper scowl. "My clan, my da, only ever wanted a simple thing."

Her eyebrows arched, and her expression turned wry. "I suppose ye are going to tell me whether I wish it or nae."

The lass was cheeky. A trait I happened to admire. It showed she had a strong backbone. "We desired, we still do, the assurance that the channel would nae be used to control our clan, to make us weaker, or beholden to whoever occupied Eilean Donnan. Yer da would nae ever give the assurance, thus the war began."

"That is nae how I heard the war started," she said, her tone unbending.

I understood. I felt just as unbending. "Well, 'tis the truth. When the king ordered the alliance, I was glad of it. Having lost so many I—" I could no longer say the word. It was a casualty of losing Magy. "I entered us into the alliance in all good faith. The alliance is over, but I would have peace over war. Over death."

Another snort was volleyed at me. "And yet ye have kidnapped me."

I had to resist the urge to bellow. With another long breath, I said, "I offered yer da a new alliance."

"What?" She frowned and shook her head as if she did not believe me. I understood. That was likely easier to accept than the truth that her father had failed her. "When?"

"During Samhain. I told ye."

"Ah, when ye entered our stronghold pretending to be an envoy."

She gave me a challenging look. I suspected she was trying to bait me to argue. She was angry and wanted a fight. I needed to avoid that. "Well, aye," I answered honestly. "He rejected it."

"Of course he did!" she said. "He can nae trust ye."

"That's simply nae true, lass. 'Tis I that should nae trust him. Yet still, I have sent a raven with another offer of an alliance and informed him that I have yer sister and ye and that I will wed ye to seal the alliance. There should nae be any reason for him to keep attacking this stronghold. It would endanger ye and yer sister."

"He will attack still because he can nae trust that ye will nae try to control the channel of passage, given ye already broke the treaty once."

Her blind refusal to see the truth stirred my temper. "'Tis funny," I said, "that ye place so much faith in a man who made alliances with the men who took ye!"

She bit her lip and turned a vivid scarlet. I hated that my words had humiliated her. "He had to, to protect the clan," she said looking down, her voice barely above a whisper now.

I stared at the top of her lovely red head. I did not want us to be enemies, but I feared it inevitable. I had not understood something that was now suddenly clear. If she admitted her da had not protected her as a loving da should, had not fought her enemies for her, then she had to accept the truth that she was not one of the most important things to him. That he would sacrifice her for power.

She picked at what, I did not know. I saw no tear in the coverlet. No thread loosened. I suspected she plucked at something imaginary to avoid looking at me. I didn't contradict her. That would be futile. And I did not tell her that I'd never put the needs of the clan above my sister or brother. If they were in danger or taken, I would give all, right down to my life, for their safe return. I did not utter this truth because that, well, that would be cruel, like plunging a dagger in her chest and twisting it.

I cleared my throat, hoping she would look up, and it took a moment, but she finally did. "We will wed, and if yer da will nae make a new alliance with me, then I will destroy him."

"Ye can nae force me," she bellowed, "I do nae have perfect control over the visions. I can nae bring them on command."

"And yet they come," I countered, feeling smugly triumphant. "Ye have had visions that saved men who were cruel to ye, so I will trust that ye will have visions to aid me."

"Are ye nae fearful," she asked, giving me a menacing look, "that ye will die? All my other husbands have?"

"I will heed yer visions. I gather they did nae."

"Maybe I'll lead ye wrong!" she spat.

Something in the way she looked quickly down as if to hide a truth made me certain of a fact I had not even considered. "Ye can nae lie about yer visions."

Her widened gaze collided with mine.

"I will nae wed ye!" she bellowed. "I hate ye!" She scrambled out from under the covers to her knees. Her hair was a halo of fiery disarray around her heart shaped face to contrast her pale pure skin. The night clothes Katherine had put her in were too sheer on top. The hard peaks of Freya's firm high breasts pushed against the material of the night rail. I hardened all over, struck dumb by the instant shaft of lust this lass caused within me. Not once since Magy died had I been moved to lust by a woman.

I'd had them strip their clothes and appear in my bed uninvited. I'd had them "accidentally" be naked in the loch when I went to wash myself, and I'd even had a lass press her ample chest to my face and refuse to remove it until I gave her a pet.

I'd felt only sadness and loss. I'd assumed the desires that made a man want a woman had died with Magy and my love for her. I'd not minded. I still didn't. What I minded was this new hunger for a woman I had no intention of ever taking to my bed other than to consummate our marriage. I bent down, picked up the dagger, and sheathed it once more. "Ye will wed me," I said, allowing no trace of compromise in my tone, so she would release the hope. It would be easier for us both that way.

"Will ye threaten to kill my sister as the others did?" she spat at me.

I already knew they'd used the little lass, Vanora. She'd told me as much at supper. She was a chatty bit and reminded me of how Katherine had been before life had hardened her with pain, loss, and the basic need to survive.

"Nay," I said. The next part would enrage her, I knew, but it had to be done. "If ye will nae wed me, I will wed yer sister to my brother and offer the alliance that way. But until ye aid me with visions, ye'll remain imprisoned."

She turned white as snow then red as blood, a tempest in the making. "Ye would nae dare."

I would not, but she did not know that, and the little lass Vanora had been the one to give me the idea. She'd overheard Katherine and me speaking at supper, and she'd said, looking longingly at Connor, "If Freya will nae wed ye, I'd be happy to wed Connor." Connor had spit out his wine, and who could blame him? Vanora was not yet a woman at thirteen summers, though I knew well there would be many men who would argue that. And setting that aside, Connor seemed to be giving it his best effort to tumble in the hay with every lass who batted her eyelashes at him. Katherine said he was searching for something. I didn't know about that, but I did know, he did not need to wed until he could keep his cock in his braies.

"I will dare," I lied through my teeth, because that's what I had to do to get what I needed to protect my home, my family, my clan. I was already bending my honor, but by the gods, I would not break it. There were lines I would not cross, but I would find a way over them with grit and determination.

"Ye are a horrible man!" she screamed and then before I knew what was happening, a wine goblet came flying my way. She missed again, and by her bellow, it enraged her. She scrambled to her feet, grabbing up a pitcher to throw it at me, a comb, a shoe, and a glass bottle that likely had contained a tincture Katherine had created. The objects flew toward me, never making it, hitting the floor in thuds and crashes. Shards flew and pottery broke off, and Freya raged. "I despise ye!" she bellowed with each object she threw. "I will kill ye!" she said, shaking her fists at me, before crumpling to the bed.

I knew her acceptance of her situation before she voiced it. One word. "When?" Small. Defeated. Yet there was a trace of defiance that underlay the word. I should not want her to keep the defiance, but I found, I did. I did not want to defeat her spirit. It gave me no pleasure.

"Tomorrow evening," I said, thinking to be generous. Thinking to give her time to fully accept things. "I will teach ye how to throw the dagger," I offered. I would prefer her to be able to defend herself, though never again would I leave a woman of mine without my protection. *Of mine.* I frowned fiercely. She would be mine. I would have to find a way for us to get along, bound in marriage by necessity.

"Excellent," she said, glaring at me. "As soon as I've mastered it, I'll kill ye."

I turned toward the door, so she wouldn't see my reaction. My lips had pulled up into a smile that I could not stop. I was amused that she wanted to kill me. I'd lost my senses.

Chapter Twelve – Freya

I could not say how long I sat on my bed, alternately fuming and worrying, but I was shocked when a knock came at my door, followed by, "Freya, 'tis Katherine and Vanora. We've come to fetch ye for supper."

I glared at the door. I'd rather eat poison than break bread with Laird MacDonald. Whatever generosity I'd felt toward him for attempting to stop Donald from hitting me the day of Samhain and then for rescuing me from Laird Buchanan, was now lost to the heat of my vexation that he was attempting to force me to wed him.

"I'm nae hungry," I bellowed.

"Hungry or nae," Katherine said, "Colin says ye're to come to supper to meet the clan, unless ye are feeling too weary still."

I grinned at those words and the idea they gave me.

I quickly raced to the fireplace, stuck my face as close as I could stand for a moment, then scrambled to the bed and under the covers. I pulled the covers up to my chin, hoping to appear as if I hadn't moved a muscle since Laird Annoying had left me here. "Enter," I called out, making sure to now weaken my voice.

The door swung open, and Katherine and Vanora entered. "I do nae feel well still," I said, adding a little cough for good measure.

A look of alarm settled on Vanora's face as she rushed

to me that made me feel guilty for causing her concern, but the temporary uneasiness she felt would be worth our escaping. Katherine, however, approached me with a clear look of skepticism, but as she got near, I could see her taking my appearance in, and her skeptical look changed to worry. "Ye're flushed."

I nodded and sighed. I'd had a lot of practice feigning illness to avoid Yennifer trying to make me sit and do needlework. It took more patience to sit that long that I cared to use. "I feel warm."

Vanora put her palm on my forehead. "Oh, she's hot!"

Katherine was next to put a palm to my skin, and she clucked her tongue. "I'll just go down and tell Colin that ye're ill, and then I'll come back up to sit with ye."

"That will nae be necessary," I told her. "Vanora will stay with me. I think I just need more time abed."

"Ye're certain?" Katherine asked, nibbling on her lip.

I nodded. "Aye. Vanora can entertain me by telling me about the stronghold, our new home." The last line made me want to toss my accounts—if there had been any in my stomach to toss. But the lie was a necessary one to make it appear as if I was accepting of my fate. I was not! I would go down fighting until the last breath! I looked to Vanora. "Have ye seen much of the stronghold grounds?"

"Oh, aye!" she said, her enthusiasm obvious and disturbing. Did she not understand these people would use her to get what they wanted? She likely expected it, as I did, but I refused to simply accept it, and I would show her not to accept it either. "I've been all over the stronghold as well as down to the lovely loch by way of the seagate stairs."

I had to bite my cheek not to grin. One thing about Vanora—well, two—She would never make a good spy, because she could not keep a secret, and she could be counted on to give way more detail than what I had asked for, which is why I had asked that question. She'd told me, without alerting Katherine, what I needed to know. Vanora had been outside. To the loch. That was excellent because she could lead us to freedom, whereas currently, I could lead us nowhere.

"I'll send up something to eat," Katherine said.

"That will nae be necessary," I replied, thinking fast what I could say. I almost felt a tad bad about myself for how quickly a lie came to me. I would have called myself a very truthful person before my Samhain outing. Now, I seemed to be bending the truth quite frequently, though to be fair to myself, circumstances had forced this less than honorable behavior upon me.

"But I'm hungry!" Vanora protested.

"Well, 'tis a tradition in our clan for the women to fast the night before a wedding."

Vanora frowned. "I do nae recall—"

"Ye are too young to remember the last time we fasted," I tossed out, cutting Vanora off. She was really not picking up on any hints I felt I was giving her. "And anyway, ye were nae required to fast, because ye were under the appropriate age, which is ten summers." My, I was a full out liar now. I really would need to correct that when all of this was over.

"Who was wed?" Vanora asked, making me want to throttle her.

"Auntie Theodora," I said, conjuring up the name I'd not thought upon in years.

"Ye're certain?" Katherine asked.

I nodded, my heart quickening in anticipation of escaping. Katherine gave a nod and made her way to the chamber door. As soon as I heard it click, I looked to Vanora. "Do ye recall the way to the water?"

"Aye, why?"

"Because we are going to escape this place," I said, kicking my coverlet back and rising.

"What?" she gasped behind me as I made my way to the bedchamber door. "I like it here!"

I swung toward her and scowled. "Do ye have any notion how strange that is to like yer captors?"

"I do nae care," Vanora said, jutting out her chin and crossing her arms over her chest. "Katherine is teaching me to be a healer, and Connor—"

"Who?" I demanded.

"Laird MacDonald's brother. He's teaching me the bow and arrow, and I wish to wed him."

I rolled my eyes at that bit of ridiculousness. After I ensured the passageway was clear, I faced Vanora once more. "Ye are coming with me."

"Why?" she demanded. "I do nae want to go home and eventually be bargained away by da as ye have been. I've found the man I'm going to wed."

"Ye are a child! A mere thirteen summers!"

"I will nae always be thirteen summers. And I'm staying near Connor to ensure he does nae wed another."

"Vanora!" I snapped. "Ye are being ridiculous. Ye have kenned him all of a few days! Ye are coming with me!" I grabbed her wrists and froze as images hit me. Vanora older and standing in front of a priest facing Connor. Their hands were bound, and she was grinning. Her love was obvious in her eyes. I increased my grip on her wrists, despite her protesting and trying to tug her arm away. Each beat of my heart thumped in my ears. The swish of my blood through my veins joined the thump. I willed the vision to show me more.

Sweat trickled down my forehead, rolled along my scalp, and beaded above my lip. Dizzy and queasy, the room around me faded, blurred. Vanora's protest drifted away like a puff of smoke, and I found myself transported to their wedding, looking down upon them. I willed the scene to solidify, to form. To come into sharp relief. Who was there? What was there? Woods surrounded the clearing, tall pine trees with branches like steeples and trunks like pillars. Their shadows crisscrossed over the forest floor like a mosaic of darkness and light. Vanora wore a dagger upon her hip, its hilt glittering like a jewel in the sun. Connor had two swords sheathed crosswise on his back, hilts over his shoulders, blades waiting in readiness. Guests stood in a wide circle around them, silent witnesses. Some held elegant weapons, swords and daggers. Others carried simple bows and spears; their rough leather armor stained from battles past. All were armed, all wore gray, and all watched expectantly. The wind swept through, and the treetops swayed, rustling as though breathing. I willed the scene to move faster, to progress to its conclusion. I willed it to live and breathe and dance before my eyes. Instead, it began to waver and blur, to diffuse into nothing.

"Let me go!" Vanora demanded, smacking me in the arm with her free hand and breaking my vision.

I stood panting, still gripping her wrist as my gaze met Vanora's. "I had a vision," I whispered.

Vanora gasped. "Of me?"

"Aye," I admitted, hoping I'd not live to regret admitting this to her. "Ye must keep this to yerself."

"I will!" she replied with a vehemence that made me hopeful she meant it, still, I knew my chatty sister.

I grasped her tight as my heart raced. "I mean it! Swear it to me! Swear it on yer life!"

"I swear it!" she said. "What did ye see for me?"

I didn't want to tell her, because I knew it would only make her less inclined to come with me. Could I keep it to myself? I sat there, testing if it would simply slip out. I'd learned I could not lie about my visions, but what if I simply never uttered them aloud? I counted to ten. Then twenty. Then all the way to one hundred. I could keep the visions in by not uttering what I'd seen.

"Ye promised ye'd tell me!" Vanora whined.

"Ye will wed him eventually," I said. "When ye are older. A woman."

"I'll wed him!" Vanora said, her excitement palpable.

I nodded. "Unless something changes. Unless I've changed the future by telling ye."

A wary look settled upon her face. "I need to stay," she said, crossing her arms over her chest.

"If ye refuse to come with me, I will have to stay. And if I stay, I will have to wed Laird MacDonald. I do nae wish to wed again. Ever. But if I do nae wed him, he said he will wed ye to his brother."

Vanora grinned like the senseless lass she was. "I want to wed him."

"Aye. I ken ye think ye are in love after a few days of kenning the man, but he is a man. Ye are a child. He does nae love ye. And ye are infatuated with him. My vision is for ye as a grown woman. That means yer love will take time to grow. I will nae be the reason ye are wed as a child, but if ye stay, ye will be the reason I'm forced to wed again to a man who only wants to use me. Ye have seen how that has been for me."

Vanora bit her lower lip. "I'd nae be the reason ye are hurt again."

My heart expanded with her words I knew were true. "I

ken ye'd nae."

She nibbled on her lip for a moment. I knew she was trying to come up with a way to get the end result she desired. "Mayhap," she said, the word hopeful, "Laird MacDonald is a gentle sort of man?"

I snorted. "He is willing to wed me for my visions. I think nae, sister."

She nibbled on her lips again as she stared at me. "I will go with ye. Ye are my sister."

I hugged her to me, and then took her hand, and squeezed it.

"How will we get home?" I could hear the concern in her tone. I had the same concern, but I shoved it away. I had to be fearless and strong for both of us.

I motioned for Vanora to follow me out of the room. We were wasting precious time. When we entered the empty passageway, I turned to her. "I do nae ken yet. First, we must get away from this castle."

Vanora chewed on her lip, a sign she was thinking. "They keep a dinghy tied at the back of the stronghold in case there's need of escape." She grinned. "Katherine told me so. 'Tis hidden in brush. And," she said, the word ringing with triumph, "Da's attacks have sorely depleted the stronghold guards. They do nae currently have enough men to guard the stronghold all the time. I overheard Connor direct the channel guards to watch the bridge tonight. He'd gotten word to expect an attack, which means—"

"There will nae by anyone keeping watch at the back, at the loch," I said, smiling.

"Aye," she said, grinning back at me.

I threw my arm around her shoulder and pulled her toward me. "We have our escape."

Chapter Thirteen – Colin

"Where are the lasses?" I asked my sister as she sat down beside me upon the dais.

Katherine scowled down at her trencher. "Porridge again?"

"Just be glad there's anything to eat," I growled. "With the constant attacks on the stronghold all available hands have been fighting nae farming."

"Freya's da is nae going to have to breach the stronghold at this rate," she said, sopping up some porridge with a hunk of stale bread, sniffing it, frowning, and tossing the dripping gray mess onto her trencher. "We're all going to starve this way."

I inhaled a long breath for patience and asked again, "Where are the lasses?"

"In Freya's bedchamber. She did nae feel well, so she did nae want to come to supper, and her sister stayed with her."

"Did ye instruct the kitchen lasses to send a tray up for them?"

"I offered to," Katherine replied, "but Freya said they've some tradition in her family about the women fasting the night before the wedding."

"That's an odd tradition," Connor said from my right.

I nodded, considering. "Did Freya look unwell to ye?"

Katherine shrugged. "I suppose."

"What do ye mean ye suppose? Ye're the healer of our clan."

Katherine glared at me. "Her eyes were bright indicating good health, and her color seemed good, and her speech was clear, but her skin was hot, indicating a fever. Why?"

"I would nae put it past that lass to try to escape the castle."

Connor snorted at that. "I do nae see how she'd do that. The drawbridge is up and manned, and the storm prevents anyone from leaving by the loch or getting near. The waters are rough, high, and dangerous."

"Aye, I suppose that's true enough," I said. Mayhap I was worrying without cause. "Even if the lasses were foolish enough to try to escape by way of the loch, they do nae ken the way down—"

"Actually," Katherine said, "I took Vanora with me to the loch."

"Why the devil did ye do that?" I asked, a twitch starting near my right eye.

"Because ye told me to keep her with me at all times that she was nae in her bedchamber, and I needed to fetch some water down at the loch."

"Fine, fine. It does nae matter, I suppose if the lass kens the way to the loch. They still can nae flee without the dinghy, and that's well hidden."

"Well," Connor said in drawn out tone that made me know I was not going to like what I heard. "I took the lass Vanora out on the water yesterday morning in the dinghy."

The twitch beside my right eye increased in speed. I reached for my goblet of wine and consumed the entire contents in one gulp to douse the spark of my temper. "Please tell me ye did nae let her see where the dinghy is hidden."

"Fine," Connor said, in his typical glib tone, "I'll nae tell ye."

I was already rising when the alarm horn cut through the noise of the clan talking in the great hall. It blew in three short bursts and one long one. The chatter of the clan increased immediately as cries of concern rang from table to table and my warriors stood, drawing swords, preparing for what they believed was another attack.

"Do ye think MacLeod is already returned?" Connor asked, drawing his own sword.

"Nay, nay I do nae, ye clot-heid," I snapped. "Ye just said yerself the waters are too rough for anyone to be in them."

"Then who—"

"I've nary a doubt that the lasses are trying to escape," I said, stomping down the dais. I raised my hands and let out a shrill whistle for silence as I strode toward the Great Hall doors. Behind me, footstep fell, and I glanced over my shoulder to see Connor rushing toward me. I swept my gaze over my clan. "Calm yerselves," I said. "We are nae under attack, so ye can return to yer supper."

With that, I strode out the doors as Connor fell into step beside me.

"If it's them—"

"It is," I cut him off. I couldn't say why I was so certain, but I was.

"Then, I'm sorry."

"Aye," I bit out, shoving through the door into the back outer courtyard. A biting, wicked wind drove the rain sideways, lashing it against me with the force of a hundred small whips, as I hurried to the narrow staircase. Chilled water snaked down my neck, but I could not stop. I raced, nearly stumbling, toward the stone steps that led to the seagate.

The worst of the night had not fallen yet, and patches of late twilight lingered over the dim sky like a gauze of bruised silk. This faint, failing light gave me just enough visibility to make out the loch below. When I reached the top of the staircase, I squinted to see the water beyond the break wall, where a single dinghy bobbed and spun and heaved through the rough churning water. The small vessel held two women, and despite the growing shadows, I knew them both with no need for a closer look. "God's blood," I cursed, thankful that I'd been able to put Nigel on guard duty at the back of the castle.

"Do ye think they'll get far?" Connor yelled over the howling wind as we now raced down the slick steps.

Right at that moment, a wave crashed into the dinghy overturning it, dumping both lasses into the water, and spurring me into an all-out sprint. I hit the land, heart pounding and breath coming fast and hard, and as I ran toward the water, I stripped off my sword, my dagger, and my plaid, dropping them as I went. I hit the water with a shout, my teeth immediately clenching against the coldness. As I dove, Vanora bobbed to the surface, screaming. Then all sound disappeared but that of the waves crashing overhead. I cut my arms as fast as I could through the water, and as long as I could, until my lungs burned, and I was forced to the surface.

The moment I surfaced, water smacked me in the face and filled my nose, my mouth, my lungs. I spit and coughed, blinking my eyes, and then took a moment to locate the lasses. I only saw Vanora, circling round and round, still screaming, but now I was close enough to hear her. "Freya!" she called, the sound choked and tormented. Vanora dove under the water, and I understood then—she was looking for her sister.

I dove, to, swimming to where Vanora had just been. I kicked furiously and swam, arm over arm, muscles burning. The water churned too violently for me to see anything clearly. When my hand brushed against a body, I hesitated, uncertain who it was. But as I grasped it and felt no resistance, dread settled in. It had to be Freya. God's blood, was she dead? I kicked us to the surface, breaking it, and coming face to face with Vanora. Behind her, Connor had managed to overturn the dinghy and was swimming it toward us.

"My sister!" Vanora screamed, trying to grab a still Freya from me.

"I've got her," I yelled. "Get yerself to the dinghy." I waited a beat, relieved to see she did as told. I flipped Freya on her back as water washed over us and then, flipping on my own back and circling her waist with my arm, I swam us to the dinghy. Connor helped Vanora into the small boat, and then they both reached down to grasp Freya. I did my best to lift her to them as we rose and fell with the waves. Up we went then back down as the water covered my head. When I came up, Freya was being tugged over the side of the dinghy by Connor and Vanora. Once I climbed over, I scrambled to my knees and to the lass.

"Move aside," I said, giving the crying and screaming Vanora a gentle push. I didn't know much about the healing arts, but I had seen my sister once revive a drowned woman at the village. I turned Freya on her side, whacked her on the back several times, and when that didn't produce any results, I leaned down, tilted her head back, pinched her nose shut, and blew as hard as I could into her mouth. The lass lay unmoving, her skin cold, her pallor graying.

"She'd dead!" Vanora screamed, starting to pound me on the back. "Ye killed my sister!"

I repeated blowing breath into her mouth once more. And again. And finally, Freya began to cough and spit out water. I exhaled a ragged breath and helped the lass to sit up. I didn't want the water she was spitting out to go back into her lungs. Under my fingertips her body started to tremble and then she began to shake with a violence that clanked her teeth together. I gathered her into my arms and pulled her close to wrap my arms around her in an effort to give her whatever warmth I had to offer.

"Do nae mind me," Connor said, winking as he leaned over the side of the boat, attempting to paddle us to shore.

"That's nae going to work," I offered, my lips turning up in a smile that loosened a few of the knots in my shoulders and neck that fear for the lass had put there.

"Ye do nae say?" Connor snapped. "Ye just sit there holding the lass. I'll do all the hard work."

"Since it's yer fault we are out here that seems just."

He opened his mouth no doubt to protest, then clamped it shut, turned and jumped over the edge of the dinghy as he held the ledge.

"What's he doing?" Vanora cried out, getting on her knees to look over the ledge at Connor.

"He's swimming us in, lass, so we do nae all drown thanks to yer and ye sister's ridiculous escape attempt." Now that the fear had abated, my irritation was rising. I felt Freya tilt her head back and look up at me. Her color had returned a bit, but not all the way, so her eyes looked especially dark against her pale skin. Water dripped from her long lashes, and I had the urge to run my thumb over them to dry them.

"If ye'd nae have taken me," she bellowed with surprising strength for a lass who'd nearly just drowned, "I'd nae have had to try to escape."

Her body still shook, so I didn't set her on her arse on the cold hard dingy bottom, as I had the desire to do. Instead, I said, "Might I remind ye, I saved ye in those woods, and then I saved ye just now. I'd think ye'd be thanking me, so I do nae dump ye back into the water."

"Nay!" Vanora gasped. "She can nae swim!"

My lips parted at that astonishing revelation. The lass had wanted to escape me so badly she'd gotten into a dingy in the middle of a storm, even though she could nae swim. "I will nae hurt ye ever. Ye do nae need to put yer and yer sister's lives in jeopardy to escape me."

"I've had three husbands in less than a year, each worse than the other, so ye must understand, if I do nae believe the promise of a man who is wedding me against my will." With that, she shoved out of my arms and moved as far away from me as the dinghy would allow. She pressed her back to the edge, drew her knees up, and wrapped her arms around them. The rain had slowed to a drizzle, but her hair, still sopping wet, was plastered to her face. Fiery strands streaked like spreading vines across her cheeks and down her neck. Even though I knew my promise to be true, guilt hardened in my belly. I was wedding her against her will. That was something I'd never thought I'd do, but to save my clan, my brother and sister, and this stronghold so many had died for, I had to do it. I had no desire to have a wife in the truest sense of the word anymore, but I did nae want another enemy either. "Ye will see I'm a man of my word."

She snorted.

I ground my teeth together but tried again as we neared shore. "I will prove it to ye."

Her eyes lit with my words. "Ye wish to prove to me ye'll nae hurt me?"

"Aye," I replied, though I had no notion why. Why

should I care? It wasn't the first time I'd asked the question, and an answer still did not magically appear.

Her lips formed a smug smile. "Then give me yer word ye'll nae bed me."

The request was so ridiculous I laughed. "Believe me I do nae want to bed ye."

"Excellent," she said, "then we are in agreement."

I shook my head. "I have to consummate the marriage to solidify the union."

"Then ye will hurt me," she said, her voice shaking.

I couldn't ignore her fear, but I also could not ignore that the marriage had to be consummated. "I will nay bed ye until ye are ready. Until ye ask me to," I said, as Connor pulled the boat to the shore.

"Then we will nae be bedding at all," she said, climbed out of the boat and went marching away in the wrong direction with her sister scrambling after her.

Connor shook his head at me. "That was a foolish vow to give."

"Aye," I agreed. "But I did nae have a choice. The lass has been abused. Apparently sorely so. I'll nae be responsible for causing her fear and more pain. And currently, she is afraid of me. She does nae trust me. And until she trust me, she will nae be relaxed enough for the bedding."

"So what will ye do?"

"I suppose I'll have to gain her trust, so I can consummate the marriage."

"Seems a lot of work for man who does nae intend to actually live as a true husband and wife."

"Aye," I agreed. "It certainly does."

Chapter Fourteen – Freya

"Ye can nae wear that to be wed in," Vanora cried out the next night as I picked up the only gown I had.

"What do I care?" I muttered. "I'm being forced to wed, yet again."

"Ye can hardly compare Colin to yer other three husbands," she said as a knock came at my bedchamber door, and she turned from me to see who was there.

"We shall see," I said, not willing to trust his word. But he was the first man who had taken me against my will to give me any sort of promise. In fact, my other husbands would have smacked me across my face for my insolence.

Vanora opened the door, and Katherine swept in holding a gown in one hand and a head wreath of flowers in the other. "Ye did nae need to do that," I said, refusing to feel thankful for the kind gesture. I knew it was churlish of me, but she was an accomplice to her brother keeping me here.

Katherine chuckled. "I did nae. I ken verra well ye do nae appreciate the gown, but Colin insisted."

"Colin? Why would he do such a thing?" And before Katherine could answer I said, "Ah, I see now. He does nae want to be embarrassed by my appearance in front of his clan."

Katherine shot me a smirk. "Colin does nae care what the clan thinks of yer appearance, Freya. They all ken this is a union of necessity."

My cheeks heated at that revelation. It wasn't surprising, still, that didn't make it any less embarrassing. "Then why the gown and the headdress of flowers?"

Katherine walked toward me and set the gown and the wreath on the bed. "He thought ye might wish a fresh gown, instead of the one ye have been wearing for seven days. And the flowers, well—" Katherine shrugged. "I can only guess that he was trying to soften the blow of forcing ye to wed him by offering ye the flowers."

"That hardly makes what he's doing any less dishonorable," I snapped.

Katherine narrowed her eyes at me. "My brother is the most honorable person I ken. If there was another way to protect our home, to protect our clan, he'd take it. Believe me."

She sounded so impassioned, that the tiniest part of me, considered what she said, and I was irritated that I could not dismiss her words outright. "I'll wear the gown," I said, because frankly my own gown was stiff and itchy from dirt and loch water, and it smelled something terrible. I may not want to wed Colin, but I didn't want to smell horrid either. "Ye can take the flowers with ye."

"Suit yerself," Katherine said, starting to pick them up, but Vanora snatched them up before Katherine could grab them.

"I'll wear the headdress if Freya does nae wish to."

"As ye like," Katherine replied. "I'd hurry and put on the gown, if I were ye, though. Connor will be here to fetch ye shortly to make yer way to the chapel, and he's been instructed nae to dally."

"I do nae need a guard to the chapel," I protested.

"He is nae sent as yer guard," Freya. "He is sent as yer escort."

"Oh," I replied, my cheeks heating yet again. This was entirely different than my other weddings. Maybe… just possibly… but no. I was not ready to extend the benefit of the doubt.

After Katherine departed, Vanora helped me into my gown, and when I turned to face her, she exclaimed, "Freya, ye are a vision. Colin will be beside himself with desire."

Her words made me suck in a sharp breath and sent a shiver through me.

"Oh, Freya," she whispered, hugging me to her as if she were the older sister and I the younger one. "My words were unthinking. I ken ye have been hurt."

She didn't know the depth of my fear or pain, and I wanted to keep it that way. At least one of us should have their innocence, their trust, intact.

She patted me as our mama would have, and longing to see my mama, talk to her, feel her loving arms around me, made me ache. "I feel certain Colin will keep his word to ye about the bedding."

"We shall see," I said. "I admit at least he bothered to give me a promise. All my other husbands simply took, though I did nae want to give." That was the most insight I wished to give, so when a knock came at the door, and Connor announced his arrival, I rushed to open it.

He grinned at me. "Ye smell much better than yesterday."

I laughed at his unexpected words. "I suppose I do."

His gaze went past me to rest on Vanora for the briefest of moments. "Ye clean up nicely, wee bit."

Vanora frowned. "I told ye nae to call me wee bit. I'm nae a child and we will—"

"Vanora!" I cut her impending revelation of my vision of the two of them wed. I didn't want to give Colin any reason to wed them instead. The future could change, and I wanted Vanora to have the time to be young, to mature as only the passing of time could allow for, so that if she did someday wed Connor, it would be for love and not some silly girl crush.

Vanora glowered at me and plopped the flowers on her head but thankfully kept her silence. Then Connor extended an elbow to each of us and we started toward my dark fate. As Vanora chattered, I tried to breathe steadily and deeply to calm the fears rising inside of me, but it was useless. Trying to abate my worry was like trying to hold back a storm. By the time we got to the outside courtyard that was filled with clan members who I supposed wanted to get a look at me, my legs trembled so much I could hardly put one foot in front of the other.

"I've got ye," Connor whispered to me, making me tear my gaze away from all the curious onlookers to him.

"Beg pardon?"

"Ye're nae moving."

I hadn't even realized I'd stopped walking.

"Colin told me ye'd likely be sore afraid, and nae to rush ye and to offer ye words of comfort."

I frowned. Those actions bespoke of honor, and I was in no way ready to grant the man any good characteristics at all. Yes, he'd saved me twice, but he'd had selfish reasons for doing so, so I said, "I'm certain he thinks to soften me to get me to want to bed him—"

"Aye, of course he does," Connor said, making me gape at him. He seemed to be unusually blunt, and I begrudgingly liked him. It was easier to like him than his brother, given Connor was not trying to force me to wed him against my will. "But he also genuinely cares for yer welfare, Freya. The sooner ye accept that, the better for ye both."

Was that true? I didn't know, but what I did know was that if I did not let him bed me, and he kept his word not to force me, then our marriage could be annulled. I didn't say that, because I was not foolish. Instead, I took a deep breath, and said, "Lead me on."

The procession through the courtyard was almost leisurely, and it seemed as if the clans people parted like the sea to make way for us. As we advanced, I heard the whispers of ban-druidh, and it made me laugh out loud. The clans people shot me strange looks as I stifled it to a chuckle. If I had the powers that Morgana possessed, I would not have been standing here, almost a bride again. If I had any say in it, I would have never been forced to wed in the first place. My pride would have never allowed it. No, I was no witch—though I had certainly been cursed by one. Bitterness at how twisted my fate had become soured my tongue and made the tears sting my eyes with their sharp tang. I blinked furiously, determined not to cry, especially with all these people staring at me with open curiosity.

Ahead, a small chapel finally came into view, and I sucked in a sharp breath at the sight of all the torches that had been lit to lead to the chapel door. The light flickered against the worn stone, stretching long across the ground. Colin stood in the doorway, waiting for me with an expectant look, calm and still. It was a small thing, really, but a gesture none of my other husbands had offered on our wedding days. My resolve wavered and my heart flipped, and for one ill-advised moment, I nearly slipped. Oh, I didn't want it to move me, but it did nudge me ever so slightly toward softening.

I forced myself to focus away from him, to concentrate instead on the path to the chapel. Uncertain and weak was no way to approach this new life. I wouldn't be taken in by false kindness. No, this time, I would be the one in control. I picked up my pace. I'd been fooled before by this frail thing called hope, as fragile as a bloom and just as easily killed. With the distance between us closing, a bright flare of resistance burned away the confusion. I would not let him fool me.

The flames of forty torches matched the glow of the setting sun in a warming brilliance. They lined the walk like sentries, marking the way to the chapel door. Their heat flushed my face; I lifted my chin. The clans people fell in behind me, the curiosity in their glances almost more than I could bear. I stepped into the chapel, and my resolve hardened in my chest against the longing for all the dreams I had lost.

Yet, I sucked in a sharp breath at the picture Colin presented of barely leashed power. His long, heavily muscled legs were spread like branches of a rooted tree, and his broad chest strained against the confines of his tunic. His hair curled at his neck in wet tendrils, as if he had just emerged from the loch. He glanced at me and the somberness in his eyes matched the grim line of his mouth. It was so clear in that moment that he didn't truly want to wed me any more than I wanted to wed him. I couldn't decide if that made me feel more at ease or worse.

Connor handed me off to Colin, and the gentleness with which he took my hand was like nothing I'd experienced with my other husbands. Every touch had been rough. Every move ordered, as if I were a hound. Colin drew me to his side, his heat enveloping me, his large stature nearly overwhelming. My heart leapt at the thought of what his body could do to mine. I'd known pain, and none of those men had been near as large as Colin. He glanced down at me, his lips softening in the hard line and his eyebrows arching. "Are ye ready?"

"Nay," I croaked, to which he nodded and set his hand on top of mine, making me jump at the contact.

"'Tis all right, lass. I vow on my life I willnae break my promise to ye."

I nodded, because there was nothing else I could do. I was glad to find that only Katherine and the priest stood inside the chapel. Behind us, Vanora and Connor entered and then the priest commenced the ceremony. I heard the words. I spoke when I was supposed to, but I was floating above myself, looking down, as if I were a bird observing strange creature far below me. I found myself wishing I was a bird. Wishing I could fly. I would fly away from here, mayhap to a convent where I would be protected. The thought made me blink. My da protected me. Except, well, except he had failed, multiple times. I could forgive his failing to protect me from the men who had stolen me. He could not have known, but a knot of resentment had grown in me, I realized, that he had wed me to Donald. I don't know why this anger had grown. Well, I knew, but it was not fair to my da. What choice had he had? I tried to imagine my life at a convent. Without a husband. That was fine. Without children. That thought made me frown.

"I suppose congratulations is nae the thing to say."

The words made me blink. In front of me stood Vanora. The priest was gone and Colin stood looking as if he too wished he was a bird. I laughed at that, and Colin, his brother and sister, who'd been patting him on the back like someone had just died, all looked to me. "What's amusing?" Katherine said.

"My life," I answered without fear, and that struck me. I did not fear to speak my mind. It was the first time that I could remember in a very long time not feeling as if I had to hold my tongue. "If I do nae laugh, I'll cry. I set out to steal a goblet to drink from it and make a wish to nae be forced to wed a man I did nae love, and look at me now? On my fourth husband!" Hysteria was rising inside of me like a wave. "I wonder how many more husbands I'll be forced to wed?"

Colin took me gently by the elbow and turned me toward the door. "I'll be yer last, lass. Ye need nae fear ever again. I will protect ye from any man who tries to harm ye," he said. As he walked me out the door of the chapel a thunderous cheer rang out from his clan.

He paused, smiling, then glanced sideways at me. "They love ye already."

"They'll nae love me when my da denies the alliance and attacks yer stronghold again. Men will die. Yer men. Their husbands. Das. Lovers. Then they'll come to hate me. To blame me."

His eyes widened. "Is this a prophecy?"

"Ye did nae need the sight to see this future," I said, my bitterness overflowing. "This is the legacy between our clans." My heart thundered in my chest. "Ye say ye will protect me from any man who tries to harm me. Ye are harming me. I fear ye. Who will protect me from ye?"

He flinched as if I had struck him with something, and then he scrubbed a hand over his face. When he brought it down, I could not deny the weariness in his gaze. "Ye do nae need protection from me, Freya. I will nae lay a hand upon ye until ye ask."

I did not bother reminding him I would not ask, but when he set his palm to my lower back to guide me, I arched away from him and glanced up at him. "Ye have already broken yer word. Ye touched me." I knew I was being ridiculous, but I didn't care.

His lips pressed together in a hard line once more, but he did not hit me and did not yell or threaten. He moved his hand, motioned to the path and said, "By all means, lead the way to the Great Hall for the wedding celebration."

I glanced around the crowded courtyard, having no idea which way to go, but I refused to ask, so I decided to turn toward the right. "To the left," he said, his words warm with gentle laughter, and I felt the embarrassment that heated my cheeks, neck, and chest. And that's how it went. Me marching ahead, and him so close behind me that his body heat rolled off him to singe me, but he did not break his word and touch me. I got to the Great Hall with his directions, and when we approached, another cheer rose. This time it was all the serving wenches and lads, who greeted us at the door with goblets of wine.

I took mine and downed it in several gulps, despite Colin beside me saying, "Slow down, lass. The wine is strong." He was right but I liked the way it burned a path down my throat and warmed the ice in my belly. When I was finished, I lowered the goblet, saw he was still holding his full one, and I plucked it out of his hands while shoving mine toward him. I marveled at my behavior. Something strange had come over me. He didn't stop me, and I marveled at that, too. He stood watching me, eyebrows arched, and a smile tugging his lips upward into a half-grin that would have made my belly flutter in the days before I'd been thrice wedded and bedded.

"Do ye ken," I said, my tongue tingling, "that ye look like the gods paid special attention to carving ye to please the lasses?"

His grin grew larger. Had I just truly said that? "Do ye think so, lass?"

I nodded. No sense taking it back now. Then, I poked

him in the chest. "That does nae mean I want to bed ye."

"Certainly nae," he replied, "but do ye think ye could find it in yer heart to dance with me. 'Tis a wedding tradition of my clan, and they are waiting on us to dance before we can all sit to supper."

I frowned, breath tight in my chest, and swept my gaze over the now full great hall. Servants darted between clansmen. The minstrel had ceased to play and was regarding us with bemusement. The entire assembly seemed to have decided it had better things to do than chat or dance, for they all now had their attention focused on us. His clan was gathered in every corner and nook, standing all around the great hall like a rising tide. They were waiting, I supposed, for us to dance. They must have entered the room when I was drinking the wine. Even my sister was there, standing between Connor and Elizabeth, looking happy like the traitor she was.

"Well, lass?" he asked, the question a gentle one.

I glanced at Colin—my husband. Yet again, I was a bride. The wine had loosened my nerves apparently, because I did not tremble, and my heart did not race ahead. "I'll dance with ye, but only because I love to dance, and it has been so verra long since I got to, and I'm famished and want to eat."

A deep chuckle rumbled from his chest, making me wonder how much heartier it would sound if I had my ear pressed to his chest. I hiccupped at the thought.

"When was the last time ye ate?" he asked, his eyebrows dipping together and setting a crease between his brows.

I reached out and pressed my thumb to it, causing him to smirk at me. "I do nae recall," I said. "When I awoke yesterday?" I offered with a shrug.

He smiled at me, and it made my breath catch. For

whatever else he was or wasn't, he was a compellingly handsome warrior. "The wine has gone to yer head."

"Aye," I agreed. "'Tis lovely. Ye may touch me now to dance."

His hand encircled mine, fingers gripping as though never to release, and he pulled me across the room, both of us breathless. At the last possible moment, he twisted me under his arm, unexpectedly turning me to face the same direction, my body drawn close to his, with his firm right hand still clasping my left. Suddenly, music filled the room with life, and his clan shouted their approval once more, clapping in a pounding, almost feverish rhythm that set the tempo of my heart. A mischievous grin spread across his face as he danced me in one direction, then pivoted to twirl me round. Skipping side by side, our feet hovered above the ground, strings of instruments propelling us, before he spun me down the other way, and the clapping grew so loud, it thundered in my chest like a wild creature, nearly deafening. I turned to face him, and he gripped my waist, circling it with both hands, and lifted me up. I had wanted to be a bird, and now, like magic, I was flying.

He spun me until the world became a whirl of hovering, dizzying colors. I was suspended in mid-air, and my laughter broke free, untethered, the kind that echoed joy, the kind that had nothing to do with hysteria, rising or otherwise. Heat and elation and something else, something foreign and familiar, something more, infused me, a warmth that melted my limbs, melted the room, melted us together, until the spinning stopped. Then slowly he slid me back to earth, hard against soft, flesh against flesh. He didn't release his hold, just pulled me tighter and tighter. As my pulse spiked, I stumbled backward while pushing him away.

He held his hands up, palms facing me. "I'm sorry, lass.

I only meant to steady ye."

I nodded. His words sounded sincere enough as did the look upon his face. He extended one hand toward me. "Come, let us sit at the dais."

"I'm more than capable of walking to the dais on my own," I said, took one step, and tripped. Biting my lip, I stole a look at him from under my lashes and found him fighting not to laugh. Something about the obviousness of his trying to protect my feelings, eased me enough again, that I took his extended hand and allowed him to lead me past his clan to the dais. I sat, stomach growling, in front of my trencher, and had just ripped a chunk of bread to sop up some gravy, when a serving wench appeared before me holding a pitcher of wine.

She started to take my goblet, but Colin shook his head. The lass laughed and winked. "Aye, laird, of course, we want the lass to be in her wits for the bedding!"

My appetite instantly disappeared, and the chunk of bread slipped from my frozen fingers. I thought of my clan and the tradition of the public bedding where everyone always watched at the new couple consummated their marriage. The wine I'd drank threatened to come up, filling my mouth with a sour taste. "Ye promised!" I hissed at Colin.

He frowned. "I promised what?"

"Ye promised ye would nae ye ken until I'm ready to—"

"Och, what's this?" the serving girl demanded, scowling. "The bedding must be public, so we all ken the marriage is consummated." Her words were like a spark to wood. The lit the room with "ayes" that became a chanting chorus of "Bed her. Bed her."

Colin's nostrils flared, and he glared at the serving wench, before he stood, and let out a shrill whistle that brought his clan to silence. "There will nae be a public bedding and anyone who cries for it again will be on watch duty tonight." I exhaled a slow shaky breath, feeling all eyes upon me but not caring. "Go back to yer supper," Colin commanded and sat.

He looked to me. "There. Ye can eat now."

I had no appetite, but given what he'd just done for me, I shoved the piece of bread in my mouth and forced myself to chew. It could have been wood for all I tasted of it. My mind had begun to replay all my wedding nights, and the more memories that came, the harder chewing became and breathing.

Colin's sister leaned behind me. "Does it feel strange to be wed again, brother?"

I stilled at that. Wed again? I turned to Colin. "Ye've been wed before?"

He nodded but offered no more. The knots in my stomach grew tighter. I did not know this man. I did not know him at all.

Chapter Fifteen – Colin

I rounded the passageway to the bedchambers and when Freya made to turn to the right, toward her bedchamber and away from mine, I sighed, knowing my next words would make her even more skittish than she already was. I grasped her as gently as I could by the elbow to still her retreat. She flinched, turning toward me and jerking her arm out of my hold.

"Why did ye grab my arm?" she demanded, her chest heaving with likely fear.

"Ye need to sleep in my—our—bedchamber."

"What?" The word was a squeak. "Nay! I—"

"Listen to me lass," I said, trying to gentle my tone. "We did nae give the clan the public bedding, but if we do nae even sleep in the same chamber, they'll talk and doubt my leadership if I can nae even get my wife to sleep in my chamber. I ken I'm asking a great deal, but we do nae even have to sleep in the same bed. I'll take the floor."

She stared at me a long moment, eyes wide, and wringing her hands. "Ye vow it?"

"Aye."

"Fine," she said.

We walked in silence to the bedchamber, and when I opened the door, I was pleased to see chamber lasses had laid out gowns for Freya as I'd instructed them to do. For a moment, looking at the gowns on my bed and seeing such feminine trinkets beside them like the hair comb and small gloves, reminded me of Magy and sent an ache through me.

"What's wrong?" Freya asked.

I blinked the memory away. "Beg pardon?" I asked.

"Ye grunted as if ye had an ache."

"It was nae anything."

She snorted audibly then trudged across the creaky floorboards in our bedchamber, slippers echoing like judgments, until she got to the fire. It was crackling low in the hearth, the way it did in the mornings when the cold had crept in, and the dampness sat heavy over everything like a wet cloth. She whirled then in a motion that sent the skirt of her gown flaring out and pinned me with a look that was the sort of look that'd start a rockslide. Her lips were pursed like a quiver drawn too tight, and her chin jutted up with a stubbornness that was as old as time.

Those looks boded trouble. I knew from past experiences with my sister and Magy. I'd been pitted against them both in arguments enough to know these looks meant they would not bend unless by force, and I was not a man to use force against a woman. Any man who said women were weak was a fool or a liar. When a woman set her mind to something or got something stuck in her head, she was a more formidable foe than the best trained warrior in the world.

"Are those ye're last wife's gowns?" she demanded, motioning toward the frocks on the bed.

"Nay," I said, my jaw twitching. I didn't want to talk of Magy. I had, in fact, purposely exited the Great Hall for the bedchambers abruptly in hopes to end any further questions about her. I could see now that had been futile. To ease the lass standing before me I suspected I would have to offer some details. Knots formed in my shoulders with the thought of it. "Magy was much taller than ye." Each word felt ripped from me. I didn't speak of Magy, because it brought back the guilt of having failed her.

A hopeful look came to Freya's face. "Will ye tell me about her?"

"Nay," I bit out. I didn't mean to be harsh, but talking of Magy was like opening up my chest with a serrated dagger, so someone could dig around, find my heart, and rip it out.

A dark look settled upon her face. "I do nae ken ye! Ye made me wed ye, and I do nae ken ye at all! I did nae even ken ye had been wed before."

I slid my teeth back and forth thinking. She was right. I knew she was, but I would nae speak of Magy. By the gods, I could not. "Ye may ask me one personal question, but—"

"Oh, laird," she said, rushing to me and dropping to her knees as if she were groveling at my feet. "Ye are so kind, so kind," she said in an exaggerated tone of fawning. When she glanced up, she had a smirk on her face. Her merriment warmed me, and I had to fight the desire to throw back my head and laugh. She was astonishingly lovely when she was happy. The thought bothered me, because it meant she had affected me, and I wanted no part of that. I reached down to tug her up, but her eyes went wide, and she scrambled back and against the bed like a cornered animal.

Anger rushed through me at what she'd endured. I immediately dropped to my haunches, setting my forearms on my legs to let my hands dangle before me, so she understood I had no intension of striking her. "I only meant to tug ye up, so we could talk. I told ye, I will nae ever lay a hand on ye to hurt ye."

She bit her lip as color flooded her cheeks, making her even lovelier. There was a vulnerability showing that made me ache for her. "Ye were nae supposed to touch me without asking. Remember?"

"I forgot," I said. "I'm sorry. I've nae ever had such a request."

"Well," she replied pushing herself up to sit on the bed. "I suppose ye have nae ever been with a lass who endured what I have."

The desire to know was so strong, I could not hold in my question. "What did yer husbands do to ye?"

She arched her eyebrows at me. "What happened to yer wife?"

I felt my nostrils flare. She was a pushy lass. It was both annoying and good to know she had backbone. "Ye're one personal question can be about anything but Magy." I hadn't meant to say her name, but it had slipped out. The guilt, as always was sharp.

She nodded. "Fine. And yer one personal question for me can be about anything but my past marriages."

If I didn't agree, I'd move one step away from getting Freya to relax around me and accept me as her husband. I needed to move one step closer, so I nodded. "Fine. May I sit?"

The wary look on her face at such a simple request made me angry for her. It took her a long moment, but finally, she nodded.

I closed the distance between us, but made sure when I sat on the bed that there was enough space between us that I would not touch her. "What do ye want to ask me?"

She tilted her head and crinkled her nose. I found myself wondering, as I waited for her question, if these were gestures she often used when contemplating something.

"Oh!" She gave an excited bounce on the bed which made me smile. "How did ye come to be such a good dancer?"

Of all the questions she could have asked me she had managed to hit on one that instantly reminded me of Magy, and why I had lost her—Freya's father. Here I sat in conversation with my enemy's daughter. About Magy. It was not acceptable. "A lass taught me."

She twisted her lips in obvious frustration. "That's a verra short answer."

"'Tis all that's required," I growled, thinking upon how I was sitting here with the daughter of the man that was responsible for my wife's death.

"Are ye always so cranky?" she asked, rising and going to the table where the serving wenches had set out wine goblets and a pitcher.

"Aye," I replied, irritated that I felt a twinge of guilt for my rudeness. I was trying to loosen her to make her willing to bed me. Simple. We did nae need long discussions where we learned each other. As she extended the glass to me, I stared at her hands. So small. So dainty. Fingers long and slim. Lash scars crisscrossing the back of her hands. I swallowed the knot of rage that had formed in my throat. "Did one of yer former husbands do that?"

She followed my gaze to her hands, and a blush stained her cheeks. "Aye. My laird did nae like the future I foresaw, but he liked my face and did nae want to scar it."

It was said as if she were explaining how to bake a loaf of bread. No emotion. Just facts. There was enough emotion raging through me for both of us. "Which husband—"

"Ah, ah, ah." She waggled her finger in my face. "Ye can nae ask me about my former husbands unless I can ask ye about Magy."

I weighed my options for a moment, then suggested, "A question for a question?"

"That seems fair."

"I'm glad I've finally hit upon something ye deem fair," I teased to which she allowed the smallest of smiles. I would count it as a step toward victory. I had to take my wins where they presented themselves. I knew the laird who had hurt her was dead, but I would have his name and never make an alliance with his clan. They were, from this moment forward, my enemies. His counsel, his clansmen, should have stopped him from hurting Freya.

"Which husband?" I asked, unable to stop myself.

"Laird Matheson."

I didn't know I was going to rise until I did so.

"Where are ye going?" she asked, her voice pitched upward.

"To attack Laird Matheson's home." My jaw twitched and flexed under the pressure of my clenched teeth, and my hand now gripped the hilt of my sheathed sword.

"Ye'd attack his stronghold for me?" she asked, astonishment in her voice. "For what he did to me?"

I nodded.

"But he's dead!" she gasped.

"Aye, but the men that stood by and watched him ill use ye should pay as well."

She narrowed her eyes upon me. "Are ye trying to win my favor to make me willing?"

"Nay." And that was the truth, currently. "'Tis an injustice that needs to be righted."

She quirked her mouth in a funny half smile and half frown. "And ye're the righter of all injustices."

"Nay. But the ones levied at ye, I am."

"Because?" Her eyebrow arched higher.

"Because ye are now my wife."

Now her eyebrows dropped, and her gaze narrowed.

"Therefore, I am yer property?"

I heard the irritation in her voice. Understandable. I'd want to be no one's property by law. Only by choice. "By law, aye. But to me, ye are my responsibility to keep safe." Thoughts of Magy filled my head and put a catch in my throat.

"I see," she said, slowly, as if she were turning over a possibility in her head. "Did ye fail to keep Magy safe?"

The lass had an infuriating ability to get right to the heart of matters I did not wish to discuss. "Aye," I forced myself to say. When she opened her mouth as if to ask more, I said, "And that is the last question I will answer about her. I must get up early in the morning and train, so I need sleep." That was as good of a reason to give to end this conversation as any.

"'Tis fine by me," she said, but I did not miss the fear that sparked in her eyes.

I sighed. How many times would I need to assure her? I rose and made my way to lie in front of the fire. "I'll be here. On this hard floor. Nay touching ye as I vowed until ye ask."

The floor was hard.

Much harder than I'd thought it would be. I tossed and turned, my muscles tired from all the training and the swim in the loch to rescue the lass. I lay on my right, but sleep did not come. With a grunt, I turned to my left. It was no more comfortable than my right. I flipped back to my right with another grunt. That's how it went until the fire died out. I flipped and grunted, flipped and grunted.

"By the gods!" Freya bellowed. "Ye are keeping me awake!"

"If ye care to take the floor," I growled, "I'm more than happy to trade."

A long silence stretched in which I was certain she did not care to take the floor. Not a surprise. But then she said, "I'll trade ye the bed for the floor if ye'll answer any one question I wish to ask."

I thought about that for a moment. I was certain she'd ask of Magy, but this ground was hard, and I had a question of my own. I could answer one question. "Fine. One question," I said, sitting up only to realize Freya was sitting up as well. In the moonlight that streamed in from the window, I could see her profile. She had a long slender neck, and an image popped into my head of my kissing my way down it. Then unwanted, inconvenient lust hardened me. Of all the women to awaken the desire I'd thought dead, I could not comprehend why it would be the daughter of my enemy. I swallowed, trying to ignore the throb of yearning that had started. "Then I get a question as well."

"Fine," she said, scrambling to her knees. The coverlet fell to reveal that she'd been too fearful to even strip to her underclothes beneath her gown. Somehow, that made me not only desire her in this moment but feel protective of her. I gritted my teeth against all the new disturbing feelings. "Where did ye meet yer wife?" she asked.

Instantly, I had a mental picture of Magy as a child. All thin limbs and long blonde hair. And freckles everywhere, unlike Freya with her perfect skin. Mag. Both women were beautiful in their own different way. The thought made me blink. "I knew her as long as I could recall," I replied. "She was the daughter of the clan vessel builder."

"Ye chose her?" she said carefully. Purposely. "Aye? And she chose ye."

"Clever," I said. She'd had a reason for her question. The lass was smart.

"Thank ye," she replied, not denying she'd been strategic.

"'Tis my turn," I said.

"I suppose it is," she replied.

"Did any of yer other husbands besides Matheson and Donald hurt ye?"

"Aye," she said, the one word stiff. "But they did nae beat me as ye might be thinking."

"I was nae," I replied, thinking upon Magy and how she'd been ill abused. "There are worse things in this world than a beating."

"Aye," Freya replied, "there are." The heaviness of her words confirmed what I'd thought. Her experience with the marriage bed had not been good.

"Stay in the bed," I said, as I heard the squeak of it with her making to rise. There was no room in war for softness, and I was in a war with her father. And yet, a softness for her, for what she'd endured had appeared. Aye, I would use her for her gift, but I would never abuse her or cause her pain. "I will keep the floor."

"That's the least ye can do after snatching me and forcing me to wed ye," she snapped.

I was glad for the darkness and the cover it provided for the smile her irritated reply had caused to come to me. I didn't know what was happening to me, and I certainly didn't want her to see it, and think I would be weak with her. I could not be. I had to wield her, if it came to that, like the weapon she was.

Chapter Sixteen – Freya

"Ye promised nae to touch me," I reminded Colin the next morning as he tugged off his tunic at the water's edge. Every muscle he possessed moved fluid like water, I thought as I watched him bring his arms up to rid himself of the tunic. His forearms bulged with every simple movement he made. I was not a silly girl. I did not wish to feel his arms or hands on me, but I did appreciate the way his body was crafted like a fine weapon.

"Ye must take off the gown," he replied.

"Are ye purposely ignoring my reminder?" I asked him, crossing my arms over my chest and not making a move to take off my gown. Far down the beach, the clank of swords filled the silent morning. No one was up yet except the warriors in training and Colin and me.

"Aye, I am," he said, the words short, but when I glanced at him from under my lashes, I caught him smiling before he looked away. He was very handsome when he wasn't scowling. In fact, I could have sworn in that moment I had seen his smile that I'd seen tell-tale signs of a great deal of past laughter. There had been lines of humor around his mouth and near his eyes. There was an inherent strength in his face, and his bronzed skin pulled taut over the elegant ridge of his cheekbones.

He finished ridding himself of his astonishing number of weapons—two swords and two daggers—and then looked to me. "Ye should be taking off yer gown."

Just the thought of taking a layer of protection off made me queasy. "Ye should be training with yer men if ye intend to keep this stronghold," I shot back.

"Ye can nae swim in the gown, Freya." His tone was surprisingly patient. "It will weigh ye down, and yer legs will get tangled in it."

"What care ye if I ken how to swim?" I demanded, not wanting to learn now that I realized I needed to take off my gown.

He smirked at me. "I would prefer ye nae drown."

"I will simply avoid the water," I pronounced, pleased with my quick wit.

"And if per chance ye needed to escape by the water and ye fell in?" he demanded. "Or what if someone dragged ye into the water, and ye needed to swim away from them?"

As he talked, I found my gaze dropping to his legs. They were long, muscled, and reminded me of solid tree branches.

"Freya!" he snapped his fingers, and I jerked my attention back to his face. "Did ye hear me?"

"Of course," I lied. "Ye said..." My face heated that I had no notion what he'd said.

"I said, I would feel better kenning ye could swim away from danger."

"So ye will nae lose yer weapon," I growled, angrier at myself that I'd been caught staring at him than I really was at him.

"Lass, everything I do is nae because of yer gift. Ye are my wife now, and I will see ye as protected as possible."

"Who will protect me from ye?" I demanded, not liking the way his words made my heart flutter like a silly naïve girl and not a woman who knew better than to believe lies.

He gave me a frustrated look. "Ye do nae need protection from me."

"Nay?" I demanded. "Ye wed me to use me, aye?"

"Aye," he said with a growl.

"Then I need protection from ye."

"Fine." He threw up his hands. "Do nae learn to swim." He bent down and started to gather his weapons.

"Wait!" I protested. My fear and my pride were causing me to make a foolish choice. "I'll take off my gown if only to learn to swim to escape ye."

"There's the spirit," he said with a wink that made me laugh. It burst out of me with a merriment I'd not felt in a very long time.

Colin went still and stared at me in way that made my belly clench. It was a heated look. Not like the way my other husbands had looked at me as if I were an object for their pleasure. He looked at me as if he were imaging pleasuring me. I swallowed, and he said, "Ye've a lovely laugh."

"Thank ye," I managed, turning away, glad to have the excuse of taking off my gown to do so. My heart surged in my chest with a furious rhythm, pulsing faster than it had a mere moment ago, and it was not fear that drove this wild tempo. No, it was something else. A tingling sensation churned in the pit of my stomach, a sensation that terrified and thrilled me in equal measure. Could it be desire? I could not let myself want this man. If I let myself want, the risk of open wounds was too great. Too many scars under the thin fabric of my gown. I was far, far too afraid to be touched, and yet here I was, remembering my past hopes and wanting.

I recalled a time before reality crushed my dreams, when I would lie alone in my bed, in the dark, and wonder what it might be like to be truly, deeply connected with my husband, the man I thought I would love. The fantasy was tender, the dream shimmering; I rolled my eyes to the sky, expelling the ghost of wistfulness. How terribly foolish I had been! As if love could protect me. What I knew now of being with a man was that it ended in pain and betrayal. As if it ever felt good. As if it ever could. What I knew now was enough to make me resolve never to feel want again. Yet here it was. This trembling. This ache. Here it was, and I was helpless before it. I knew it, and I hated it, and I hated myself more. And still, my heart would not stop its frantic beat, and still, the tingling in my stomach would not subside. It consumed me, leaving me ragged. If I let it undo me, what would be left? Only terror upon terror, only hurt. I remembered his hands on me, the way I trembled, and the way he laughed. I forced myself to think of nothing now but the task at hand.

Once I had rid myself of my gown, I turned back around and blinked to discover Colin had already entered the loch. The man moved with a frightening quietness. I walked to the water's edge and allowed a gentle wave to roll over my toes. "What should I do?" I called out, as he swam away from me.

"Get in!" he called out. "But do nae go further than yer calves."

"For what purpose?" I said, taking a step into the water.

"For the purpose of seeing how the water makes ye feel. For the purpose of allowing yer body to get used to the temperature difference before we begin. I'll swim closer if ye dinnae mind?"

"Aye," I said immediately, having no wish to drown. I moved further into the water and watched him swim toward me. The sun glistened off his arms and back like icy beams of radiance. He seemed a very steady swimmer with his sure measured strokes and the speed at which he ended up before me. When he was standing in front of me, I asked, "Who taught ye to swim?"

"My da," he replied. "Come further. To yer thighs."

I nodded, proceeding slowly. The water crept up, as did my heartbeat, but I was determined not to be fearful.

"How is it that yer sister kens how to swim, but ye do nae?" he asked.

"When I was a lass, Bran offered to teach me. His idea of teaching me was to throw me in the water from a cliff and shout, 'swim.'" The memory made me shiver. I shrugged. "Needless to say, I did nae learn to swim that day, and after nearly drowning I was terrified of trying again."

"I imagine yer da was angry at Bran."

I frowned, recalling suddenly that I'd felt upset because Da had not seemed as angry at Bran as I would have thought he'd been. But I did not reveal that memory. Instead, I said, "Aye," and nodded.

"Did he punish him?" Colin asked.

"Well, nay." The disgusted look on Colin's face caused me to rush out more words in my da's defense. "Only because Yennifer, my stepmother, begged him nae to."

"Does yer da always do what yer stepmother asks?" Colin inquired.

I guessed immediately where he was trying to lead my thoughts. "My stepmother did nae ask my da to attack yer castle!"

"Maybe nae," he shrugged. "But maybe she begged yer da to cover up the fact that it was her son who broke the treaty."

I opened my mouth to deny it, but I had a sudden sick sensation in the pit of my belly that the possibility he'd just suggested could be true. I thought back through the years, and all the things Bran had done that he'd not gotten into trouble for whereas I'd constantly been in trouble with Da telling me he expected more from me.

Bran had failed to water a horse after a long ride, and it had gotten terribly ill. I'd once forgotten to brush my horse and been sent to bed without supper for the transgression. Bran never showed up for supper on time, but if Vanora or I were to do that, we were denied our seat at the dais or supper. And Bran slept through his shift at the guard tower more times than I could count without punishment. I got smacks on my hands quite often for failing to show up to needlepoint with Yennifer.

I could feel the heat of Colin's gaze upon me. "My da would nae have done that," I whispered. My emotions swirled within me. If Bran really had been the one to break the treaty, and if my da had covered the truth up, then Da had chosen to protect the needs of one over the clan. Over Vanora. Over me. And in doing that he would have restarted a war that had already taken so many lives. And he would have been willing to wed me away when it could have been avoided by admitting the truth. But the truth would have cost him Eilean Donnan. Power. Mayhap Yennifer's affection. Had my da sacrificed me for power? For Bran? For Yennifer? I shook my head. "Nay. Nay, he would nae do that to me."

Colin nodded, but his face held a skeptical look. "As ye say, Freya."

I scowled at Colin. The words were right, but the knowing tone, the look of pity was not. "Are ye going to teach me to swim or nae?" I bit out.

"Aye. Cup yer hands like so." He held up his hands to show me and I mimicked what he did.

"Verra good. Now use yer arms like this," he said, arcing one arm over his head, and when his hand cut through the water, the other arm started the progression. "And turn yer head side to side as yer doing it."

"For what purpose?"

"For the purpose of nae dying. Ye turn yer head to take a breath," he said with a deep hearty chuckle that made me want to laugh with him, so I did.

When our merriment died, I tried what he'd shown me. "Is that right?"

"Aye. The last part is to kick yer legs."

"But if I kick my legs, I'll nae longer be standing on them."

"By the gods ye're an astonishingly clever lass," he teased with a wink.

I scowled, but this time, it was pretend. I was surprised to find I was having fun. "I mean to say, I'll drop under water."

"Nay if ye kick hard enough and use yer arms like I showed ye. And if ye should drop under water, ye kick yer legs to propel ye up and ye use yer arms to cut through the water and aid yer legs. Beyond that," he said, "ye currently could simply stand. We are nae that deep."

And yet, even knowing that, I could nae make myself try. Fear had a grip on me and kept me standing and not moving.

"I could hold yer hands while ye get used to kicking yer legs," he offered. "Of course, that means I'll be touching ye."

"I'll make an exception for this," I said, smirking.

He grinned, and my heart squeezed oddly. Nay. Nay. This man was teaching me to swim because he wanted to ensure I was safe, because he needed me alive to use me.

Not because he cared even the smallest measure about me. I needed to remember that. Yet, as he extended his hands to me, I took them. For one moment, I tensed as an image of him flickered at the edge of my mind, but then I squeezed my eyes shut and willed it to come. Instead, I saw nothing but black as I did every time I tried to conjure an image of my own future to use.

"Lass?"

I opened my eyes and met his concerned gaze. "The sun was in my eyes," I lied, as my heart thudded. Why could I not conjure that image of him? Before, I had not willed the vision I had of him saving his sister to come. It simply had. Morgana's words rang through my mind. *Ye will have the power to manipulate futures. But nae yer own.* The image that had tickled my mind must have somehow been a vision that I could use to manipulate my own future. I had seen visions of my past husbands, but in not one instance did my vision give me the opportunity to change my future. I was physically incapable of holding my visions back when they came or lying about them, and each time I'd had a vision of my husbands, I had been touching them. And they had demanded to know the vision.

"Are ye ready?" he asked, thankfully taking me at my word about the sun.

I nodded and lifted my legs to kick. He pulled me sideways through the water as I did as he instructed, and soon, he let go of my hands and yelled, "Use yer arms as I told ye!" Immediately, I started to sink, and tensed, but he reached under me to put his forearm underneath my belly and push me up.

"I have ye," he assured me. "I willnae let harm come to ye."

I nodded and tried to do as he'd showed me again.

When I felt I had mastered it, I said, "Ye can let go." I kicked my legs furiously and arced my arms over my head with my palms cupped as Colin had showed me, and I swam four strokes. I got so excited about it that I shouted, forgot to kick and sunk under the water in a flash. Terror gripped me but then strong hands grabbed me.

Colin pulled me up out of the water, slid his arms under my legs, and looking down at me with a smile, said, "Ye did it."

"I did it," I said between coughing because I'd gulped in water.

"Do ye want to try again?"

I nodded enthusiastically. He released me, and this time, I did not yelp when I began to swim. Instead, I concentrated on doing as he had told me, and I swam back and forth, savoring the feel of my body gliding through the water. Soon, though, my arms and shoulders started to burn, and my legs felt heavy. I turned to find Colin, suddenly fearful that I was too weak to keep swimming, and there he was directly behind me.

"Tired?"

"Aye," I said.

He swam right up to me, and said, "I'm going to flip ye on yer back to swim ye to shore."

I nodded, but when he did as he said and slipped his arm around me, and my body was pressed to his, I went rigid.

"Lass," he said. His mouth was near my ear and his warm breath wafted over my sensitive earlobe. "Ye dunnae need to be tense. I fancy myself quite a capable man, but I do nae think I'd be able to ravish ye in deep water whist attempting to swim ye back to safety."

I burst out laughing at that, and my body immediately relaxed. "I'm sorry, 'tis just—"

"Ye need nae explain, and ye certainly do nae need to be sorry," he said, swimming us with sure quick strokes toward the shore. "'Tis yer dead husbands who were sorry. They should have protected ye, nae hurt ye."

"Oh, they protected me, all right," I said, not hiding my sourness. "Just nae from them."

When we got to the shallow part of the water, I went to stand up, but he said, "Hold on."

"For what?" I asked, glancing up at the clear blue sky.

"I want to give ye a gift."

"A gift? What sort?"

He grinned. "Close yer eyes, lean yer head back, and put out yer arms. Ye're going to float on yer back. 'Tis the most relaxing thing in the world."

I nodded and was quick and eager to do as he said. "What now?" I asked when my eyes were closed and my arms out to my sides.

"Now, ye float!" He moved his hand from my lower back, and when I didn't sink under, but stayed atop the water, I opened my eyes in amazement. Our gazes collided, and the intensity in his, put a flutter in my chest.

"Why are ye watching me?" I asked, self-conscious.

"To keep ye safe," he answered immediately. Then frowning, he added, "And because ye are beautiful."

His begrudging tone and deep scowl made me laugh when the day before I might have become fearful at him calling me beautiful because I knew full well men wanted what they were attracted to. "Ye do nae like that ye find me fetching?"

"Nay," he replied. "I do nae like it at all. Come along," he said, his voice now gruff. "I want to teach ye to throw the dagger, and I do nae have all morning to waste."

I trudged behind him through the water to the beach,

and when he hit the sand, he quickly dressed and was sheathing his weapons while I struggled to get my gown on as I stared at his back. He'd turned away from me to allow me to dress I presumed, and when he faced me once more, his gaze stopped on my face before dropping downward. With a half groan, half grunt, he said, "Can ye nae dress quicker?"

"Nay, I can nae!" I snapped at him, because he'd snapped at me.

"Turn around," he barked, just as I got one of my arms fully into my gown.

"Whatever for?" I demanded.

"Ye are wet. The material of yer gown is thin. And I can see all the ample gifts the gods gave ye."

"Oh!" I squeaked and jerked around. Once I had the gown on and tied, I turned slowly back and blinked to find him gone. Looking around I located him at the foot of the stairs that led to the outer courtyard.

"Hurry up," he bellowed.

"Brutish man," I muttered under my breath as I strode toward him only to have him leave me again the minute I got to the foot of the stairs. He was halfway up before I had even gained two steps. When he reached the top of the stairs, he glanced back at me, and I did get the sense it was to ensure I was coming still, but then he gave a nod, swiveled around, and banged through the gate to the inner courtyard.

I clomped up the last of the steps and through gate, seeing from the distance that a serving wench had approached Colin. The lass was laughing and holding a goblet of wine to him which he drank from before smiling and handing it back to her. He looked my way, and the smile left his face to become the scowl again.

"Do nae mind me," I said, finding myself surprisingly irritated to watch the lass fawn over the man I did nae even want to be wed to. "I'll just stand here whilst ye two carry on."

Colin gaped at me, but then turned to the lass and said, "Thank ye, Letha. My thirst is quenched."

She eyed me then smiled up at him and said, "If there is anything else ye require—anything at all—ye ken where to find me."

"He gets yer verra loud, verra clear message," I growled. "So go on with ye."

Glaring at me, the lass turned and stomped away. I pretended to be watching her, but really, I was embarrassed to look at Colin. I had no notion what had come over me. What did I care if a lass flirted with him, or if he flirted back or bedded her? I did not want to be bedded by him, and I was under no illusions that he wed me out of any sort of affection or loyalty, so I expected nothing. And still...and yet...my heart suddenly ached. I supposed it was for all I had dreamed of, had wanted, and would never have.

There was a faint glint of humor in his gaze. He knew, damned the man, that I'd acted strangely.

"Jealous were ye?" he said, the humor in his tone matching what I'd seen in his eyes.

"Certainly nae," I said, trying to sound bored as I watched him unsheathe his dagger and then mine, which he'd insisted on holding since I did not yet have a sheathe for it. He held my dagger out to me, hilt first, and I took it.

"Do ye still wish a lesson?"

"Do ye still wish to give it? Seems to me ye could nae get away from me quick enough."

His response was a grunt. "Aye. If ye were nae jealous, what was that behavior?" he asked, motioning in the air with his dagger.

"I am far too used to my husband's nae keeping their wedding vows to bother with jealousy," I snapped.

His intense stare riveted me to my spot. "I am nae one of yer former husbands. I will nae ever break our vows."

"Nay?" I said, allowing all my disbelief to come through. "Nae even if I do nae ever agree to let ye bed me?"

"Do nae have a big head," he huffed. "My bedding ye is about duty nae desire. I will nae be pining for ye and needing to bed another lass because of unchecked desire."

My pride felt as if he'd hit it hard. I flinched inwardly. "Well, that's certainly good to know, because I do nae desire ye at all either. Now teach me how to throw this dagger, so I'm better equipped to kill ye with it."

Chapter Seventeen – Colin

"Well?" Connor said as I finished reading the response to my offer of an alliance to MacLeod.

"It will be war," I said, throwing the missive on my desk then slamming my fist against the wood.

Connor arched a brow. "Did that help?"

"Aye. Nae. Possibly?"

"Ye kenned MacLeod would likely nae agree to an alliance, despite yer having wed his daughter."

I nodded. "Aye, I kenned it."

Colin eyed the missive on my desk. "'Tis unlike ye to allow yer anger to overcome ye."

It was. I stood and went to the window that overlooked the courtyard. Below, there was Freya practicing with the dagger as she had done dutifully since our first lesson two fortnights ago. My chest tightened oddly, as it had been doing more and more lately when I was looking at her. With a start, I realized my anger was for her. I knew her father had attacked our home, but once again he would trade his daughters for power. I was angry for her.

I turned slowly back to Connor. "I offered more than a simple alliance."

"What?" Conor asked, sitting upright now. "What did ye offer."

"I sent another raven a sennight ago and offered to send Vanora and Freya back to him if he would confess before the king that it was his men who had attacked Dunscaith, so that the king would end this war for Eilan Donnan and send troops to us to hold the castle."

"I thought ye said ye would nae do that," Connor sputtered. "Was that even wise to offer to send the lass back to him? Have ye gone soft? What if she had a vision that could aid him in defeating us?"

"I thought about it, and if MacLeod were to confess that he broke the treaty, and then go to war with the king, which he'd have to do as the king would then be backing us to hold Eilean Donnan, the other highland clans would turn against MacLeod. They'd nae want to court the wrath of the king. I saw I could send them back, and my marriage has nae yet been consummated, so…"

"Ye have gone soft." He pointed at me. "She has made ye soft."

"Nay. I simply did nae wish to be yet another man who used her." And having her here, spending so much time with her, was feeling more like a curse than a gift. I wanted her. But I did not want to desire her. I feared soon I'd want other things—like her trust for more than a bedding. What of my vow to Magy then?

"I can nae believe ye offered to send them back without even speaking to me!" Connor bellowed.

Just then I saw a flash of bright red in the crack of the open solar door, and I cursed the ill timing. "I see ye, Freya, so ye might as well enter."

Slowly the door creaked all the way open, and she stood, eyes wide, chest heaving, skin rosy and glowing and her hair in tumbling waves. A primitive desire to protect her from the truth rose up in me.

"Ye offered to send my sister and me home?" she asked.

"Aye, in exchange for a confession from yer da that it

was his troops that attacked Dunscaith and broke the alliance."

"My da can nae confess to what he did nae do," she said, nibbling on her lip. I had no desire to have the same argument we'd been having, so I stood silently and waited for her to speak. "He will nae have peace?"

"Nay," I said.

She frowned. "Did he say anything else?"

I watched her. She was wringing her hands in front of her. "He said he looked forward to giving me a slow, torturous death."

She bit her lip so hard that she winced and released it. "If my da had captured yer sister, and he offered to release her for ye confessing to something ye did nae do, would ye confess?"

"Aye," I said without hesitation. "There is nae anything I'd nae do to protect my sister."

Her shoulders drooped, and she nodded. "War will come here."

"Aye."

"Many will die," she whispered.

"Aye," I agreed and the knowledge was a like rocks in my stomach.

"I would... I would offer a bargain to ye."

I felt my eyebrows arch in surprise. "What sort of bargain?"

"Return my sister to my da, so she'll nae be in danger during the attacks, and I will sleep with ye."

Her words rendered me speechless. She backed up a pace so that her back was pressed against the door, and she wrapped her arms around her waist. A primitive desire to shield her from physical harm as well as harm to her feelings rose in me. I did not want to think about what it might mean. I couldn't, so I shoved it down. I could feel Connor's stare drilling into me. "I will return yer sister, but nae for the price of yer submitting to me when ye do nae truly want it." No matter how much I needed the marriage consummated, I would not lay with Freya, knowing she had submitted for fear of her sister's safety.

"What is yer price then?" she whispered.

"I will send yer sister home, and if she discovers the truth of the attacks on Dunscaith, she agrees to send us a raven, so that ye may ken ye can trust me. Is there a way she could do this?"

"Aye," Freya said with a nod. "Our lady's maid can sneak out a raven."

"Do we have an agreement?"

She tried to press further against the door, but there was nowhere left to retreat. "Aye. Let us find Vanora and tell her the plan."

Chapter Eighteen – Freya

I missed Vanora greatly after she departed with Colin's warriors to return home, but I was surprised to find I did not feel alone. Between the swimming and dagger lessons with Colin in the afternoons, and Katherine allowing me to aid her in the healing room every morning, one sennight turned into another, and I stayed busy. But at night, lying in my bed, listening to Colin's deep breath in sleep from the floor where he lay or his grunts when he could not get comfortable, I found my thoughts going to him and his offer to my da. That always led to my thinking upon Colin's refusal of my bargain to sleep with him for Vanora's sake.

I could not reconcile the things he'd done for me with a man I should fear and think of as my enemy. But he was Da's enemy. Who should I believe about the breach in the alliance—my da or Colin? The question haunted me, and after yet another sleepless night of tossing and turning, I decided that when the sun rose, I would question him about the attack. What had the warriors worn? When had they come to Dunscaith? Had he actually seen my stepbrother leading the troops? And if not, what made him think they were MacLeod warriors, given the clans had been at peace? Had he seen a MacLeod flag? A tartan? Our emblem? I lay there, thinking of all these questions, and eventually my eyes grew heavy.

I awoke to utter quiet and bright light. As I lay there wondering exactly when I had fallen asleep, I remembered I was going to speak with Colin. I sat up and sighed when I saw that he was gone. I stared at the crumpled plaid he'd used to keep warm, and guilt pricked me at how uncomfortable the hard floor surely had to be. He'd not asked once to share the bed with me. Not that I wanted him to ask. I certainly did not. And yet, for one moment, I wondered what it would feel like to have him sleeping next to me, so solid and powerful. He had shown himself to be quite careful with me, and that had been a new experience for me. None of my other husbands would have slept on the floor or waited to consummate our marriage. Certainly, they would not have taken time out of their days to teach me to throw a dagger or swim. Perhaps it was a strategy, Colin's way to make me think he was good and could be trusted. I still felt my defenses lowering.

He wouldn't come to fetch me to break my fast and have my lessons as he had for the first month of my captivity. Since Vanora had departed, he'd failed to return to the bedchamber for me in the mornings, and I'd had to seek him out in the afternoons to ask if he could train me. I found him always with his warriors going through drills. I rose from bed and put on my gown, and I was shocked to realize I could call up a perfect mental image of him as he trained.

On those days when the skies were crystal blue and the sun shone with a fierce brightness, light would catch in his brown wavy hair and reveal red undertones that flickered like flames. His skin was bronzed and golden from hours spent beneath the sun's unyielding gaze and his muscles were lean and taut, chiseled by the punishing repetition of mock battle. Beneath furrowed brows, his eyes were fixed with intense concentration. A frown carved deep lines across his face as he trained, his brows knotting together like clenched fists, and his lips drawn into a taut purse.

Each time his movements failed to satisfy him, he shook his head with grim determination. He repeated the motion so often that those who trained beside him came to recognize it as a sign of his dissatisfaction. But more than anything, his warriors—and indeed anyone within range— knew he was displeased by the sharp and sudden outbursts, cutting through the air as swiftly as any sword. Whenever he believed the warrior he was training was not heeding him, he would yell with a voice bellowing like thunder, a voice that rattled through armor and pierced even the strongest helmet: "God's blood, ye clot-heid. Do ye want to die?"

Such cries were not infrequent, for his demands were high, his expectations higher, and his patience, like a blade that had seen too much use, severely worn. These outbursts continued, whipping the air like vicious gales. The words were harsh, but they served as a warning, a call to take seriously what he taught, to strive harder, to think and act as if life were truly on the line.

The force of Colin and his warrior's hits was astonishing, and the sounds of swords clashing and whistling through the air echoed through the courtyard. At the end of each session, he always patted his opponent on the back when they were done, and he did it with a smile.

I shook the image away and strode out the bedchamber door to the Great Hall to break my fast and discover where Colin went every morning. As I reached to open the Great Hall door, it swung out and Katherine came to a stop so we wouldn't collide. "Where does Colin go every morning," I blurted, my impatience getting the best of me.

"Well, good morning to ye, too," Katherine said with a smile.

"I'm sorry," I replied as she exited the Great Hall.

"'Tis just that every morning I wake up, he's always gone, and I'm wondering where he goes."

She arched her eyebrows. "Why do ye care where he goes?"

Heat singed my cheeks. "I, well, I am trying to understand who he is really. I, I am trying to reconcile him being the man who broke the alliance, which would make him dishonorable, with the man who has shown me consideration and kindness."

She smirked at me. "Ye can nae reconcile those two things because Colin is nae dishonorable. He did nae break the alliance. Yer da did." She set a hand on my shoulder and gave it a squeeze. "But I do understand why ye may nae wish to accept that, given then ye would have to accept all that yer da has done for power and greed. He's lied and killed and he's sacrificed ye all for his own gain."

I did nae like that her words hit so close to my own private thoughts. I hated the doubt in my da that was growing. I shrugged her hand off my shoulder. "Can ye please just tell me where Colin goes every morning?"

Katherine eyed me for a long moment, as if she were trying to decide something, then she nodded. "He goes to the bridge to mend planks with the others. He goes to the wall to carry stones to rebuild it. He goes to the gardens to help replant the crops that were burnt. All these things were destroyed in various attacks from yer da."

"But he's laird," I said. "Why does he nae appoint men to see to these things?"

"Because he is nae that sort of laird, Freya. He would nae ever ask one of our men to do a task he's nae willing to do himself."

I nodded, thinking about my da and about my brief marriages and husbands. Neither my da nor any of my past husbands would have worked alongside their men to do tasks they could assign.

"He's different, Freya." The words were soft, and I could hear Katherine's love for her brother in her voice. I was starting to question myself, my beliefs about Colin. I was starting to wonder if perhaps his sister was not correct, and Colin truly was different. I didn't want to face what that might mean in regard to my da, so I looked to Katherine and said, "I'd like to help, too."

"Ye'd like to help rebuild that which yer da destroyed? Ye'd like to help us gain strength to fight yer da?" She stared at me with obvious skepticism.

"I am nae thinking of it that way. I do nae want to see children starve. Women lose husbands. Bairns lose their das." I shrugged, feeling suddenly foolish for my offer to help.

"Come along then," she said, surprising me. "We can use an extra pair of hands, even if it is the hands of our enemy."

She started to walk away from me, but I said, "Is that how ye see me? As yer enemy?"

She swung around to face me once more, a serious expression on her face. "Until I ken ye will nae hurt my brother, ye are my enemy. He's been hurt enough by yer family. We have lost our parents. Friends. He lost Magy who he loved with all his heart."

"Did she die during one of the attacks on Dunscaith before our alliance?" I guessed.

"Aye," she said, her eyes glistening with unshed tears.

"What happened?"

"That's nae my place to tell ye, Freya. Ye'll have to ask Colin."

He'd never tell me. I nodded, but my agreement was lost on Katherine. She'd already dismissed our conversation and was striding away. I glared at her back as I rushed to catch up to her. The MacDonald siblings were a cranky lot. I'd lived with warfare as well, though the strategic position of my home meant that Dunvegan had never been breached as Dunscaith had. But keeping Dunvegan secure had meant heavy losses of warriors for my clan as well, which was the main reason Da had needed an alliance—to gain forces to defeat Colin's clan once and for all.

These thoughts and a jumble more swirled in my head, like the fluttering wings of restless birds, as we made our way out of the shadowed castle through the expanse of the courtyard and over to the stone wall at the far west side of the stronghold. Dozens of men and women moved breathlessly in a busy line, carrying piles of stones back and forth and everywhere to the gaping holes in the wall that protected the west side of the stronghold. With grim determination they worked with urgency, their voices mingling with the clatter of stone and the dust rising in the dim light.

A strange mix of desperation and hope permeated the air around us, buzzing as loud as the activity itself. I glanced around with purposeful intent, searching for Colin, but did not see him. The air felt heavy with waiting, as though something was about to happen but was not yet ready to show itself. I turned in search again, my eyes darting over each blurred face, anxious for some sign of him. But still, I could find no trace.

"Connor!" Katherine bellowed, making me jerk. "Where's Colin?"

Connor paused in trying to help a lass up to stand on top of the wall and looked between the two of us. "I think he's gathering stones down by the shore to carry up here to help rebuild the wall and bridge."

"Connor!" the lass on his shoulders cried out. "The height is making me dizzy! I do nae think I can stand up on the wall and position the stones."

He rolled his eyes but immediately lowered the lass to the ground and then flicked his gaze between Katherine and myself. "Nay!" Katherine said before he'd spoken. "Ye ken I can nae abide heights."

He grunted, scrubbed a hand over his face, and looked around the gathered group before turning back to us. "I've already asked most of these lasses. Nae anyone can abide heights. How can that be?"

Katherine shrugged. "Where's Murieal? She does nae mind heights."

"I dunnae ken, and I need another set of hands now," he growled. "I need someone to stand on the wall and position the stones!"

"I do nae mind heights," I offered.

His eyes lit as he looked at me. "Excellent. All ye need to do is let me hoist ye to the top of the wall and then grab the stones from me as I lift them up and position them on the wall."

"Colin will nae like this," Katherine warned, her tone sharp. "'Tis dangerous at this corner with the fall to the rocks below." It warmed me instantly to imagine Colin fearful for my well-being. I had become a silly fool like Vanora.

"I'm nae a clot-heid, Katherine," Connor snapped. "I'll keep hold of her ankle when she's positioning the stones. I ken how important the lass is to Colin with her gift of sight." The warmth that had infused me turned to ice. Of course, they had been speaking about Colin being worried for me because of my sight and not simply me.

"I'll nae fall," I said, wanting to end the mortifying conversation. "I climbed trees and balanced on branches quite often as a wee lass. I've got verra good balance." And before anything else mortifying could be said, I moved to stand directly in front of Connor and said, "Hoist me up now."

His eyebrows shot up and then he started laughing.

Katherine flung up her hands. "I'm nae lingering for when Colin returns and sees this. He'll be furious, and I do nae wish to be in his path."

Shaking her head, Katherine left us, and Connor said, "Ye're certain ye have good balance?"

"Aye, excellent."

Nodding, he threaded his hands together, and I stepped onto his hands and then onto his shoulder to reach the top of the crumbling wall that needed repair. The wind felt stronger up at this height, and for one moment, as it pushed on my body, rustling my skirts and hair, my breath did catch with the slightest bit of trepidation.

Connor raised his hands to his forehead to shield his eyes from the glare of the sun. "Are ye alright up there?"

"Aye," I said, forcing myself to take measured breaths until the unease slithering through me settled. Once I felt sure footed, I knelt and extended my hands to Connor. "Hand me up a stone."

"I'll start with a light one until I'm certain ye have yer footing."

I nodded, and he handed me a stone. "I'm nae a weakling," I said, laughing at the small stone he'd handed me. "If ye give these pebbles all day, we willnae make much progress."

He stooped to retrieve yet another stone, this one much larger and heavier than the first. Lifting it as if it were nothing, he held it for me to take. When I grabbed it in both hands, the sheer weight tugged me forward with its full force. I yelped as it slipped from my grasp and tumbled to the ground. My right foot slid off the wall. Connor seized my hand in the nick of time, steadying my fall and keeping me upright.

"What in the name of the gods are ye doing up there?" came Colin's booming, unmistakable voice.

I didn't need to look to know where he was. He appeared next to Connor in the blink of an eye, his brows knitted in a worried scowl as he glared up at me with tempestuous eyes. "Get down," he commanded, thrusting his hand in the air for me to seize.

"I'm nae a hound to be ordered about," I retorted, my patience with husbands and their demands long worn thin. "So, nay," I snapped, my tone as sharp as a blade, defiance sparking within me with a rebellious edge. Fueled by insolence, I pulled back from Connor and regained my footing, my glare piercing Colin's brother like an arrow. "Hand me another stone."

"Dunnae ye dare," Colin growled, his voice tempered with steel and warning, sending an involuntary shiver through my bones. His eyes, serious and forbidding, locked with mine in a silent challenge. "What the devil do ye think ye are doing?" he asked, the air around him brimming with frustration and disbelief.

"Helping, ye clot-heid!" I bellowed, my voice echoing with righteous determination.

"There are a hundred other ways ye can help, lass. This is too dangerous."

"Stop yer fretting. I'm nae going to fall and get killed, so ye do nae have to fear ye'll lose my visions!"

I felt the gawking of his clansmen, but I did nae care. I

wouldnae ever dared with my other husbands to defy their orders, but with Colin, well, I knew I could without repercussion. The thought had me suck in sharp breath. I felt safe with Colin. I mean safe in the sense that I trusted him not to lash me or punish me. When had that happened?

"It's nae the damned visions I'm worried about, ye stubborn lass. 'Tis ye! My every thought is nae for yer visions," he growled. "Please, get down."

It was an effort to stop my jaw from sliding open. Please? He'd just said please. The grin started slowly and then became so big I could not stop it. "Well, that's all ye had to say," I finally managed and clasped the hand that he'd been holding out to me. He steadied me, and I squatted and sat on the wall.

He reached up, and his hands came to clasp my waist, strong and sure. I scooted off the edge toward him as he pulled, and then I was dangling in the air, above him slightly, skirts falling between us in a puddle. I immediately tugged them to the side as he began to lower me down slowly to the ground. All the way we were skin to skin, body to body, and it wasn't until my feet touched the ground and settled beneath me that I realized I'd not even flinched or tensed with his touch. My chest had passed against his, the warmth of his body against mine, and I'd not had the slightest bit of fear. Standing so close before him, I did feel something, but it was like nothing I'd ever felt before. There was a tingle in the pit of my stomach and a strange, exhilaratingly overpowering energy humming through my veins. A dizzying, electric current that seemed to come from nowhere and everywhere all at once. My gaze met his, and the smoldering flame I saw in the depths of his gray eyes made my heart skip and jolt.

But then I had a flash of a memory of Donald's lust-filled eyes. The look he'd given me before the first time he'd taken me to consummate our marriage and had left me empty and broken. He'd looked at me with the same fiery, hungry eyes.

The memory washed over me, sharp and sudden, and I went stumbling backward over a stone and would have tripped and fallen to the ground had Colin not reached out and grasped my arm. His hand was strong and unyielding, reassuring, and as he pulled me back to my feet, I realized I'd been holding my breath. He righted me, and then said, "I had to touch ye." He looked to the wall, and I realized he thought my reaction was from his helping me down.

"Aye, 'tis nae—" I shook my head, swallowed, and tried again. "'Twas nae ye. It was, it was—" I could feel his clan watching us.

Colin leaned toward me and brought his mouth close to my ear without touching it. "Ghost from the past?" he whispered. The soft hiss of the wind and the distant hum of the water were the only sounds around us, but Colin's whisper was clear and distinct in my ear, sending a shiver down my spine.

"Aye," I rushed out grateful that he'd understood without my having to spell it out for him. "Ghost come back to haunt me."

"Do ye want to aid me in the gardens?" he asked.

I nodded eagerly and when he held his hand out to me, I took it with little hesitation. His long fingers curled around my hand, and then he turned to his brother and said, "Ye train the men today. I'm going to be with Freya."

I blinked in surprise. "Ye're taking the day to be with me?"

"Aye," he nodded and then led me past his gaping clansmen, through the courtyard, and down a pebbled path to charred grounds.

I stared in dismay. "This was the gardens?"

"One of them," he said with a nod.

There were a dozen women working in the garden, and I saw many of them look up and wave. I could tell by their lingering looks that they would not mind having Colin's attention at all. He led me to a small plot that looked better than the plots around it. The soil had been prepared, and there were holes for new seed. He released my hand and scooped up a hand-turned wooden tool with a metal cutting tip and held it out to me. "What's this?" I asked.

"'Tis a wimble for digging," he said. The look of astonishment he gave me made my face heat with embarrassment, but he quickly hid his surprise. I was moved by his concern—genuinely grateful. This man was unlike any I'd ever known. There was a gentleness in him, hidden behind a gruff exterior, but unmistakably there. That gentleness had chipped away at my fear, and now I stood on the edge of something uncertain, both hopeful and afraid of what might come if he banished the rest. He was my da's enemy. And yet, no man had ever shown me such kindness.

Was it real?

Could I trust it?

Did I even dare?

Chapter Nineteen – Freya

I determined to keep my distance from Colin after our afternoon in the garden. Only a fool would lose her heart to her family's greatest enemy. Yet, when I entered the great hall that night, the sight of Colin by the dais twirling a young lass around stilled me and tugged at my heart. And despite myself, I watched him and thought he would make a good da. He was just as gentle with the little lass as he was with me.

Behind me came the sound of someone clearing their throat. I glanced over my shoulder to find Katherine staring at me. "Ye like him."

"I do nae," I protested and started toward across the Great Hall toward the dais, but I was hobbling from having kneeled all day. To my irritation, she quickly caught up with me. The problem was, I did like him, but I did not want to. I could not allow it.

"A raven has come with a missive for ye from yer sister," Katherine said.

I stopped in my tracks and looked to her and the scroll she clutched in her hands. She extended the missive to me. I took the missive; aware I should wait to open it. I was standing in the middle of the great hall, after all. But I couldn't wait. I trembled as I opened the missive. Whether my sister revealed Da had known of the attack or he hadn't, the news would hurt me. I loved my da, but I wanted Colin to have been truthful as well. It could not be both ways. I knew that well.

Freya,

Bran attacked Dunscaith without Da's knowledge, but Da learned the truth from Yennifer right away and lied for Bran, thus starting the war anew. Da kens Colin was nae the first to break the alliance, but he will go back to war instead of confessing it and losing Eilean Donnan to Colin. Use the information as ye must. I discovered the truth by eavesdropping, so there is nae proof for the king but my word. Yennifer is horrid as ever, but I am fine.

I looked up, surprised to see Colin standing in front of me beside his sister.

"Freya?" he asked, extending his hand slowly to my face and brushing away—I realized with a start—tears. "What does yer sister say?"

I could not answer. Too much emotion choked me. I looked down to finish the missive.

I am safe. Do nae forget me. I want to be with you when the war is over.

Love,
Vanora

"Freya, what did yer sister say?" he repeated gently.

The betrayal, the sadness choked me. I looked up and met his questioning gaze. I had been forsaken by my da for this stronghold. I had been kidnapped. Abused. Wed first for the alliance and then for the power of my terrible curse. Never for me. And was Colin any different? He'd kidnapped and wed me for my visions, just as the others had. Heat rose in me and with it my heartbeat. Yes, he had been kind and careful with me, but what sort of fool was I to think that had to do with any sort of feelings for me? If I never could conjure a vision again, he'd not want me. I had been disposable to my own da, after all. I shoved the missive at him, desperate to get away, be alone. When he took it, I turned and fled. I ran down the length of the rows of tables of Colin's clansmen, burst through the doors of the Great Hall, and ran down the torch lit passage toward the courtyard.

I needed air. I was suffocating.

"Freya!"

Colin's voice filled the great hall, but I pushed myself harder, wanting to get away from him, from any man who had used me, who had wanted me for nothing more than what they could gain. I would never have the love I'd wanted. I'd taken what didn't belong to me, and I would pay the rest of my life for that terrible decision. I burst into the courtyard gulping the air, but it wasn't enough. I could not breathe. I doubled over, grabbing at my throat, crying.

"Freya," Colin said. I felt his presence behind me, close enough to touch, close enough to suffocate me. His heat. His breath. I could feel it all. Concern threaded through his voice, but to me, it rang as false as the words of my da. Lies upon lies, lies all of it, and nothing more. A surge of anger engulfed me, the heat of it searing through me like molten iron. I whirled to face him, fury lancing my body into motion.

The anguish carved into his features served only to stoke the fire of my rage, feeding it, making it blaze. The truth of his words—that he had not broken the alliance—did not penetrate my haze of hurt. No, not when all I could feel was betrayal. Not when all I could feel was the pain of treachery. It lay too thick upon me, the double betrayal of

Colin and my da, as if they conspired together to wound me as deeply as they could. Their combined deception cut all at once, a sharp, unbearable blade. I had no true home to return to, I had no husband to comfort me, to love me. The anguish of it swamped my senses, and I could not withstand it.

"Ye want my visions?" I shrieked, my voice breaking over the words. "Take them. Quit pretending with me. Ye do nae care for me. Ye care only for how I can be used for yer advantage. Just like my da."

Cruel desperation fueled my words, despair and heartbreak mingling in the wild intensity of my cry. "Here are my visions," I screamed. "Here are yer precious visions!"

I clasped my hands to his face, forcing the visions to come, forcing my gift to unleash itself, to pour forth. Light, harsh and blinding, consumed my sight. I was drowning in it, a world of nothing but light. I willed it to be so. Light became everything, everywhere, and for a moment, it was all I saw and all I knew. I fell, twisting inside it, directionless and lost. I fell, and when everything finally went white, an army of horses appeared, thundering…

Flapping in the wind at the head of the army was the MacLeod crest. The warriors rode hard, faces grim with determination. Suddenly, Eilean Donnan appeared in the distance under the full moon. Then I was looking at Bran. "Taking the castle will be easy," he crowed. "The fool has nae rebuilt the wall. And look, the bridge is down."

Everything went back to white, then blinding light, before I stared at Colin, looking down at me, his gaze full of false concern. I dropped my hands from his face, heart thundering as hard as the horses had been. Exhaustion swept over me as I stared at him. "Ye must fix the bridge immediately and the wall. Bran will attack on the next full moon, and if the bridge is down, he will ride in and take the stronghold."

"Freya," Colin said, reaching for me.

I stepped back out of his grasp. "I will give ye my visions when they come. I will try to conjure them, too. I do nae have loyalty for my da now. But stop the lies," I begged, inhaling a sharp breath, understanding only in this moment, Colin had given me hope. I'd started to hope that between us, maybe, possibly—I was a fool. A naïve, gullible, desperate fool. "Go away," I said, my voice low and so weary to my own ears. "Ye have what ye want, leave me b—"

"Damn ye," he said, took me gently by the arms and pulled me to him. "I do nae care about the visions anymore. I care about ye. I want ye. And nae for the damned visions. I crave ye. I do nae want to, but I can nae seem to stop it. I'll let ye go this moment, if ye ask it of me, but if ye do nae, if ye do nae tell me to release ye, I'm going to kiss ye. I'm going to kiss ye if ye'll let me, if ye do nae fear me still, because kissing ye fills my every thought. I wake with it in my head. I go to sleep with it in my head. And then I dream of it. The desire haunts me. Ye haunt me."

"Kiss me then," I said, my voice husky, stomach fluttering, and my body tingling. I flung caution to the wind, and I allowed the hope that he had created to flow through me. His hands came to my face, so gentle, so careful. My belly tightened with the glide of his fingertips against my skin.

Ever so slowly, he traced my upper lip and then my lower with his thumb. The tightness in my belly increased and a pulsing yearning sprang up in my core. He pressed his lips to my forehead, then my nose, and then his lips whispered across mine like a caress. There was no fear in me. Only desire. He was, I understood, going slowly to ensure I was not scared. That made me want his kiss more. I raised my hands to his body and trailed them slowly up his powerful forearms, over his biceps and to his shoulders. Never had I willingly touched a man. The heat in me burned so hot for him I panted.

He ran his tongue over my upper lip, then the lower one, and then across the crease of my mouth. I opened it instinctually. I wanted him there inside my mouth. I wanted to taste him, learn him. The ache he had sprung within me grew more intense with each caress of his lips to mine and when our tongues met and swirled, the need grew almost painful, unbearable. He sucked my lower lip between his teeth and then my upper lip, and I gripped his shoulders, digging my nails into his flesh and pulling him closer until he was pressed fully against me—hardness to softness.

"I want to show ye pleasure," he whispered at my ear.

I nodded, because I could not speak. The need in me for him was too great. I did not fear what was to come. This was different than any encounter I had ever had. He had sparked something in me I had only ever dreamed of. His lips captured mine fully, and his kiss became more intense. But I met the passion he showed me with a depth of need and want that surprised me.

When he broke the kiss a muffled cry of protest came from me, but then his lips came to my neck to trail hot kisses down it all the way to the top of my chest and the skin that was exposed there. I felt the bodice of my gown tugged down ever so slightly and for a moment I tensed as memories of rough touches flooded me, but then his tongue traced ever so lightly over the burning sensitive flesh of my breasts and pleasure exploded within me. It flooded my veins to go to every limb, my heart, and my head. I threaded my hands in his hair as my nipples hardened and pressed his head down wanting him to go lower.

"Nae here," he whispered, capturing my mouth before I could protest and lifting me into his arms. He was walking, I knew, by the movement I felt, but I didn't care. I didn't care who might see us. I cared only about feeling his lips on mine, his body on mine, and experiencing pleasure instead of pain, desire instead of dread, hope instead of despair.

He broke the kiss at the castle door and slipped one arm out from under me to open the door. We were inside in a breath, up the stairs and to the bedchamber door without seeing another person. He paused at the door, set me on my feet, then captured my hand, as he opened the door and gently pulled me inside. I hadn't been nervous, but in that moment, I tensed.

He paused and turned to me, releasing my hand to face me and brush my hair back from my face to tuck it behind my ear. "Lass, if ye have changed yer mind that's alright. I will—"

"Nay," I said, taking his hand and placing it over my thundering heart. My other husbands had never tried to earn my trust, but Colin had. He had told me the truth about the alliance, and I believed he would never hurt me. I trusted him. I could trust him. As I stared into his eyes, I saw only concern and tenderness. "I have only known pain in the marriage bed. I want to know pleasure."

He nodded slowly. "Ye're certain?"

I was. My heart had been crushed by my da's betrayal, but his betrayal, I now realized, had opened a new door. I was wed to Colin. I wanted our marriage to have the chance to be real, and true, and something wonderful. He lowered his lips to mine and brushed a gentle kiss on them before the kiss turned more urgent and exploratory. Our tongues tangled as they had before in the courtyard, and the thrill of it shot through my body and started a pulsing need at my core.

He kissed his way down the right side of my neck and up my left then down again until he was at the edge of my bodice, and there he ran his tongue along the edge of my gown, over the exposed skin until I was moaning, and a sweet torturous pain grew in me. I ran my hands over his back, reveling in the strength I felt there and committing how his body was shaped, how he felt under my fingertips, to memory.

My breasts grew heavy, and my body trembled with an aching desire that his lips and hands were creating. He turned me slowly, whispering words to me as his hands came to the back of my gown to undo the laces. "Ye are so beautiful, lass," he whispered, slowly slipping my gown from one shoulder then the other. It hung at my arms until he turned me toward him, and the desire on his face took my breath. "Ye have a smile that lights up the room," he said, taking one of my arms out of the gown. "And yer laugh is the most magical sound," he said, taking my other arm out of the gown then sliding it down over my hips to drop at the floor.

Cool air instantly hit my skin, causing gooseflesh to pop up on my arms. He pulled me close and enfolded me in the circle of his arms until our bodies were molded to each other. I pressed my cheek to his chest and was shocked at the hammering beat of his own heart. I smiled to think I had the ability to cause desire in him like he was in me. His heat slowly warmed me, and I wrapped my arms around his waist wanting to somehow get closer. That's when I felt the faint trembling of his own body. I pulled back and looked up at him to find him staring down at me with a look that promised pleasure to come. "Are ye cold?" I asked.

"Nay."

"But yer trembling."

He smiled slowly. "Aye. I tremble with need for ye, lass. I want to be slow and mindful, but my body wants ye now."

That he was restraining himself for me was the greatest gift and emboldened me. I untangled myself from his arms, stepped back, and slowly drew my underclothing off one shoulder and the other. The material fell to the floor around my feet in a puddle. Never had I undressed out of a desire to for a man. I felt exposed but also freer than I ever had in my life. My blood rushed through my veins to pulse at my temples and roar in my ears.

"Ye have given me a gift," I told him.

He cocked his eyebrows up at me.

"Ye have given me enough confidence to stand here in front of ye without fear."

"Lass," he said, "I'm going to give ye many more gifts tonight and each and every one will be my pleasure." He rid himself of his braies and plaid in a breath, and then he stood before me naked. I had never looked truly at any of my other husbands. I'd almost always squeezed my eyes shut and wish to be anywhere else, but here with him, I took him in slowly, bit by bit, savoring the ability to do so. He stood still, as if he knew I needed this moment, and I did.

I allowed my gaze to move down, a slow and hesitant descent like rainwater trickling, over the broad expanse of his chest, gliding across his taut abdomen, and following along to his narrow hips. There my eyes stopped and lingered, and heat kissed my face, blooming with warmth and a tell-tale flush. Between his legs was the proof of his desire for me, bold and unashamed, and it nearly took my breath away. I knew this would be different. I understood it absolutely and deeply, to my core and my marrow and my blood. Colin was powerfully built, but that was not the whole of it. He would be gentle, gentle in ways that no one else had been, tender in his strength.

I stepped to him, a timid step then another more assured, and traced my hands over his chest. My fingers caressed his stomach, and with bolder abandon ventured down to his staff. My breath caught in my throat, and I gasped, the ache between my legs growing almost unbearable, a delicious torment, as I touched him there. He was hot, smooth as river stone, and it was wondrous to me, astonishing and dazzling, to think what it might be like to have him in me. He made no sound save a sharp intake of breath when I first touched him, but when I began to run my hand up and down the length of his staff, an animalistic, raw, guttural groan ripped from him. He became harder, thicker, and longer, and more alive in my hand. A wild feeling of control ripped through me as well, like a storm or a surge, and with it came a realization, bright and profound. This was one of his gifts to me—power over him, power over how we proceeded, the assurance that I would not be powerless, not in this nor ever again.

A new ache sprang up within me, but it was in my chest. Colin had breached my defenses, and I was in danger of losing my heart to him. I raised on my tiptoes with the new frightening knowledge, and I pressed a kiss to his lips. He returned it with a passion that took my breath, but he did not make a move to touch me. "I want to pleasure ye," I said and glanced down at his manhood before meeting his gaze once more. "Will ye tell me what to do?"

His eyes widened and then he offered a sinful smile. "Lass, ye were already doing it."

"The rubbing ye up and down?" I asked.

"Aye," he said, the word husky. "I want ye to do all ye

wish, but I warn ye, it will take me a moment to recover if ye bring me to full pleasure, but there are things I would do for ye in return while I recover."

I frowned. "What sort of things?"

His lips parted, and he stared for a moment, before he closed his lips and then spoke. "Have ye nae had any pleasure in the bed ever?"

I shook my head.

"If ye will allow me, I'll touch ye with the greatest care and give ye pleasure with my mouth and hands before we join, which will make ye all the more ready for me, and that, lass will make the joining verra good."

"I'll let ye," I said, "but ye'll tell me what ye're doing as ye do it?"

He grinned. "For as long as I can talk. Ye have my vow."

I started to stroke him once more, and as he groaned and grew even thicker and harder, I had a desire to replace my bad memories of the past with new, good ones. "Would ye like me to pleasure ye with my mouth?"

He had his eyes closed and his head thrown back. It took him moment to lift his head and look at me. "Aye, but I do nae want ye to feel—"

I pressed a fingertip to his lips, knowing even though I'd not let him finish the sentence that he was thinking of me and my fears. "I'm in control of what I'm doing. What I'm offering. Do ye wish to take me up on my offer?"

"By the gods, aye," he said.

I kneeled then slid my hand up his muscled thigh and around to his firm buttocks to grasp him there and tug him close. He groaned again, but I knew it was a sound of pleasure. I took him into my mouth first by the tip, testing my reaction, but it was one of excitement, wonder, and unchained desire. With a slide of my mouth, I found the boundaries of what I could take, and then I began to pleasure him. But the more pleasure I gave him, the more pleasure I gained, until I was panting, aching, and bursting with need. When he gave a shout and pulled back, I knew he was at his release. I held tight and took him in, wanting all of him because I had chosen it.

For one breath silence fell, and then he kneeled before me. "Thank ye," he said, holding out his hands to help me up. I placed my hands in his, and he helped me to my feet, released me immediately, and then fetched a goblet of wine. I thought it was for him, so when he handed it to me, I blinked in surprise.

"Thank ye," I said, taking it, once again touched by his consideration for me.

"'Tis the least I can do after what ye just did for me." He took my hand and walked me to the bed and helped me onto it. I lay on my back, and he stood at the edge of the bed looking down at me.

"Is it like this always with, with ye. Give and take? Gentleness?"

His eyes became hooded for one moment, before he blinked and looked directly at me again. "I have only ever been with my wife, but it was like that with her. And it will be like that between us."

"Ye have nae had a woman since yer wife's death?"

"Nay. I did nae have the desire to—until ye." That breach upon my heart grew bigger in that moment. "I'm going to kiss ye now. All over. And I'll be needing to spread yer thighs—"

"What for?" I interrupted, not alarmed, but a tad nervous. I knew what for, truly, but still… I wanted his words, which I knew would calm me.

"For loving ye properly."

I knew he meant pleasure, yet my heart tugged at his use of the word love. I was like dough in his hands at this moment. I nodded. "Alright."

The bed dipped, swaying beneath the weight of him as he settled on it, coming to me with a tenderness that could melt the hardest heart. For a moment, he was still, a soft breath escaping his lips as he lowered himself to me, his need so evident in the way his hands trembled ever so slightly. True to his word, he took my foot in his hand, lips pressing with the gentleness of a spring breeze on its tender arch. One of his hands gripped the curve of my ankle as he began to move slowly upwards, traveling a path of soft, insistent kisses along my legs. Without breaking rhythm, he paused only to wrap strong arms around me, pulling me closer. His lips burned warm as embers against my flesh, up over my stomach with the fire of him and the heat of his mouth, until my breasts ached with the desire he sparked. I shivered beneath him, head tossed back, wanting him utterly and without pause.

"Now I'm going to—" he began to speak, but I could not wait any longer.

"Just do it!" I pleaded, cutting him off in desperation. "I do nae need more talking. I need yer mouth upon me. I trust ye. I trust ye. Do what ye will."

Satisfied by my words, he grinned, a glint of pure wickedness in his eyes. He resumed his attentions with increased fervor, lips returning to my skin His answer was to take my nipple into his mouth. My answer was a scream of pure ecstasy. Never had I imagined such a thing. Never had I experienced such a thing. I wanted more. And when he swirled his tongue around my nipple while using his hands to rub my other nipple, I wanted more. I wanted all of him.

In me. Right then. "Take me!" I commanded.

"Such an impatient feisty lass," he teased. He raised up and kissed my mouth, sucking my lips between his before releasing them to lower himself between my thighs, which he gently spread. His fingers came to my private bits, and he spread them as well, making me gasp. Before I could decide whether to voice a protest, his tongue slid down the center of my sex, and then he suckled at a spot that made me lose my mind.

Pressure built within me so strong that I raked my nails over his scalp, thrashed my head side to side, and cried out. His tongue tantalized me at my core as passion pounded the blood through my heart, chest, and head. I grew taut as a bow, my body flaming with need, and my impatience growing to explosive proportions. "Colin!" I begged and insisted in one breath. He suckled the secret spot he had found in one long pull and waves of pulsating ecstasy flowed through me making me arch my back and scream out my pleasure.

But it was not enough. I wanted all of him. To know every inch of him. To take all the pleasure he wanted to give me. I tugged at his head and his shoulder until he was sliding up and over me. Then I grasped his back and attempted to push him closer, but he stilled. "Ye are certain? Ye are ready?"

"Aye, aye!" I assured him. He came between my thighs and catching my lips with his, he slid into me in a long slow motion filling me in a way I had never been filled before. He stilled for a moment, allowing me to get used to him, and then together, we found the tempo that bound us. We moved in exquisite harmony as the room around me disappeared, and all I could hear, feel or smell was him. Again, a pressure began to build, and the heat of his body coursed down the length of mine. My desire for him overrode all memories, all pain, all longings, and I moaned with erotic pleasure as I yielded to the searing need that he had created.

A guttural cry escaped him at the same time it did me and passion exploded, sending fiery sensations through me. His arms locked around me, and then he poured his life into me before he became heavy on top of me, his heart pounding against mine, and his ragged breaths rhythmic in my ear. We lay depleted and silent against each other, until my skin started to cool, and our breaths had evened. Then Colin rolled off me and somehow brought me with him so that I was nestled in the crook of his arm and my head was pressed against his chest.

His hand came to my back, and he traced his fingers back and forth on my chilled skin and without a word, he drew the rumpled coverlet up over me with his foot. I glanced up at him from underneath my lashes, and I found him looking at me. "Did ye find pleasure?" he asked.

I laughed. "Could ye nae ken that I did?" It seemed to me my screaming made it obvious.

"Well, I would say, aye, but I do nae want to ever assume."

I placed my hand on his heart. "Ye shatter me into a million pieces."

His mouth came over mine in a tender kiss. When he pulled back, he said, "Good. Now ye take those million pieces and create a new fierce ye."

I stared in amazement at this man and his words. A hot ache grew in my heart, but this was a new yearning. I wanted to know him fully. Reaching up, I traced the white line on his forehead that I had noticed before. "What happened here?"

His entire body went tense underneath me.

"If ye do nae wish to tell me…" I offered, but I hoped he would.

Moments stretched, and my heart grew heavy that he would not share, but then he inhaled a long breath. "I got this scar during one of yer da's attacks on Dunscaith three years ago." He breathed deeply for a moment and then continued. "During the attack I chased some of yer da's men into the woods to vanquish them from our home, but I did so against the advice of a witch who I had encountered the day before in the woods. She'd been cornered by a pack of wolves, and I came to her aid. For that, she offered a vision of my future, which I dismissed, because I did nae believe in magic at the time."

My curiosity was instantly sparked. "What was the ban-druidh's name?"

"Morgana."

I raised on my elbow, my heart lurching. "Morgana is the witch who cursed me."

He frowned. "I did nae ken that."

I nodded. "Aye."

"She's the one ye stole the goblet from?"

"Aye."

"Why did ye steal the goblet? I heard ye speak of it at yer da's but with the noise in the courtyard and my own tumbling thoughts, I did nae catch all ye said."

"I will tell ye," I said, "but first tell me how ye got the scar."

"As I said, I chased the men into the woods, and upon my return, Katherine told me Magy had been snatched, just as the witch Morgana had warned me would happen if I did nae guard her. I rode hard after Magy's captor, and in the process, I rode straight into a low hanging tree limb. It hit me straight across the forehead. When I came to, I found Magy." He paused, and I did nae speak as his chest rose and fell in short breaths. His fingers had stopped tracing lines over my back, and he turned his face away for a moment, but when he looked to me, I could see the unshed tears in his eyes. "She had been ravished by one of yer da's men," he continued, his words low and throbbing with so much pain that my heart twisted with it. "And she had fought him and gotten stabbed in the gut for it."

He inhaled a sharp breath as if the pain were still so fresh and raw and shocking. "I held her as the life blood poured out of her, and that's when she told me she was with child," he said, his voice cracking in anguish. "I lost her, and I lost our child. She was but a breath away from her last when I realized it. I could see the life leaving her eyes when she told me she carried my bairn. I saw the light of two souls flicker and fade right before me, and I was helpless and weak, and I could nae stop it. I was as good as dead myself at that moment, for what was left of me? I was a hollowed-out shell."

A silence heavy with all that lived and died and lived again in his words fell between us. The horror of his story pressed down on me and filled the space between us. "I'm sorry," I whispered, barely able to speak through the lump that clogged my throat, horrified by the suffering he had known.

He looked down at me, his eyes a sea that threatened to drown me. "I am the one who is sorry that I did nae take heed of what Morgana told me. I dismissed magic. I doubted the one thing that might have saved her. I was a disbeliever. I was a stubborn fool who refused to see the truth until it was too late. And I lost the only woman I ever loved for it and my child. I would have gladly given my life for Magy to keep hers. There was nothing I would nae have done to keep her alive."

Tears filled my eyes, brimmed until they were too heavy to hold, and spilled over them onto my cheeks. That was the sort of love I had always wanted. That fierce, reckless, and unending sort of love that would sacrifice anything to hold on until the very end. What woman would not want such a thing? What woman would not give anything to have love like that? An undeniable and dreadful thought froze in my brain even as my heart surged with want. I was already falling in love with him, and he still loved Magy.

Chapter Twenty – Colin

When tears slid down Freya's face, I feared I had hurt her with the truth of my words, but before I could ask her she said, "Do ye want to ken now why I stole the goblet?"

"Aye. This is what I heard ye say the day ye were found by Donald. Ye said ye stole it so that yer wish to have visions to control yer future would come true. Ye said ye wished to see the future, so yer da would defeat his enemies—me."

"I wanted my da to defeat his enemies, so that he would nae have to use me in marriage to protect our clan," she said, her words shaking. She sat all the way up, pulling her knees to her chest, and wrapping her arms around her legs to hold them tight. "I desired to wed for love. To be wanted only for me and nae what I could bring a man. So, I wished to have visions to manipulate my future. I have been wed four times now," she said. Her fragile shaking voice made my chest hurt. "Never for love. I see now," she said, each word a broken whisper, "that my fate is to never be loved as I wanted to be."

I feared asking her how she wanted to be loved, and I feared not asking. I felt either way, I would face a problem, but I could not ignore her words. We had come too far for that. "How did ye want to be loved?"

"Like ye loved Magy," she cried out, burying her face

down into her knees so that I could not see it. "I wanted to be loved so greatly that my husband would give his life for me, and I would for him."

"I would give my life for ye," I said, because it was true.

She jerked her head up, and her gaze impaled me. "Out of duty," she accused.

"Nae simply duty," I responded. I did nae want to think too long on that. She was not mere duty anymore for me. Where did that leave my vow to Magy? How could I even reconcile this?

"Ye have taken away my fear and given me hope."

Her words sounded accusatory. "And that is bad?"

She nodded. "Aye. And nae. In doing these things, ye reopened a door I closed. I had resigned myself to a loveless marriage, a life of despair. But now, well now, I want more. I do nae want to be resigned."

"Freya," I said, the weight of my vow heavy in my mind and upon my chest. "I do nae ken if I can give ye that."

She nodded as the tears continued to roll down her cheeks.

"I am giving ye my protection, my honesty, my passion—"

"'Tis nae enough," she said, laying on her side and curling herself into a ball. "I want to give my heart, and how am I to do that to a man who will nae give me his?"

"I do nae ken," I replied. I felt torn as she stared at me with longing. I felt myself needing her. Caring for her. And I certainly wanted her. But more? "Can we nae just go along like this?"

"Well, we will have to, won't we," she said, her words terse. She turned from me, giving me her back. "Ye stole me!" she flung out, her voice rising. "Ye wed me!" said, her voice even louder now. "And then ye built this desire in me, so now we are good and truly wed. I'm stuck with ye!" she bellowed.

She scrambled suddenly to her knees. "I am stuck in marriage with ye. I want to be loved completely, and ye do nae think ye can give me that ever." She shook her fists at me. "I have no choice but to resign myself to this fate, now do I? Where am I to go?" She poked me in the chest. "To my da?" she laughed at that. "He threw me to the wolves for this castle. I believed in him! I trusted him! I gave my future for him! I gave my body to protect our clan, but it was his greed, his need for power that I gave it all for!" She shot up and off the bed, yanking the coverlet with her. She stomped over to the fireplace and faced me. The dancing flames threw shadows across her naked, magnificent body. "If ye can nae give yer heart to me," she seethed, "then, I will nae give my heart to ye." With that, she plopped onto the ground in front of the fire grate. Her labored angry breathing joined the crackling fire to fill the room.

I lay on my side, fighting the urge to go to her. She was a tempest rising. A woman on the verge of discovering truly her own strength. My desire for her had made me step on a slippery path that experience had shown me led to pain. I was torn. The emotion she invoked in me was not welcome. It was a tide that I was struggling to outrun.

I awoke with a plan in my head to avoid further attachment to the lass, more unwanted emotional ties, but keep the passion between us. I would avoid Freya during the days, but at night I would give her my full tender attention and passion. I smiled at my cunningness, sat up, looked to the fireplace, and frowned. She was gone. Fear jolted through me, and I scrambled out of bed, yanking on my braies, and snatching up my plaid, as I headed for the door.

Moments later, I burst into the great hall and found it nearly empty. Where the hell were all my clansmen and women? I stormed toward the dais where Katherine was sitting. "Where is everyone?"

"Good morning to ye too, brother," she said, with a smirk. "Ye should break yer fast. Mayhap it will improve yer mood."

"My mood is just fine," I growled. "I—"

"I would have thought," she said, interrupting me, "that ye would have been so pleasant this morning. After all," she said, giving me a knowing look, "ye did sleep past sunrise."

"Did I?" I had been too preoccupied by Freya being gone from the bedchamber to look out the window and take note of where the sun was in the sky.

"Aye, ye did," Katherine replied, licking her fingers and then standing. "And I can nae recall ye sleeping past sunrise since, well, you were married to Magy—"

"Cease this, Katherine," I said, aware of what she was trying to do.

"Cease what?" she asked, her tone and face innocent, despite the fact that she was anything but.

"Ye ken what. Have ye seen Freya?"

"Aye," Katherine replied, but annoyingly offered no further information.

"Well, where is she?" I demanded, having to work not to snap at her.

"She's with Connor helping to plant crops. Her mood was fouler than yers is."

I thought immediately of our conversation last night. She was vexed at me for not being able to give her the words she wanted, but I'd soothe her tonight with my touches. Katherine moved down the dais past me. "Where are ye going?" I asked her.

"To aid Freya and Connor," she replied.

"I'll come with ye," I said.

"I'd nae if I were ye. When I told Freya I'd let ye ken where she was when I saw ye, she said nae to bother. That ye were the verra last person she wished to see."

"Fine," I said and nodded. That suited my plan anyway. In her anger, the lass had just done me a favor. My instinct had been to go to her, but my plan had been to keep a distance in the day. I needed to remember that.

Despite my resolve to stay away, I found myself looking for Freya at every moment. But I explained it away, again and again, with a thin urgency to make sure she was safe, and that she was not suffering because of me. I kept my distance. I didn't speak to her or move near. I just waited until I could tell she was well, until the hammering of my blood grew less wild, until my worry eased its grip on my mind. When the sun was high in the sky, I lingered behind the half-cracked kitchen door, where I caught glimpses of her preparing a stew for supper, her sleeves rolled up, her hair tied back, her brow shining with sweat.

In the late afternoon, while the sun spread its golden cloak over the damp hills, I stood unseen on the seagate stairs and watched from afar as she waded in the loch, surrounded by children and adults who gathered close to learn the same swimming lessons I'd once given her. At night, I made a pretense of shunning her still, sitting far away at the other end of the dais, but I took comfort in her merry laughter, in the sound of her voice soaring above the drift of conversation, in knowing that she was joyful and untroubled.

After the meal, she departed the Great Hall, yet I sat, determined to keep up the ruse. The torches burned low, and the hall echoed with the din of chairs being pulled back from the long tables. Tired from my pretense, I rose heavily from my seat and slipped quickly out, into the drafty corridor, avoiding eyes, passing those who lingered, whose cheerful voices followed me like shadows.

Once I was out of sight, I slowed my pace, and my footsteps clattered on the stone floor as I headed toward my bedchamber and tried to outrun the noise of my own thoughts of Freya. I climbed the stairs, running my fingers through my hair as the echoes of the day teased in my head.

I had decided to stay away, yet I could not stop seeking her out, tracing the sound of her laughter, wanting to breathe in the air she stirred. I felt the threads of my resolve unravelling, and my chest ached with what I could not name.

I paused in front of our bedchamber, shoring up my resolve one more. I knew what I wanted—her. I would seduce her with passion and gentle touches. When I opened the chamber door, the sound of her deep breathing filled the room. I frowned. Surely, the lass wasn't asleep yet? I'd not been far behind her. "Freya?" When she didn't answer, I walked to the bed and bent to peer closely at her. Her eyes were closed, and her chest rose with the steady measured rhythm of sleep. "Poor, lass," I said. "Ye're wore yerself out today." This was best. This would give me the night to strengthen myself against weakening. I smiled to myself as I climbed into bed. My plan was not so ridiculous. It was working, albeit not perfectly.

She turned over with a soft murmur and tossed off the

coverlet to reveal her long slender leg and her gown tugged low over one of her perfect breasts. Desire so hot gripped me, I grunted. The night part of my plan needed some adjustments. Tomorrow night, I would come to the bedchamber with her.

The next day went along the same with Freya somehow rising before me, and it seemed she had thrown herself wholeheartedly into our clan life. That was good, though. That boded well for the division of our lives into separate days but passionate nights. Except that night, she went to the healing room with Katherine after supper, and by the time she came to our bedchamber, I had fallen asleep.

On the fourth night, she retired from supper not feeling well, and when I finished supper and went to check on her, she was asleep. On the fifth night, she did not appear for supper and neither did Katherine. It was Connor who let me know they were both helping to birth a bairn. When I awoke that morning, and she was already gone, I realized, we had not actually spoken more than five words in five days. My plan was working too well and seemed to need some extreme adjustments. I determined that night to sit by her at supper, talk with her, and walk her to our bedchamber to retire, so when I arrived in the Great Hall to find her seat empty, my irritation rose. "Have either of ye seen Freya?" I demanded of Katherine and Connor.

"I lunched with her," Connor offered.

"Aye. I gardened with her today, worked in the healing room, and then I aided her in swim lessons."

"Well, where is she now?" I demanded, hearing the surliness of my tone.

Katherine's smirk did nothing to improve my mood. "I imagine she's avoiding ye as she's done all week."

I frowned. "Avoiding me?" Realization clicked in my

mind and as my sister stared at me with a knowing look, it only increased. "I thought I was avoiding her."

Katherine chuckled at that. "Mayhap ye were, but it was made easier by the fact that she was avoiding ye as well." Katherine gave a long hard stare that reminded me of one our mama would have given me before a lecture. "I see what ye are doing," she said.

"I do nae ken what ye are talking about," I lied.

"Ye do. Mayhap ye do nae ken why, so I'll tell ye. Ye like her. Ye more than like her, I suspect. And ye do nae want to. Ye fear it. Ye fear the strong feelings she invokes in ye, because ye had them once for Magy, ye lost her, and ye fear that same pain."

"Nay," I said, unwilling to discuss how I felt with Katherine.

"Ye can say nay all ye want, but the truth is aye. Mayhap ye do nae even realize it yet, but I do. Ye stare at her with intense longing, brother."

"That's desire," I snapped.

She narrowed her eyes at me. "That's a lie ye are trying to tell yerself to avoid facing what ye fear the most—loving and losing again. But I tell ye this, ye will lose Freya anyway, if ye refuse to give yer heart to her. She will be here, living amongst us, but lost to ye."

"Ye dunnae ken what ye speak of," I bit out.

"I ken what I speak of because I've watched ye. And I ken a woman's heart, because I am one. And I will tell ye one more thing. Magy would nae have wanted ye to live out the rest of yer life nae ever really loving again. She would nae have wanted it, because that way is loneliness, and she loved ye and would nae have wished ye to be lonely. She would have wanted ye to have children. And love."

"I made a vow," I said, my temples pounding with Katherine's speech.

"I ken yer vow. But ye will nae forget Magy or stop loving her by loving Freya. Ye carry Magy in yer heart, and yer heart is big enough to make room to love Freya."

I did see images in my head then. And they were of Magy dying. The pain sliced through me as if it had just happened. It shredded my insides and left a hollow ache. It engulfed my body in a tide of weariness so strong that I could imagine it drowning me. "Ye are wrong," I snapped at my sister. "Freya and I will rub along fine as soon as she settles into how things will be." Even as I made my way down the dais and stalked away, I heard Katherine's derisive sound. I didn't turn around. I strode out of the great hall, through the passage, up the stairs, and to my bedchamber, determined to wait there awake until Freya returned and then bring her to pleasure.

When I threw open the door, I stopped short at the site of her, standing up in a washbasin with steam rising around her. She had her hair piled on top her head, and water ran in rivulets down her breasts, belly, and hips as she sung a loud bawdy tune while washing her arms. Desire hardened every part of my body. I kicked the door closed, and her head snapped up from ministrations. Our gazes collided, and I blurted, "I need to touch ye. To feel ye. I—" God's blood, I didn't know what I was, but I knew one thing for certain. "I can nae go another breath without touching ye."

"Come to me then, husband," she whispered. "Let me love ye."

Chapter Twenty-One – Freya

*M*y defenses crumbled when faced with the unbridled yearning in Colin's eyes and the naked desire in his voice. I didn't want to avoid him any longer than I already had. Every day apart had been its own sort of torture for me. I'd seen him watching me, shadowing my every step and move, and I had started to wonder if he would ever say something, anything to me at all. Wherever I went, he somehow seemed to find me, and that gave me hope that he might finally reach out, but at the same time, it left me irritated. Each day that passed was agony in its own way, and I hated that he could be so stubborn, so silent, so maddeningly patient.

And now here he was, filling the air around me with the warmth of his presence. He was not giving me exactly what I had hoped for—a small sign that he could one day let me into his heart, so I could fully open my own to him—and yet, this was something.

And beyond that, I burned for him from the time I woke up until sleep claimed me, and even in sleep the insatiable hunger he'd created in me appeared in all my dreams. So no, I would not deny him or me this joining. I would embrace it. Revel in it. And hope it led to something more. He closed the distance between us with shocking speed, but then as he reached for me, he hesitated, his hand suspended in midair halfway to my waist.

"Sorry, lass," he said, dropping his hand, taking a deep breath, and stepping back. "I'll gain control of my need before I touch ye. The hunger for ye is so great, I fear I'll devour ye."

I was shocked at the thrill his words sent through me. "Devour me then," I replied, shocking myself yet again with my own words. "Touch me. Take me. Do with me what ye will as long as it brings us both pleasure."

The instant his clothes were strewn about the floor in a reckless whirlwind, his hands were sliding over my stomach, eager and warm, burning with need. They moved up my body, rough and tender at the same time, cupping my breasts and teasing my nipples until they hardened as solid as granite. Desire pulsed and spiraled in my belly, pooling swiftly and wrapping around my core, setting everything in my chest straining and heaving with a wild, breathless yearning.

My fingers dug into his shoulders, the strength of them firm and unyielding, as he lifted me from the basin. He slid me, slippery and aching, down the length of his unrelenting body, pressing and thrilling, only to hoist me up again, holding me steady, with an arm beneath my legs and another under my backside. "Wrap yer legs around me," he whispered in my ear, urgency and longing mingling in his voice.

Immediately, I did as commanded, finding his lips with my own and plunging my tongue into the hot recesses of his mouth. Our drugging kiss ripped a moan from me and elicited a guttural sound from him, and a moment later, the wall pressed firmly into my back as he broke the kiss. His mouth descended to my nipple, and his tongue caressed the sensitive swollen bud as his hand delved between us to part the flesh between my thighs as he'd done the first night.

Instantly, he found that secret throbbing spot, and he caressed his finger over it once, twice, a dozen more dizzying times. Each gentle massage sent a current of desire though me, built pressure within me, and coiled me so that I was certain at any moment I would unwind in a burst of need or pleasure. Our mouths met and retreated, met and retreated, each kiss becoming more urgent and demanding. We were two people starving for each other.

His lips continued to tease my nipple as his fingers teased my sex. My thighs trembled, and my insides coiled tighter and tighter. I grasped at his back, grinding my teeth, wanting to prolong the sweet torture, but I was being swept up in searing emotion that I could not control. He brought me right to the edge of fulfillment, then drew his hand away. I cried out and punished him with a hard demanding kiss. He returned my demands by sliding himself fully into me and beginning the ritual of consuming me body and soul.

As his tip came fully in, the need in me mounted until I could not take anymore. "Give me what I need," I demanded. And he did. He pulled nearly all the way out then slid back in, increasing the pace with each retreat and return. His heat enveloped me. His body overpowered me. My own world slipped away, and he became my world just as before. The friction of every slide within me rippled pleasure through me, and his lips came back to mine with a savage intensity that pushed me over the precipice we'd been climbing together. I clenched around him, as he drove into me once, twice, two more times. Then he clenched my buttocks and filled me with himself before his head fell to my shoulder, and we stood heaving breaths and racing hearts.

Silence descended and time stretched and with it the

roar in my ears dulled, my skin cooled, and my heart slowed. Colin drew his head up, and his gaze locked on me. "Ye are mine," he said, his voice raw with need and unbendable with possession. I had been avoiding him so he would not take my heart in case he was never willing or able to give me his, but I understood in that moment, he'd already taken it. I was his. I loved him fully.

I could not turn back time. I could not undo what had been done. I could not take my love away to protect myself. There was no great love without vulnerability. No joy without sorrow. No pleasure without pain. You had to experience one part to recognize and appreciate the other. "I am yers," I replied, pressing my lips to his, and praying that eventually he would be truly mine.

I was strong. I hadn't realized just how stiff my spine was, until my other husbands had attempted to break me. Colin had given me back my confidence in myself and my hope for that love I'd always dreamed of. I could wait for his love for a time, but I did not think forever. There was a difference between being strong and being a fool. I kissed him again, and when I pulled back, I said, "I will wait." I knew he understood me. "But nae forever. Eventually, yer coldness and yer walls will become mine."

His answer was to kiss me. It was a stalling tactic, but one I quite enjoyed. He carried me to the bed, lay me gently upon it, and then retrieved a rag from the basin, which he used to clean me. Then he pulled the coverlet over me and brought me wine. I watched him do all of these things and a new understanding settled in me. He could not give me the words I wanted, but he was showing me with his actions what his mind was afraid to let him embrace.

He offered me caring, consideration, and tenderness at every turn. I had to believe love would follow. He settled on the bed beside me, but did not yet lay down. "Do ye need some supper? I'll fetch it for ye if ye do."

"Nay," I replied. "I grabbed a hunk of bread from the kitchen."

"Oh, aye," he said. "Did ye grab it and rush up here with intentions of avoiding me?"

"Aye," I replied, not holding back the truth.

He laid down beside me and brought me into the crook of his arm. I settled my cheek against his chest and listened to the steady solid beat of his heart. I loved this man. It was wondrous and frightening at once. His fingers traced back and forth over my shoulder. "I do nae like that ye were avoiding me."

"Ye were doing the same to me," I pointed out.

"'Tis different," he replied, his words groggy with sleep.

I frowned at that ridiculous reasoning. "How?"

It took him a long moment to answer me. I suspected it was more sleep that was lulling him, by the way his breathing had already turned to slow, deep breaths, than his not wanting to discuss it.

"I've a plan," he finally said, then released a long sigh before he began to snore.

I tried to imagine what sort of plan he'd come up with, as I listened to him sleep, but my own thoughts grew heavy, and soon I was lulled into darkness myself.

I jerked awake from the nightmare, but as the castle warning horn started to blow, I understood with sick dread that I had not had a harmless nightmare. I'd had a vision of the future, and that future was now here. Snippets from the dream flashed in my mind as Colin bolted upright in bed in one breath, and in the next he was on his feet, sword in hand. There was just enough moonlight that I could see the confusion on his face as sleep lifted, and then his mouth set in a grim, determined line. "That's the horn for an attack," he bit out, setting his sword down long enough to jerk on his braies and arm himself with all his weapons.

"I know what the horn means," I said, rising and hurrying to don my gown. As I tugged on my laces to tighten them, Colin sheathed two daggers and a sword in the leather holder crisscrossing his bare torso.

He strode to me, swung me in the circle of his arms and his large hand took my face as he held it gently. "Bar the door from the inside," he said, "and do nae open it for anyone but me, Katherine, or Connor."

Before I could speak, he covered my mouth with his in an urgent, abrupt kiss. When he broke away, he turned as if to leave me, but I grabbed him by the forearm. "I had a vision," I rushed out, marveling how he had not asked me to try to conjure the future to tell him how to win the battle. He had taken me for my visions, but I realized in this moment, he had never once used me for them. He loved me, the blasted man. He just hadn't yet accepted it. And likely because he loved me, or simply because he was the most honorable man I'd ever met, the guilt he felt over how asking me to conjure a vision might make me feel would not allow him to ask it.

"When?" he asked, his gaze clinging to mine.

"In my dreams just now. I awoke a breath before horn began to sound, a breath before ye awoke. Bran attacks from the front today, but when the mist rises thick, my da will attack," I said, my pulse racing.

"Did ye see anything more of today?"

I nodded, fear making me shiver. "I saw Bran aiming to

shoot ye. Ye are in his line of sight, but I could nae see where ye stood or where he stood. Colin, I saw ye fall." In truth, I'd seen a faceless blurry body fall, but I was certain it was him. "I'll attempt to conjure another vision, and as soon as I do—"

"Nae," he said. The one word shook, and he gripped me by the arms. "Do nae attempt to come to me. 'Tis too dangerous."

"The reason ye took me was for my visions!" I bellowed. "I'll nae sit in here if I conjure information that will keep ye safe."

"I do nae care about the damned visions if it means risking ye," he bellowed back. "Vow to me ye will nae endanger yerself," he said, his tone hard.

I had to lie. If I didn't, I could see by the wild look on his face that he'd lock me in here from outside. "I vow it," I lied not feeling a twinge of guilt. I could not manipulate my own future, so I knew with certainty my vision would not show me if I was endangering myself or not.

"Freya, are ye lyi—"

The door slammed open, and Connor stood in the threshold "Ye must come now. MacLeod's men are at the bridge."

"Tell me it was nae down," Colin said. My gut clenched. I knew the repairs on the bridge were almost done, but I also knew if Colin's men had put the last of the stone on the broken bridge, it would have been down to allow the stone to set in place.

"I'm sorry, brother," Connor said, shaking his head. "I had it down, so the bridge would be repaired by tomorrow. "The MacLeods are pushing forward. We need ye."

"Stay here!" Colin bit out one last time to me, before striding out of the room with Connor.

I wasted no time. The weight of the moment hit me. I barred the door quickly, so if the trance overtook me, I wouldn't be vulnerable. I'd be safe. Closing my eyes, I forced my thoughts to fall in line, to concentrate all my will on Colin. On the way I'd seen him fight. On the way he moved, the way he made me feel, like a fire catching. Everything dissolved under this urgent act of will. The edges of the room began to fade, and the swish of my blood filled my ears, moving through my veins up to my head. My pulse ticked up, and my breathing rose. A bright light threatened to blind me, and the room split itself in two. I saw nothing but white, and then, emerging, the bridge that led to Eilean Donnan.

There stood Colin at the head of a group of men, battling my clan back off the bridge.

Chaos reigned. Arrows flew and men shouted. Swords clanked and horses whinnied. Blood spurted from cuts and men fell from both sides onto the bridge. But Colin was winning. His men—our men—were winning. A scream from behind had me turning, and there stood Katherine, sword in hand, but she was not wielding it. She was facing the castle, pointing toward the rampart and screaming a warning. Sounds came at me from every direction, making it nearly impossible to make out her words. I strained to hear her, my heart thudding with fear that I would not, could not.

"Kill him!" she shouted, pointing. The man beside Katherine raised his bow, only to be struck in the chest by an arrow before he could release his own. And as I glanced around, I saw men lay at her feet all with arrows protruding out of their chest. My gut pitched to the ground, and I scanned the rampart.

There.

I narrowed my eyes trying to make out the figure and inhaled a sharp breath. Bran. He stood barely visible upon a high tower, well away from the guards. He was shooting arrows, killing men one by one. He raised his bow and aimed again. Panic rioted within me. I knew. I knew who he was aiming for. Katherine knew, too. She was running now toward Colin, screaming for him to take cover. My stomach clenched tight, as Colin swung his sword, cutting down MacLeod warriors, unaware that he would be the next to fall. I turned back toward Bran as he released the arrow, and it flew straight and true to lodge into the back of Colin's neck. He pitched forward to his knees before falling to his stomach where he lay unmoving on the ground as the battle raged around him.

I blinked and the vision disappeared. Then I bent over and lost the little food in my stomach. When I quit retching, I jerked upright, wiped the back of my hand over my mouth, and unbarred the door, swinging it open to go save Colin.

Chapter Twenty-Two – Colin

"Colin, to yer left!" Connor shouted.

I jerked to my left, bringing my sword up just in time to parry a blow from another MacLeod warrior. The battlefield was filled with the stench of blood, sweat, and fear. My own sweat mingled with the metallic scent of my sword as I swung it in front of me. The smell of charred wood and smoke from the castle fires added to the intensity of the moment. Iron met iron, and the force of the contact sent vibrations down my arm. I slid my blade away and slung low, hitting the man across his legs. He fell at my feet, and I wasted no time ending his life. There was no room for mercy in the heat of battle. It was kill or be killed. The bridge was finally being raised, which would save the castle, but it made the fighting more difficult with unsteady ground. I did not doubt we would be victorious in this battle, now that the bridge was being raised, but we had to finish the enemies who were on it before they finished those of us fighting them.

I glanced around, assessing. My gaze passed over Connor fighting, and two dozen other of my men locked in battle with MacLeod warriors. We were moving backward toward safety from the bridge rising, but every step backward we took was a step that brought the MacLeod warriors closer to the outer courtyard. We had to stop them before they reached the entrance to the courtyard.

One of my men fell to my left and then another fell on my right—both struck with arrows. The roar of the battle was near deafening, and I turned behind me to search the dark night for the enemy who was shooting my men. Someone had gained the castle. I scanned the shadow as I parried blows, but I could not locate the perpetrator. I ducked when a sword came at my head, then jumped when another aimed toward my feet.

Like a hammer, the pain gripped my side as I landed with a heavy thud, but another cry of terror reached my ears, chilling me. Katherine's voice? A wave of apprehension, sharp and biting, swept through me. My sister had promised to stay in her bedchamber and bar the door; she had sworn to me that she would do so. But she was a stubborn lass and rarely did as she was told. She was strongwilled and as wild as the wind. A quick glance over my shoulder showed my foolish sister to me. She stood there, fragile and defiant, at the other end of the bridge near the courtyard entrance. Her panic was clear, her back turned to me. She pointed, then turned around suddenly, screaming my name. Tears threatened her voice as she cried out to me. I gave a quick shake of my head, desperate to stop her, and as she started to run toward me, I bellowed, "Make to yer chamber."

"Colin, in front of ye!" Connor bellowed.

In the madness of the fight that churned around me, I jerked back toward the front just as a MacLeod warrior materialized where I had been a moment before. His sword lunged with the force of all his anger, and the sharp point aimed toward my gut. I whipped my weapon up, catching the oncoming blow in the nick of time, just as the white blade scraped across the polished hilt of my dagger. My enemy's eyes went wide in shock and disbelief. He knew his mistake as well as I did. His blow had failed; he was just lowering his sword from the doomed attempt to gut me. Such knowledge was fatal in battle. I seized the opportunity and brought my weapon swiftly up in one clean motion, taking his head with one powerful blow. He fell. My body clenched. I turned quickly back toward the castle to see if Katherine had fled as planned. But it wasn't Katherine in front of me.

Black fright swept through me at the sight of another figure. It was Freya. She was nearly upon me. Fear tangled through my body, and then I saw it—the arrow. It was arcing through the air, coming toward me, and coming toward her. Panic rioted as I lunged madly toward her. She crashed into me, wrapping her arms around my body like a rope. And then she grunted, and her hold went slack. Her limbs unspooled and went limp as if her very bones had melted from inside her.

Icy fear twisted hard around my heart. I knew before I looked. There, lodged in her back, was an arrow. My fingers felt it as I clasped her, long and true and deep. A guttural cry ripped through me as I cradled her and met her closing gaze. It was already starting to cloud. A small smile tugged at the corner of her lips. "I saved ye," she mumbled before her eyes shuttered closed, and her body went limp.

Shock stilled everything for a moment. Time. My breath. The battle. And then a thought froze my brain. I loved her. The truth was undeniable. The clarity of it fearful. My chest ached, and I tried to push the thought away, but it pounded at me, until I had no choice but to relent to it. I loved her. I loved her, and I might lose her. "Nay, nay, nay!" I bellowed, squeezing her to me. I gripped her to me as raw, primitive, familiar grief shredded me from the inside out. "Ye will nae die, damn ye," I yelled.

"Colin! Put her down! We need ye! She needs ye!"

I heard my brother to my right. I saw him battling the enemies around us. I had to release her to save her. I knew it. Ice spread through my veins, as I lay her carefully on her side, and bit out to Colin, "Guard her. With yer life."

I was the better warrior for killing. I was faster and quicker. And I was driven now with a fury so hot it scalded my veins as my blood coursed through me. My vision tinged red over everything, and the rage clawed up my stomach and my throat to release from my mouth with an inhuman bellow. I cut through the MacLeod warriors in front of me, killing them ruthlessly. One by one they fell at my feet as I fought like a crazed man until there was no one standing to fight.

I turned to make my way back to Freya and Connor and saw him a dozen steps in front of me, carrying a limp Freya in his arms. And then I remembered the archer. I glanced up to the rampart to search for the enemy and found a body half slumped over the rampart edge, bow dangling from the still form. Frowning, I scanned the courtyard for who had shot the MacLeod down, and there on one knee was Katherine, bow in hand.

I reached her as she was standing, and the bridge was shutting. My men parted as I came, and I called orders to them to, "Man the towers and search the moat. A MacLeod breached the stronghold. Make certain there are nae others. Thor will lead ye until Connor returns."

"Aye, laird," came a loud chorus of agreement. They had each trained for these attacks and knew well, if I could not lead then it fell to Connor or his right-hand man.

"I told Connor to head to the healing room," Katherine said, having to run to keep up with me, as I was already heading that way. I knew my sister's mind. I wove in and out of people, assuring them we would be victorious and sending a prayer to the gods that we would be.

"Ye will save her," I said to Katherine, not slowing, not glancing at my sister. If I met her gaze and saw pity or fear or doubt, I was not sure I wouldn't crumble under the weight of grief. I loved her. I was terrified of that truth, but I was more terrified of losing her because I was afraid to open up to her. I began to run through the throngs of warriors and servants racing to and fro carrying water and cloth to cleanse wounds and stop bleeding. I hit the stairs that led to the healing room and burst through the door.

There, sitting up, talking to Connor was Freya. Wild relief ripped through me, and I closed the distance between us, seeing the arrow still lodged in her. It had hit the back of her arm, not her back as I had thought.

"I'm sorry," she said, tears in her eyes. "I could nae let ye die."

I gripped her around her waist, careful not to bump the arrow, and buried my head in her lap. "Connor, go finish the battle, and only if ye can nae see a way to win, return to retrieve me." Footsteps fell and then a door clicked shut. I knew, without glancing up, that Connor had gone to fulfill my command and Katherine had stepped out for a moment to give Freya and me privacy. I struggled to hold my raw emotions in check, but it was no use. I was no match for how she made me feel. I rose, cupped her face in my hands, and kissed her long and hard. When I pulled back, I said, "I love ye. I am sorry it took me so long to admit it. If ye will still grace me with yer heart, I will take it. I will protect it and cherish it, and ye can have my broken heart in return."

Chapter Twenty-Three – Freya

Tears of pleasure filled my eyes at Colin's words and a warm glow flowed through me, despite my throbbing shoulder. I raised my good arm to bring my hand to his face and ran my fingertips over his stubble. He captured my hand with his and brought my fingertips to his lips to kiss them almost reverently. "Ye have unlocked me heart and soul, Colin. Despite the gruff exterior ye tried to present, ye gave only gentleness, kindness, and understanding. Ye gave me back the confidence, the inner strength, I had lost. Do ye realize, ye did nae once ask me to try to conjure a vision when that is precisely why ye took me in the first place?"

"Aye," he said, going to my left shoulder to examine, I knew, the arrow protruding from it. "I did nae ever wish to take ye, but," he said, his gaze soft as a caress, "I'm glad I did. When I did take ye, though, I promised myself, I'd only ask ye for a vision if there was nae another choice. I felt I still had choices."

"Felt?"

He sighed. "Aye. We cannae keep doing this. I lose good men with every attack, and we become weaker and weaker. Eventually, yer da will best me, and then—" He shook his head and growled. "I ken he is yer da, Freya, but he used ye, and I'd nae see ye fall to his mercy again."

Tears spilled down my cheeks. Maybe it was that my

mother had been the best part of Da? Maybe, she had kept the good parts of him at the forefront when she'd been alive, and when she'd died, that part of him had slowly died as well, quickened with Yennifer and Bran whispering in his ear to gain more power. It was not a simple answer, but I refused to be used by my da again. My allegiance resided with the man who had loved me as I always had hoped to be loved—unquestionably, completely, and passionately.

I stared at Colin. The man I loved. "Are ye asking me to conjure a vision to defeat my da?"

"Aye," he said, his tone sorrowful. His pain for me spoke volumes of the man he was. "I am. I'm sorry. If ye do nae want to do it, we will find another way. Somehow."

There was no other way. I knew it, and he knew it too, and yet he offered to find one, because when ye loved someone, you put them first, thought about their happiness, their safety, over yers. "If I say nay—"

"'Tis alright," he said, pressing a kiss to my forehead before his gaze found mine once more. "I will send ye and Katherine to the convent for protection, and then I will come for ye both, if—nae, when—I'm victorious over yer da."

So many emotions rioted in me. Sadness. Happiness. Fear. Hope. Awe and gratitude. I had conjured a vision that had saved Colin's life. Now, I was being asked to summon one that might end my da's. "I will do it," I said, hoping when the time came, I actually could. "I will do it because if I do nae, he will kill ye or Bran will."

"Bran is dead," Colin said, matter of fact.

"How?" I asked, not having seen Bran's death in my vision.

"Katherine shot him with an arrow."

"Ye taught her?"

"Aye. That and the dagger."

In that moment, a pounding came at the door.

"Enter," Colin bellowed.

Katherine strode into the room. "'Tis all the time ye can have. Freya needs the arrow removed to help avoid infection and fever."

Colin raised an eyebrow in question then leaned forward. I nodded, giving an answer, and his lips touched mine, tentative at first, then eager and deliberate. A blinding light filled and overwhelmed my vision, and I gasped as the world around me spun and fell away. The quiet healing room vanished with startling suddenness as the warmth of his mouth swept me far, far away.

I stood beside Colin in his solar, leaning over his shoulder as he scratched out letters with an ink-stained hand, focused and intent, the room filled with parchment and the musky scent of old books. His hair shone in the candlelit glow as he wrote a careful missive, the words sprawling with urgency, meant for delivery to the king.

Yer Grace,

I beg ye to send a trusted advisor to hear a confession from Laird MacLeod of his stepson attacking Dunscaith and breaking the treaty. The war between us rages on, and I wish to end it, and have thought of a way to elicit the confession to do this. If ye will give me leave in this, I can once again turn my attention to serving ye.

Yer faithful servant,
Laird Colin MacDonald

A sharp and unmistakable flash of white light penetrated my vision again, accompanied by a sudden, searing pain that tore relentlessly across my forehead. I cried out, clutching *my temples, as my vision warped, twisted, and the agony grew unbearable.*

Now, I was standing on the far side of the bridge at Eilean Donnan, shrouded in a thick and cloying mist. The bridge was lifted, a barrier between worlds, and there stood my da, defiant, his army clustered in tight formation behind him. Alone, I faced him. To the right, concealed among the dense forest trees and emerald brush, the king's man held his station with Colin beside him, both of them straining to hear my father's confession. I was desperate to hear, too. My vision began to splinter into fragments, to break apart and reform in flashes, never constant, never certain. Me pleading with him, me sacrificing my power for his confession to only me. Slivers of him agreeing and giving the confession. Me warning him with urgency—if he did not heed, he would die, just like the others. And him laughing, unbowed, refusing to listen. But it was not my da who lay slain; the ghostly image of my own body filled my mind. It was I who fell.

I opened my eyes with a start, and I was looking at Colin and Katherine once more. I did not know exactly how my story ended, if I lived or died, but I knew without a doubt, what I had to do to protect Colin. I had wished to control my own future and now I was being handed the chance to do that. At the base of my throat a beat pulsed and swelled as the knowledge of what was to come, what I had to do, sank in.

"Are ye alright?" Colin asked, standing so close his heat washed over me.

"I'm the key to ending the war," I said.

"Ye mean yer visions?" he asked with a frown.

"Nay," I said, shaking my head. "Me. I must confront my da face to face, and ye must write to the king and convince him to send a trusted advisor to hear the confession."

"Nay," Colin said, the word hard and uncompromising. "I'll nae let ye confront yer da and risk yerself. When I thought I lost ye, it nearly killed me."

I put my palm on his cheek, even as my shoulder ached so badly I had to grit my teeth. "Ye gave me back my strength, Colin. Now, ye must let me use it. I set my fate in motion, and my gut tells me the only way to put right what I caused is to do this."

His eyebrows dipped into a deep frown. "Ye wish to be rid of the visions."

I nodded. "I do, but I wish to end this war, save lives, and atone for the death of Morgana's mother. She died as a result of me stealing the goblet. If my visions disappear, will ye still—"

He pressed a finger to my lips. "Lass," he said the one word brimming with love, "ye ken I will. I do nae love ye for the visions. I love ye for ye."

"Enough talk," Katherine clipped. "I must remove the arrow now."

After night had finally stretched its dark cloak over the castle, and when my da's men had ridden away in defeat and disgrace, I lay spent and naked in Colin's arms. I was still panting and sweaty from the intense joining of our bodies. Colin turned on his side, so he could face me, and I rolled carefully onto my good shoulder to look at him with eyes full of love and longing. He ran his thumb over my lower lip, and the touch clenched my belly with desire once more, though my body was exhausted from the events of the night—from the battle and the horrible loss of blood, and most especially from having Colin love me so completely and so thoroughly. I tried to calm my breathing, savoring the feel of him next to me, the warmth of his skin against mine. Moonlight streamed in from the window, and I counted in my mind to when the first clear night would be. I knew there were ten more to come before my da returned with more men and I had to confront him again. I would live each one of those nights as if it were my very last.

"Freya."

I knew before he even voiced the question what it would be, but I let him ask so he could hear it for himself.

"Did ye see yerself safe in yer vision?"

I swallowed the knot forming in my throat. "I saw myself fall."

Colin's entire body tensed next to me. He rolled on top of me and his heavy weight settled over me. His arms came to either side of mine, not locking me in place but sheltering and protecting me. He pressed against me, his heart frantic against my chest. "Freya, I cannae let ye do this. I cannae live without ye should ye die."

I pressed my lips to his, relishing the warmth and the fire his nearness was already rekindling. When I broke the kiss, I said, "Ye would give yer life for me. And I would ye. That is the perfect love I wished for. If I only have these next ten days of it, so be it, but I dinnae believe that is so. I believe what I needed was true faith in myself and once I found that, I gained the power to see my future. Now, it's up to me to control the outcome."

"Us," he said, brushing his lips first to mine, then delving his tongue inside my mouth. Our tongues tangled and retreated, before he pulled back to stare at me. "Tell me what ye want me to do to ye."

I loved how he always thought of me. "Ye ken what I want," I said.

His mouth moved down to my breast, his lips suckling and tongue teasing. A pulsing knot of desire tightened at my core, each flick of his tongue making my heart leap and my body blaze with more and more heat. My breast grew heavy under his relentless attentions as the need and ache built with intensity until they were all I could feel, all that I was. I shook my head and mewled, moving beneath him, desperate. He rolled to the side of me to spread my sex and find the secret spot again, his fingers coaxing even more pleasure from me with each touch.

I gasped as his fingers moved softly, like a whisper, and then more insistently with increasing pressure, until I was unraveling. The ache increased, and I was clutching at him and pulling him to me, everything inside of me throbbing with need. His fingers moved ever faster until he was expertly strumming me, and I climbed again toward the peak. Desperate, almost senseless with wanting him, I brought my mouth to his and kissed him with the message I knew he would read.

He came over me, and my body opened to him as he drove inside me to the hilt, sending a hunger spiraling through me. "Now," I moaned, my voice raw. He did not hesitate. His hands came under my buttocks, lifting me. With long, full strokes of his body, he drove into me faster and harder until we were both crying out, wild. He took me to the top of the pinnacle, to the edge of it and over, to the place where only he had ever taken me. Passion inched through my veins as we reached our release, my insides throbbing, and our bodies becoming one.

He collapsed on top of me, his head coming to the side of my shoulder, and I brought my hands to his back and traced my fingernails across his hot skin until he moaned his pleasure. "Ye are every bit the husband I wished for. Ye saved me."

He rose his head up and kissed me fully on the mouth. "Nay, lass, ye saved me."

Chapter Twenty-Four ~ Freya

Colin's eyes bore into mine as he lifted the heavy breastplate to adjust the position and insisted, "Ye will stand far enough from yer da that his sword can nae reach ye." With a determined hand, he tugged on the straps of the armor he had specially fashioned for me. I met his gaze, sensing the weight of my own doubt mirrored back.

"'Tis heavy," I protested, feeling my shoulders slump beneath the cumbersome shield that bore down like the weight of our fate itself.

"Thor says it will stop an arrow," Colin assured, conviction firm in his voice as he adjusted the fit yet again. "And if ye are shot at in the chest or back, this will save yer life," he added, tapping a nail on the surface of the plate with an urgency that heightened my fear and my resolve. I let my gaze drift toward the window in our bedchamber, where the thick, ghostly mist was rising outside, lending an eerie veil to the land, precisely as I had foreseen it would appear after ten days. Just as I had predicted, the king's advisor had arrived this morning, and it was only a matter of time before my da, always relentless in his pursuits, would come as well.

Beyond the bridge, deep in the shrouded woods, Connor had been attending to the positions of nearly a hundred men all morning long, readying them with both attack and defense. I had never in my life felt more cherished, never felt more loved. Colin had devised an entire plan around ensuring my survival. I did not wish for death, but if I were to meet it on this day, I knew I would do so having received the love I had longed for.

Though I had been betrayed and discarded without thought, used for gain and abused by wicked men, I had persevered. I had been made stronger through all my trials. I knew choices bore consequences, and I had endured more than I had thought possible, living through the ones my choices had brought upon me. I had to believe I would somehow endure this one too.

Colin fastened the last strap and lifted my chin with his hand, bringing my eyes to meet his again. "Ye're ready for what comes," he said, and his words carried a weight beyond the battle itself. His steady gaze was both love and plea, an unspoken insistence that I believe in him, believe in us, and believe in the strength we had found in each other.

I took a breath deep enough to carry all of my hopes. "Ye dinnae have to worry. I'll stay out of reach," I vowed, with a resolve that was as much for my reassurance as it was for his.

He hugged me fiercely, a brief embrace that held a lifetime of promises. "Let us go then," he said, releasing me and holding up my cloak that I was to wear to hide the breastplate.

For a moment, I stood still, wanting to etch every detail of him into memory. The intensity of his gaze, the stark resolution in his every movement, the way his presence seemed to fill even the spaces where fear dared to creep in.

"I love ye," I said, each word a piece of my heart left with him, unwilling to face the uncertainty of what was to come without first making that truth known.

Colin nodded. "And I, ye. Now we have to go." His

command was gentle but firm, and I knew it was his strength he was lending me as he spoke it.

I nodded, my mind awash with every moment that had led me to this one, each memory a thread in the tapestry of our lives, each thread binding me to the belief that I would live through this to build a long, beautiful life with him.

"The mist is almost fully risen," Colin said, bringing my attention back to him and the cloak.

I presented my back to him, he settled my cloak on my shoulders, then turned me to face him. He gave me a long, desperate kiss, before breaking contact and silently taking my hand to lead me out of our bedchamber and into the darkening sky. The servants and many of the wives of the warriors stationed in the woods were gathered in the courtyard. They each held a burning torch. "What are the torches for?" I asked Katherine as we paused at the gate to the outer courtyard where she stood with one as well.

"To light yer way back to us, Freya. Ye are part of our family."

My chest felt as though it would burst, filling me with a strange and wondrous sensation that at once surprised and consumed me. We had met as sworn foes, each of us intent on the other's ruin, but now we stood entwined in something far more enduring and rare. Against all odds, an unbreakable connection had blossomed and flourished between us, nourished by kindness, by time, by the courage to see beyond our differences. It was a bond of our own making, crafted through the moments we had shared, the trust we had built, all of it more resilient than the ones formed by kinship alone. Family was not only a matter of lineage; it was a deliberate act, a choice, a thread woven through shared experiences and tended with care.

I marveled at how we had transformed into part of each

other, and how the space between us, once filled with animosity, now overflowed with warmth. As I stood there, contemplating what we had so astonishingly become, the silence of the morning shattered in an instant, split by the ceaseless barrage of pounding hooves. The earth beneath me trembled with growing insistence, sending vibrations through the thin soles of my slippers and into the marrow of my bones.

I gave Katherine a hug, and then Colin led me through the outer courtyard and down the bridge. When we got to the end, the squeak of it being raised cut through the tense silence that had grown. Colin turned to me and cupped my face. "I will be just there to the right with a bow aimed at yer da. I willnae let ye die," he vowed.

I knew he would try. I had made choices that set my fate in motion, and Colin's too. Now, I would make a new fate for us, I hoped. Morgana had said I would not have visions that could change my future, but she had either been wrong or had been lying to me, so that I would come to see the truth on my own. Each choice I had made, each vision I had, had changed my life.

I felt certain the point had been that I had been the decider of my fate all along. If I had understood this, I would not have made the reckless decision to steal the goblet, and would have instead, refused to wed, or run away. But I had made the choice I had, because I had wanted to change the course of my life while still getting exactly what I'd envisioned for my life. I rose on my tiptoes and kissed him. When I lowered myself, I patted his chest and said, "Go now." Those were the only words I could get out. My breath seemed to have solidified in my throat, and it felt as if a hand had closed around my heart to squeeze it.

Colin slipped into the cover of the woods. And as I

stood there watching my da approach, I thought about how Colin's choices had also affected our fate. He had chosen to take me, but then he'd chosen to treat me with care, not as his enemy. He'd offered kindness when all other men I'd known had offered cruelty. He'd offered freedom when all my other husbands had offered control. He'd given desire when the others had gifted me fear.

Da rode with scores of men behind him. Enough, I knew, to take Eilean Donnan but not enough to oppose the king. As he brought his destrier to a halt in front of me and dismounted, I prayed Da would make a choice that would bring him a peaceful fate. I could not choose for him. His consequences would not be my fault. He had his men halt a dozen steps behind him, and then he closed the distance between us. "Freya? What's this?"

He did not reach to hug me, or exclaim how glad he was to see me, or even inquire if I was alright. I cast my mind back trying to remember the last time my da had shown me true care. It had been ages ago around the time Mama had died. At first, I had been too young and mourning the loss of my mama, but as I had grown older, I had chosen not to see the change, his withdrawing, his allowing his obsession with having power to consume him. I understood now, it had been too painful to face. But turning a blind eye to painful things was no way to live. I would be much more aware in my life from this day forward for myself, for my sister, for Colin, and the children we would have. "Why are ye out here?"

"I slipped out when I heard ye approaching. Nae anyone noticed because they are preparing to war with ye. I want to come home with ye after ye kill Colin." Saying the words made my stomach turn.

Da nodded. "Of course, lass. I already have an alliance

set in motion for ye."

I didn't even feel disappointment that he intended to use me again. I had expected it. He had never intended to offer me protection. I knew this now. I shook my head. "Nay. I will nae wed again unless ye speak the truth to me. When Bran was captured, he tried to gain mercy by admitting he broke the alliance." It was a partial lie, but I felt no guilt. "Bran confessed to me that it was he who attacked Dunscaith, and that ye kenned it and covered it up."

A tiny flinch was the only reaction Da had to what I said. "Who else heard this?" Da asked.

"Only me," I quickly supplied. "I am yer loyal daughter. I have wed as ye asked. Give me the truth, so I can truly aid ye in gaining all the power ye desire. So I can aid ye in how to take this castle, keep it, and control the channel."

"Yer visions are that clear?"

"Aye," I replied. "How do ye think I knew it was ye that approached?"

"Bran attacked without my consent," Da said, his tone low, but not so low that Colin and the king's advisor would not hear. "I dinnae have a choice but to claim otherwise. I cannae lose Eilean Donnan and have to bow and simper to MacDonald the rest of my life."

I inhaled a long slow breath. "Colin wanted peace. He entered the alliance in good faith. If ye will confess to the king what ye just did to me, Colin will nae try to rule the channel and cut ye off. But if ye dunnae," I said, stepping to him and setting my hand on his heart, "I see this fate for ye."

The vision came in a flash of bright light, and I knew it was but a breath before it became reality. "Ye will die."

At that moment, Da's gaze flicked past me to the

woods. I didn't have to turn to know who approached. I'd seen it. The king's advisor walked toward us, his cloak, with the king's emblem, blowing in the breeze and clear for my da to see. He reached down toward his dagger, but before his fingers could curl around the hilt, an arrow whistled past me and lodged in his heart.

I screamed as he fell, Colin's warriors poured out, and Colin crouched by me and I kneeled over my da. My stomach clenched, as I pressed my hand to the blood pouring out of his wound, but I knew it was useless. As shouts swirled around me, and the king's advisor ordered the MacLeod warriors to stand down in the name of the king, I leaned over my da, tears filling my eyes and rolling down my cheeks. "I forgive ye," I whispered, as he coughed up blood. He stared past me, but when I took his hand, he squeezed mine ever so gently, as he used to do when I was a child and my mama was alive. Then his eyelashes closed on his life.

The grief came hard and fast, knocking the air out of me with the force of it.

I could not stand to walk, my legs just would not properly work. Men moved around me silently, and Colin gathered me in his arms. My blood roared in my ears, but I heard the king's man ordering my da's men to gather my da's body and return to the MacLeod stronghold to await the king's command.

Colin carried me to our bedchamber and did not demand words from me. I crawled onto the bed and lay down, letting the tears roll down my cheeks for the loss of the love I had once known from my da, and the new love I had gained from Colin. He lay down behind me, circling his arm around my waist and pulling me against the solid length of his body. As I cried, he ran his fingers through my hair, whispering words of comfort and love.

And as my tears eventually lessened and stopped, bright light filled my sight, and a vision hit me.

It was different than all others. I was in the exact place I had been before the vision hit. I could see Colin behind me, and Morgana knelt in front of me by the bed. She smiled down at me and pressed her fingertips to my eyelids.

"The debt is paid," she said, her voice loud and clear. "A life for a life. I take yer curse, and I leave ye with a gift."

She snapped her fingers, my eyes flew open, and there I sat on the loch beach with Colin beside me. I held a new bairn and so did he—a girl and a boy.

Morgana smiled down at us. "Teach them that they control their fate."

The vision disappeared, and I gasped to be fully back in the bedchamber on the bed Colin's arms tightened around me. "What is it?" he asked, his lips close to my ear.

I grasped his hand and placed it over my belly. "A boy and a girl," I said, turning to him to find his eyes wide. I smiled through my sadness. "They will be here in the spring."

"Bairns? We've bairns coming?"

I nodded as he hugged me tight then kissed me. When he pulled away, he leaned down and kissed my belly before rising back up to kiss me once more. "Ye saw it in a vision?"

"Aye. The last one. Morgana was there and told me."

"I'm glad," he said. "Now we can live in peace."

I laughed at that. "With two bairns coming? Oh, my dear husband, this is the beginning of the chaos, of the love, of the family and fate we have chosen."

Epilogue – Freya

Ten months later

"Ye want me to do what?" I demanded of Colin, as I gripped my wailing son and daughter in my arms.

He gave me a patient smile. "I want ye to give me the bairns, and ye go down to the loch and have a nice relaxing swim, and wash—" he said, thrusting the tallow soap toward me, "and then return here where a tray of food will be waiting for ye, and ye can take a nice long nap while I watch the children."

I gaped at him while curling my fingers tighter around my bairns. "Nay," I said with a shake of my head in case he somehow did not understand my answer, because clearly the man had lost his mind if he thought I was going to leave my children out of my sight.

With a sigh, he sat on the edge of the bed beside me and put the soap down. "Freya," he said, his tone gentle. "Ye stink."

I felt my eyebrows shoot up. "I dinnae!" I protested. "That must be one of the bairns. Mayhap Magy wet herself or Roan spit up on himself," I said, laying them beside me to unravel them from their blankets and have a look.

I quickly uncovered a wailing Magy and then did the same to an equally unhappy Roan. Then I bent down and sniffed each bairn and smiled at their sweet smell. I sat up and settled a glare on Colin. "Ye are mistaken. The children smell divine. They are washed and fed." I frowned. I had seen to their every waking need since they had been born a month prior, never letting them out of my sight, so I could not understand their sudden unhappiness that had started a day ago. "I do nae ken why they will nae quit fussing," I said, warm tears trickling out of my burning eyes. I could not recall the last time I'd slept through the night.

Colin scooped up both children as I protested, brought them to his broad chest, and began to coo to them in his deep voice as he stood and walked around the bedchamber to bounce them. To my astonishment, they both fell instantly quiet. He faced me with a tender look on his face. "They like movement."

"I ken," I protested. I'd been moving since the day they were born it seemed, because they loved to be held and bounced and walked and bounced. My brain felt rattled from all the bouncing.

"My love, ye are exhausted. Ye have nae let me or anyone else aid ye. And ye have barely slept, or eaten, and I love ye, but ye do smell. When was the last time ye bathed?"

I tried to recall but couldn't to my mortification. My cheeks instantly heated.

"Let me help ye."

I wanted to, but I was afraid to leave them.

Colin closed the distance between us and bent down to press a kiss on my lips. When he rose, he said, "I vow to ye, I will guard them with my life, just as I do ye. I love them just as much as ye."

"I know. Of course I do," I said. I did feel itchy. And when I discretely tilted my nose to my shoulder, a stench rose that made me wrinkle it. Was that spit up or urine? I wasn't sure which I preferred it to be and that made me laugh. "Alright," I relented, rising off the bed and picking up the soap. "Maybe just a quick swim in the loch."

"A verra wise decision," he said in a teasing tone.

I looked at the bairns now sleeping—traitors—and said, "Roan likes—"

"To sleep on yer chest," Colin finished. "Aye, I'll put him on mine."

I pursed my lips at Colin. "Are ye trying to prove ye ken what to do?"

"Aye," he said with a chuckle. "I want ye to have a moment to yerself, so ye will want to have more bairns someday." He gave me a heated look. "Which means we will eventually join again."

My dormant desire since giving birth awakened with a burst of yearning through me. I reached out to him and traced my nails over his rounded bicep. "Verra tricky, husband."

"Aye. But with the best intentions," he said with a wink.

"Mayhap Katherine could watch the bairns for a bit when I return?" I said, the tingling of need already building within me.

"She can."

"Ye already asked her?" I said, surprised.

"Aye. It's almost as if I can read what ye want."

I gave a little mock shudder. "As long as it's because ye ken me that well, and nae because ye can read my mind." I turned toward the door, but Colin said, "I almost forgot, ye received a raven this morning."

"From Vanora?" I asked. She was the only one who had sent ravens to me since I'd been at Eilean Donnan, but she was supposed to be coming for a visit. "I hope she is nae cancelling her visit," I said, on a sigh, thinking of the raven I'd just sent her telling her that Connor was wedding the

Lord of the Isle's daughter to gain a strong alliance for Colin.

"Actually, ye received two ravens," he said. "I set the missives just there," he added, tilting his head to the washstand.

I went to them and glanced down to find that one was indeed from Vanora and one was had to be from Elena as the Clan Gordon crest sealed the missive. As Colin lay on the bed and settled both twins on his chest, I read Vanora's missive first.

I'm coming at once to declare my love to Connor. Did ye tell him of yer vision? That we are destined to wed?

"Is she coming this instant?" Colin asked with a chuckle, knowing of Vanora's feelings for Connor, or the ones she thought she had, and knowing of the vision I'd once had of Vanora and Connor standing before the priest.

"Aye," I said, rolling up the missive.

"She kens she's a child compared to Connor, aye?"

"Apparently, nae," I said. "Connor will be gone by then, so Vanora will nae be able to cause him trouble."

"Well, even if he were still here, Connor can hold his own with yer wee sister."

"Ha!" I said. "That wee lass has changed. I hear tell from my uncle that she has become quite stubborn and insists upon sitting on the clan counsel."

"And he lets her?"

"Aye, he says it's more trouble to try to stop her, and that she actually has quite the keen mind for politics." I smiled. "I believe she got that from me."

"Oh, aye, of course," Colin replied with a chuckle to which I served him the appropriate scowl.

I reached for the other missive and unrolled it.

Dear Freya,

I am still working to control my gift. 'Tis nae as easy as I had thought it might be.

I sighed in understanding of that.

I intend to use it, once I can control it, to destroy Laird Campbell and his clan.

Elena's line made my gut ache for her.

I'm going to infiltrate Laird Campbell's stronghold, pretend to be a healer, and use my power to read minds to take all he has and all he killed for. What I want to ken is this: Was there any price to pay for yer gift? It seems almost too good to be true. Morgana had said I would have the power to read minds, but I would grow to rue the day I wished for the gift. I cannot imagine that. Can ye?

I rolled up the missive and looked to Colin to find him watching me. My heart thumped hard in my chest. "I'll be a little longer than just a swim in the loch."

He nodded. "We're fine. Is all well with Elena?"

"Nay," I said, shivering when I considered her words. Was there a price to be paid for her gift? Aye. I had to warn her. Mine was a life. I had no notion what hers might be, but she needed to be reminded, before dire consequences were set in motion, that it was a curse, not a gift.

"Go have time to think," Colin said. "We will be here waiting, the three of us, yer family." I smiled as I walked out of the door. I had made a wish, and it had gone terribly wrong, but in the pain and the suffering, I had met Colin, and he had given me the gift of strength to find myself. Not who I was. But who I wanted to be, and when I had found that woman, and let go of the beliefs I'd blindly clung to, I found the love I'd longed for and so much more.

Thank you for reading *The Laird's Magical Lass*! I hope you loved Colin and Freya's story!

If you love sweeping epic romances that take you on rollicking adventures through the highlands and have interconnected family stories, then you'll love my series *Highlander Vows: Entangled Hearts*, that starts with the USA Today bestselling When a Laird Loves a Lady!

And don't miss my dark and sexy bestselling *Wicked Willful Highlander* series, starting with Highlanders Hold Grudges! *He kidnapped her to save his clan, not to lose his heart.*

If you're looking for something sexy, sweet, and romantic, you'll fall in love with my *Of Mist and Mountains* series, starting with Highland Hope! *Sometimes the one you love is the very one you cannot have.*

Sign up for my newsletter to get chances at Advanced Reader Copies, news on books, and inside scoops! Go here > juliejohnstoneauthor.com. You can also join my private Facebook group, Julie Johnstone's Literary Wenches. And you can find me on Instagram. See what I'm recommending on Goodreads. Hear about my sales via Bookbub. And get news from me about my books on Amazon by following my Amazon Page.

Read below for an excerpt from *When a Laird Loves a Lady*...

One

England, 1357

Faking her death would be simple. It was escaping her home that would be difficult. Marion de Lacy stared hard into the slowly darkening sky, thinking about the plan she intended to put into action tomorrow—if all went well—but growing uneasiness tightened her belly. From where she stood in the bailey, she counted the guards up in the tower. It was not her imagination: Father had tripled the knights keeping guard at all times, as if he was expecting trouble.

Taking a deep breath of the damp air, she pulled her mother's cloak tighter around her to ward off the twilight chill. A lump lodged in her throat as the wool scratched her neck. In the many years since her mother had been gone, Marion had both hated and loved this cloak for the death and life it represented. Her mother's freesia scent had long since faded from the garment, yet simply calling up a memory of her mother wearing it gave Marion comfort.

She rubbed her fingers against the rough material. When she fled, she couldn't chance taking anything with her but the clothes on her body and this cloak. Her death had to appear accidental, and the cloak that everyone knew she prized would ensure her freedom. Finding it tangled in the branches at the edge of the sea cliff ought to be just the thing to convince her father and William Froste that she'd drowned. After all, neither man thought she could swim. They didn't truly care about her anyway. Her marriage to the blackhearted knight was only about what her hand could give the two men. Her father, Baron de Lacy, wanted more power, and Froste wanted her family's prized land. A match made in Heaven, if only the match didn't involve her…but it did.

Father would set the hounds of Hell themselves to track her down if he had the slightest suspicion that she was still alive. She was an inestimable possession to be given to secure Froste's unwavering allegiance and, therefore, that of the renowned ferocious knights who served him. Whatever small sliver of hope she had that her father would grant her mercy and not marry her to Froste had been destroyed by the lashing she'd received when she'd pleaded for him to do so.

The moon crested above the watchtower, reminding her why she was out here so close to mealtime: to meet Angus. The Scotsman may have been her father's stable master, but he was *her* ally, and when he'd proposed she flee England for Scotland, she'd readily consented.

Marion looked to the west, the direction from which Angus would return from Newcastle. He should be back any minute now from meeting his cousin and clansman Neil, who was to escort her to Scotland. She prayed all was set and that Angus's kin was ready to depart. With her wedding to Froste to take place in six days, she wanted to be far away before there was even the slightest chance he'd be making his way here. And since he was set to arrive the night before the wedding, leaving tomorrow promised she'd not encounter him.

A sense of urgency enveloped her, and Marion forced herself to stroll across the bailey toward the gatehouse that led to the tunnel preceding the drawbridge. She couldn't risk raising suspicion from the tower guards. At the gatehouse, she nodded to Albert, one of the knights who operated the drawbridge mechanism. He was young and rarely questioned her excursions to pick flowers or find herbs.

"Off to get some medicine?" he inquired.

"Yes," she lied with a smile and a little pang of guilt. But this was survival, she reminded herself as she entered the tunnel. When she exited the heavy wooden door that led to freedom, she wasn't surprised to find Peter and Andrew not yet up in the twin towers that flanked the entrance to the drawbridge. It was, after all, time for the changing of the guard.

They smiled at her as they put on their helmets and demi-gauntlets. They were an imposing presence to any who crossed the drawbridge and dared to approach the castle gate. Both men were tall and looked particularly daunting in their full armor, which Father insisted upon at all times. The men were certainly a fortress in their own right.

She nodded to them. "I'll not be long. I want to gather some more flowers for the supper table." Her voice didn't even wobble with the lie.

Peter grinned at her, his kind brown eyes crinkling at the edges. "Will you pick me one of those pale winter flowers for my wife again, Marion?"

She returned his smile. "It took away her anger as I said it would, didn't it?"

"It did," he replied. "You always know just how to help with her."

"I'll get a pink one if I can find it. The colors are becoming scarcer as the weather cools."

Andrew, the younger of the two knights, smiled, displaying a set of straight teeth. He held up his covered arm. "My cut is almost healed."

Marion nodded. "I told you! Now maybe you'll listen to me sooner next time you're wounded in training."

He gave a soft laugh. "I will. Should I put more of your paste on tonight?"

"Yes, keep using it. I'll have to gather some more yarrow, if I can find any, and mix up another batch of the medicine for you." And she'd have to do it before she escaped. "I better get going if I'm going to find those things." She knew she should not have agreed to search for the flowers and offered to find the yarrow when she still had to speak to Angus and return to the castle in time for supper, but both men had been kind to her when many had not. It was her way of thanking them.

After Peter lowered the bridge and opened the door, she departed the castle grounds, considering her plan once more. Had she forgotten anything? She didn't think so. She was simply going to walk straight out of her father's castle and never come back. Tomorrow, she'd announce she was going out to collect more winter blooms, and then, instead, she would go down to the edge of the cliff overlooking the sea. She would slip off her cloak and leave it for a search party to find. Her breath caught deep in her chest at the simple yet dangerous plot. The last detail to see to was Angus.

She stared down the long dirt path that led to the sea and stilled, listening for hoofbeats. A slight vibration of the ground tingled her feet, and her heart sped in hopeful anticipation that it was Angus coming down the dirt road on his horse. When the crafty stable master appeared with a grin spread across his face, the worry that was squeezing her heart loosened. For the first time since he had ridden out that morning, she took a proper breath. He stopped his stallion alongside her and dismounted.

She tilted her head back to look up at him as he towered over her. An errant thought struck. "Angus, are all Scots as tall as you?"

"Nay, but ye ken Scots are bigger than all the wee Englishmen." Suppressed laughter filled his deep voice. "So even the ones nae as tall as me are giants compared te the scrawny men here."

"You're teasing me," she replied, even as she arched her eyebrows in uncertainty.

"A wee bit," he agreed and tousled her hair. The laughter vanished from his eyes as he rubbed a hand over his square jaw and then stared down his bumpy nose at her, fixing what he called his "lecturing look" on her. "We've nae much time. Neil is in Newcastle just as he's supposed te be, but there's been a slight change."

She frowned. "For the last month, every time I wanted to simply make haste and flee, you refused my suggestion, and now you say there's a slight change?"

His ruddy complexion darkened. She'd pricked that MacLeod temper her mother had always said Angus's clan was known for throughout the Isle of Skye, where they lived in the farthest reaches of Scotland. Marion could remember her mother chuckling and teasing Angus about how no one knew the MacLeod temperament better than their neighboring clan, the MacDonalds of Sleat, to which her mother had been born. The two clans had a history of feuding.

Angus cleared his throat and recaptured Marion's attention. Without warning, his hand closed over her shoulder, and he squeezed gently. "I'm sorry te say it so plain, but ye must die at once."

Her eyes widened as dread settled in the pit of her stomach. "What? Why?" The sudden fear she felt was unreasonable. She knew he didn't mean she was really going to die, but her palms were sweating and her lungs had tightened all the same. She sucked in air and wiped her damp hands down the length of her cotton skirts. Suddenly, the idea of going to a foreign land and living with her mother's clan, people she'd never met, made her apprehensive.

She didn't even know if the MacDonalds—her uncle, in particular, who was now the laird—would accept her or not. She was half-English, after all, and Angus had told her that when a Scot considered her English bloodline and the fact that she'd been raised there, they would most likely brand her fully English, which was not a good thing in a Scottish mind. And if her uncle was anything like her grandfather had been, the man was not going to be very reasonable. But she didn't have any other family to turn to who would dare defy her father, and Angus hadn't offered for her to go to his clan, so she'd not asked. He likely didn't want to bring trouble to his clan's doorstep, and she didn't blame him.

Panic bubbled inside her. She needed more time, even if it was only the day she'd thought she had, to gather her courage.

"Why must I flee tonight? I was to teach Eustice how to dress a wound. She might serve as a maid, but then she will be able to help the knights when I'm gone. And her little brother, Bernard, needs a few more lessons before he's mastered writing his name and reading. And Eustice's youngest sister has begged me to speak to Father about allowing her to visit her mother next week."

"Ye kinnae watch out for everyone here anymore, Marion."

She placed her hand over his on her shoulder. "Neither can you."

Their gazes locked in understanding and disagreement.

He slipped his hand from her shoulder, and then crossed his arms over his chest in a gesture that screamed stubborn, unyielding protector. "If I leave at the same time ye feign yer death," he said, changing the subject, "it could stir yer father's suspicion and make him ask questions when none need te be asked. I'll be going home te Scotland soon after ye." Angus reached into a satchel attached to his horse and pulled out a dagger, which he slipped to her. "I had this made for ye."

Marion took the weapon and turned it over, her heart pounding. "It's beautiful." She held it by its black handle while withdrawing it from the sheath and examining it. "It's much sharper than the one I have."

"Aye," he said grimly. "It is. Dunnae forget that just because I taught ye te wield a dagger does nae mean ye can defend yerself from *all* harm. Listen te my cousin and do as he says. Follow his lead."

She gave a tight nod. "I will. But why must I leave now and not tomorrow?"

Concern filled Angus's eyes. "Because I ran into Froste's brother in town and he told me that Froste sent word that he would be arriving in two days."

Marion gasped. "That's earlier than expected."

"Aye," Angus said and took her arm with gentle authority. "So ye must go now. I'd rather be trying te trick only yer father than yer father, Froste, and his savage knights. I want ye long gone and yer death accepted when Froste arrives."

She shivered as her mind began to race with all that could go wrong.

"I see the worry darkening yer green eyes," Angus said, interrupting her thoughts. He whipped off his hat and his hair, still shockingly red in spite of his years, fell down around his shoulders. He only ever wore it that way when he was riding. He said the wind in his hair reminded him of riding his own horse when he was in Scotland. "I was going to talk to ye tonight, but now that I kinnae…" He shifted from foot to foot, as if uncomfortable. "I want te offer ye something. I'd have proposed it sooner, but I did nae want ye te feel ye had te take my offer so as nae te hurt me, but I kinnae hold my tongue, even so."

She furrowed her brow. "What is it?"

"I'd be proud if ye wanted te stay with the MacLeod clan instead of going te the MacDonalds. Then ye'd nae have te leave everyone ye ken behind. Ye'd have me."

A surge of relief filled her. She threw her arms around Angus, and he returned her hug quick and hard before setting her away. Her eyes misted at once. "I had hoped you would ask me," she admitted.

For a moment, he looked astonished, but then he spoke. "Yer mother risked her life te come into MacLeod territory at a time when we were fighting terrible with the MacDonalds, as ye well ken."

Marion nodded. She knew the story of how Angus had ended up here. He'd told her many times. Her mother had been somewhat of a renowned healer from a young age, and when Angus's wife had a hard birthing, her mother had gone to help. The knowledge that his wife and child had died anyway still made Marion want to cry.

"I pledged my life te keep yer mother safe for the kindness she'd done me, which brought me here, but, lass, long ago ye became like a daughter te me, and I pledge the rest of my miserable life te defending ye."

She gripped Angus's hand. "I wish you were my father."

He gave her a proud yet smug look, one she was used to seeing. She chortled to herself. The man did have a terrible streak of pride. She'd have to give Father John another coin for penance for Angus, since the Scot refused to take up the custom himself.

Angus hooked his thumb in his gray tunic. "Ye'll make a fine MacLeod because ye already ken we're the best clan in Scotland."

Mentally, she added another coin to her dues. "Do you think they'll let me become a MacLeod, though, since my mother was the daughter of the previous MacDonald laird and I've an English father?"

"They will," he answered without hesitation, but she heard the slight catch in his voice.

"Angus." She narrowed her eyes. "You said you would never lie to me."

His brows dipped together, and he gave her a long, disgruntled look. "They may be a bit wary," he finally admitted. "But I'll nae let them turn ye away. Dunnae worry," he finished, his Scottish brogue becoming thick with emotion.

She bit her lip. "Yes, but you won't be with me when I first get there. What should I do to make certain that they will let me stay?"

He quirked his mouth as he considered her question. "Ye must first get the laird te like ye. Tell Neil te take ye directly te the MacLeod te get his consent for ye te live there. I kinnae vouch for the man myself as I've never met him, but Neil says he's verra honorable, fierce in battle, patient, and reasonable." Angus cocked his head as if in thought. "Now that I think about it, I'm sure the MacLeod can get ye a husband, and then the clan will more readily accept ye. Aye." He nodded. "Get in the laird's good graces as soon as ye meet him and ask him te find ye a husband." A scowl twisted his lips. "Preferably one who will accept yer acting like a man sometimes."

She frowned at him. "*You* are the one who taught me how to ride bareback, wield a dagger, and shoot an arrow true."

"Aye." He nodded. "I did. But when I started teaching ye, I thought yer mama would be around te add her woman's touch. I did nae ken at the time that she'd pass when ye'd only seen eight summers in yer life."

"You're lying again," Marion said. "You continued those lessons long after Mama's death. You weren't a bit worried how I'd turn out."

"I sure was!" he objected, even as a guilty look crossed his face. "But what could I do? Ye insisted on hunting for the widows so they'd have food in the winter, and ye insisted on going out in the dark te help injured knights when I could nae go with ye. I had te teach ye te hunt and defend yerself. Plus, you were a sad, lonely thing, and I could nae verra well overlook ye when ye came te the stables and asked me te teach ye things."

"Oh, you could have," she replied. "Father overlooked me all the time, but your heart is too big to treat someone like that." She patted him on the chest. "I think you taught me the best things in the world, and it seems to me any man would want his woman to be able to defend herself."

"Shows how much ye ken about men," Angus muttered with a shake of his head. "Men like te think a woman needs *them*."

"I dunnae need a man," she said in her best Scottish

accent.

He threw up his hands. "Ye do. Ye're just afeared."

The fear was true enough. Part of her longed for love, to feel as if she belonged to a family. For so long she'd wanted those things from her father, but she had never gotten them, no matter what she did. It was difficult to believe it would be any different in the future. She'd rather not be disappointed.

Angus tilted his head, looking at her uncertainly. "Ye want a wee bairn some day, dunnae ye?"

"Well, yes," she admitted and peered down at the ground, feeling foolish.

"Then ye need a man," he crowed.

She drew her gaze up to his. "Not just any man. I want a man who will truly love me."

He waved a hand dismissively. Marriages of convenience were a part of life, she knew, but she would not marry unless she was in love and her potential husband loved her in return. She would support herself if she needed to.

"The other big problem with a husband for ye," he continued, purposely avoiding, she suspected, her mention of the word *love*, "as I see it, is yer tender heart."

"What's wrong with a tender heart?" She raised her brow in question.

"'Tis more likely te get broken, aye?" His response was matter-of-fact.

"Nay. 'Tis more likely to have compassion," she replied with a grin.

"We're both right," he announced. "Yer mama had a tender heart like ye. 'Tis why yer father's black heart hurt her so. I dunnae care te watch the light dim in ye as it did yer mother."

"I don't wish for that fate, either," she replied, trying

hard not to think about how sad and distant her mother had often seemed. "Which is why I will only marry for love. And why I need to get out of England."

"I ken that, lass, truly I do, but ye kinnae go through life alone."

"I don't wish to," she defended. "But if I have to, I have you, so I'll not be alone." With a shudder, her heart denied the possibility that she may never find love, but she squared her shoulders.

"'Tis nae the same as a husband," he said. "I'm old. Ye need a younger man who has the power te defend ye. And if Sir Frosty Pants ever comes after ye, you're going te need a strong man te go against him."

Marion snorted to cover the worry that was creeping in.

Angus moved his mouth to speak, but his reply was drowned by the sound of the supper horn blowing. "God's bones!" Angus muttered when the sound died. "I've flapped my jaw too long. Ye must go now. I'll head te the stables and start the fire as we intended. It'll draw Andrew and Peter away if they are watching ye too closely."

Marion looked over her shoulder at the knights, her stomach turning. She had known the plan since the day they had formed it, but now the reality of it scared her into a cold sweat. She turned back to Angus and gripped her dagger hard. "I'm afraid."

Determination filled his expression, as if his will for her to stay out of harm would make it so. "Ye will stay safe," he commanded. "Make yer way through the path in the woods that I showed ye, straight te Newcastle. I left ye a bag of coins under the first tree ye come te, the one with the rope tied te it. Neil will be waiting for ye by Pilgrim Gate on Pilgrim Street. The two of ye will depart from there."

She worried her lip but nodded all the same.

"Neil has become friends with a friar who can get the two of ye out," Angus went on. "Dunnae talk te anyone, especially any men. Ye should go unnoticed, as ye've never been there and won't likely see anyone ye've ever come in contact with here."

Fear tightened her lungs, but she swallowed. "I didn't even bid anyone farewell." Not that she really could have, nor did she think anyone would miss her other than Angus, and she would be seeing him again. Peter and Andrew *had* been kind to her, but they were her father's men, and she knew it well. She had been taken to the dungeon by the knights several times for punishment for transgressions that ranged from her tone not pleasing her father to his thinking she gave him a disrespectful look. Other times, they'd carried out the duty of tying her to the post for a thrashing when she'd angered her father. They had begged her forgiveness profusely but done their duties all the same. They would likely be somewhat glad they did not have to contend with such things anymore.

Eustice was both kind *and* thankful for Marion teaching her brother how to read, but Eustice lost all color any time someone mentioned the maid going with Marion to Froste's home after Marion was married. She suspected the woman was afraid to go to the home of the infamous "Merciless Knight." Eustice would likely be relieved when Marion disappeared. Not that Marion blamed her.

A small lump lodged in her throat. Would her father even mourn her loss? It wasn't likely, and her stomach knotted at the thought.

"You'll come as soon as you can?" she asked Angus.

"Aye. Dunnae fash yerself."

She forced a smile. "You are already sounding like you're back in Scotland. Don't forget to curb that when speaking with Father."

"I'll remember. Now, make haste te the cliff te leave yer cloak, then head straight for Newcastle."

"I don't want to leave you," she said, ashamed at the sudden rise of cowardliness in her chest and at the way her eyes stung with unshed tears.

"Gather yer courage, lass. I'll be seeing ye soon, and Neil will keep ye safe."

She sniffed. "I'll do the same for Neil."

"I've nay doubt ye'll try," Angus said, sounding proud and wary at the same time.

"I'm not afraid for myself," she told him in a shaky voice. "You're taking a great risk for me. How will I ever make it up to you?"

"Ye already have," Angus said hastily, glancing around and directing a worried look toward the drawbridge. "Ye want te live with my clan, which means I can go te my dying day treating ye as my daughter. Now, dunnae cry when I walk away. I ken how sorely ye'll miss me," he boasted with a wink. "I'll miss ye just as much."

With that, he swung up onto his mount. He had just given the signal for his beast to go when Marion realized she didn't know what Neil looked like.

"Angus!"

He pulled back on the reins and turned toward her. "Aye?"

"I need Neil's description."

Angus's eyes widened. "I'm getting old," he grumbled. "I dunnae believe I forgot such a detail. He's got hair redder than mine, and wears it tied back always. Oh, and he's missing his right ear, thanks te Froste. Took it when Neil came through these parts te see me last year."

"What?" She gaped at him. "You never told me that!"

"I did nae because I knew ye would try te go after Neil and patch him up, and that surely would have cost ye another beating if ye were caught." His gaze bore into her. "Ye're verra courageous. I reckon I had a hand in that 'cause I knew ye needed te be strong te withstand yer father. But dunnae be mindless. Courageous men and women who are mindless get killed. Ye ken?"

She nodded.

"Tread carefully," he warned.

"You too." She said the words to his back, for he was already turned and headed toward the drawbridge.

She made her way slowly to the edge of the steep embankment as tears filled her eyes. She wasn't upset because she was leaving her father—she'd certainly need to say a prayer of forgiveness for that sin tonight—but she couldn't shake the feeling that she'd never see Angus again. It was silly; everything would go as they had planned. Before she could fret further, the blast of the fire horn jerked her into motion. There was no time for any thoughts but those of escape.

About the Author

USA Today and #1 Amazon bestseller Julie Johnstone is the author of historical romance novels set in the Medieval and Regency periods and occasionally modern-day times. Her novels feature fast paced plots filled with political intrigue, intricate world building, and complex characters.

Her books have been dubbed "fabulously entertaining and engaging," making readers cry, laugh, and swoon. Julie is a graduate of The University of Alabama & Springhill College. She lives in Birmingham with her husband, her youngest son, two snobby cats, and two perpetually happy dogs.

In her spare time she enjoys way too much coffee balanced by super-hot yoga, reading, and traveling.

Sign up for her newsletter here: www.juliejohnstoneauthor.com.